THE L̷ v̷E̷ OF

ST ELIGIUS

Second Edition

Tom East

Benybont Books

www.benybont.org/

First published 2018. This edition 2019

ISBN **978-1-9161198-7-1**

To *Suki, Joseph, Edmund, Ping and Annabella*

ACKNOWLEDGEMENTS

Most of the stories in this collection were written especially for it but some have appeared in various magazines and elsewhere. *THE FIRST AND LAST LETTER* formed part of the libretto of an opera produced in 2018 in Illinois, USA, *FOR THOSE IN PERIL*. Together with the composer FRANCIS LYNCH, I am co-librettist.

I am grateful to JOYCE JAMES and HUW GRIFFITHS, also to the members of the N05 Group (ROWLAND HUGHES, DOMINIQUE SPEAREY and CHRIS WILLIAMS) for their helpful comments and suggestions on the text. One of the stories, *MYFANWY*, is loosely based on an actual experience of ROWLAND HUGHES.

Contents

Guardian

My daughter-in-law says I'm the oldest man in the village.

She's probably wrong. Anyway, Thexbury shouldn't really be called a village these days. With all the new houses, the superstores and the industrial estates that magically transformed themselves into warehouse-parks about thirty years ago, the place has earned itself the doubtful status of a small town.

There's bound to be someone older than me in one of the newer parts. Although, to judge by the number of pushchair-pushers, i-Prodders and hoodies I trip over on one of my rare visits to the new shopping centres, I sometimes doubt it.

It is conceivable that I have more years to my name than anyone in Old Thexbury. If John Bolton had lived for longer, until the present time at least, it would have been he who might have been the oldest man in the place. John was one week older than me on the night it all happened.

Back then, soon after the Second World War ended, Thexbury was definitely a village. Where I live still is no more than that. This is why they call it 'Old Thexbury'. It's a sop to the old stagers like me.

*

'So you're saying you won't come with me are you, John? You're telling me if I've got to go, I've got to go on my owny-own. I always counted you as my friend.'

'No. I'm not saying I'd leave you to do this all by yourself. I don't think you should go near the place, either.'

I could sense a weakening in John's resolve. Now was the time to press home my advantage. Right through the war Thexbury had stubbornly remained boring old Thexbury, even though our nearby city had been heavily bombed. The German bombers had merely flown over our village. Now the war was over and the fifteenth birthdays of the pair of us were due later that month I was hoping life would brighten up. During the war, we'd seen nothing more exciting than what our ridiculous scoutmaster had the nerve to call 'special manoeuvres'.

'You're scared, John, is that it?' Yes, I was taunting my friend. This, I thought, was my best tactic. 'If you are, all you have to do is come out and say so. I won't tell anyone.'

'Of course I'm not scared. All I'm trying to say is that The Manor isn't a place where anyone should go. Especially at night.'

"The Manor" was what the boys in our gang called Hartlebury House and its grounds. The old house had been locked up ever since I could remember. It was supposed to be haunted. This was the attraction for me, naturally. I fixed John with the most knowing smile I could manage and delivered the best punch line I had. Right between John's eyes. Or between the thick lenses of his glasses, at least: he was a small, weedy boy, forever blinking away behind those oversized specs.

'Old Man Hartlebury isn't there any longer, you know,' I said, even though I knew John was aware of this. I was trying to make him feel like a scaredy-cat. 'He died a week or two before we were born. He left no family. There'd be nobody there to chase us away, don't worry. That's why they've locked the place up for all these years. They're still trying to find a great-niece somewhere, is what I heard. Doesn't seem like they've been trying hard.'

Lord Hartlebury had died in November, 1930. The local story was that, back at the end of the nineteenth century, when he was still a fairly young man, he'd been given a copy of the new book by HG Wells, *The Island of Doctor Moreau*. Reading it over and over again had turned his mind, so the gossip went. *Doctor Moreau* was, so they said, a horrible story about a mad professor performing surgery on all sorts of animals to try to make them more like men. The vivisection of human beings came into it somewhere as well, so I heard. I should think it was enough to turn anyone's mind, that story. I'd never read it. Still haven't.

At first, all this meant was that the younger Hartlebury used to tramp around Thexbury and its surrounds muttering odd things like "His is the hand that heals" or "Are we not men?" But, when his old parents died and he inherited everything, things took a more sinister turn.

It was claimed he'd even tried to replicate some of the experiments of the fictional Doctor. In those days, there were plenty of tramps and stray animals around. It was easy to get wild creatures from the colonies, if you had the money.

His weird fascinations, so my Grandmother used to say, had finally driven him completely off his head. All these strange goings-on were even supposed to have had something to do with the old man's death. Ever since I'd heard the story, Hartlebury House had held a strong appeal to my youthful imagination. I wanted to visit the house or, at least, to walk in the grounds. And of course I wanted John to come with me. I was afraid to go on my own.

'What do you plan to do when you go there, then?' asked John after a few minutes of glum silence.

'Nothing much,' I said. 'I'm only going to walk through the grounds, for goodness' sake. We won't try to break into the house.'

*

It was a few weeks before we were able to get to The Manor. In fact, all of what I'm going to tell you happened on the eve of what should have been John's fifteenth birthday. We found ourselves standing before the rusting, padlocked gates of Hartlebury House looking at each other. My earlier bravado was evaporating as the November night became darker and gloomier. John never had any bravado to begin with.

'It's locked,' he said. 'There's no way we can get in. We may as well pack up and go home.'

'Don't be such a coward,' I said. 'We knew the gate would be locked. You didn't expect it to be left wide open for us, did you? I planned for us to go over the wall. That's why I've brought this rope. I found this old bike lamp, too. It still had batteries in it. See?' I flicked it on briefly. The beam wasn't very bright but I hoped it would bolster John's confidence.

In truth, there was nothing I'd have loved more dearly myself at that moment than to go home. It was a cold night and one of those slimy, clinging fogs we used to see back then, even in places like Thexbury, was in the air. The mist was already starting to creep across the damp ground. This wasn't the sort of night anybody should choose for exploring the Manor grounds. Still, I was determined not to show the weakness I was feeling in front of John. So, I put my hands on my hips in the way my granny used to do whenever the butcher tried to palm her off with short meat rations. I even tried to imitate her gentle, mocking laugh.

'The wall is a bit high,' said John, when he saw and heard me doing my granny imitation. 'Is the rope going to be long enough?'

I knew I'd won the argument.

'Of course it's going to be long enough. I'll climb up to the top of the wall on your shoulders and then use the rope to pull you up. Then we'll jump down into the grounds. Simple, see? You're not still windy, are you? We'll go home if you are.'

It didn't prove to be as straightforward as I'd tried to make it sound. The rope was certainly long enough. In fact, carrying the heavy rope made it more difficult for me to clamber up the wall, even with the aid of John's bony shoulders. But at last we were over, and scrambling to our feet on the uncut lawns of the house. There was a full moon, and the light it gave was at least some compensation for the rapidly-thickening fog.

'Well, what now?' said John. 'I'm not going anywhere near the house. I vote we climb back over the wall and get away. I twisted my ankle a bit when we jumped. The thing is bloody painful.'

John wasn't normally one for even mild profanity, so I knew he must really have hurt himself. But the last thing I wanted to do was to cut and run now. I looked up at the old house. The building, smaller than I'd imagined, was in complete darkness. It seemed to glower down upon us. Wild horses wouldn't have dragged me one step nearer.

'Don't worry, John,' I said. 'We won't try to break into the house. The grounds here are supposed to be quite big, so I've heard. Let's take a look around the back. Your ankle seems fine to me. You can walk on it at least, can't you?'

The grounds were even more extensive than I'd expected. Although the moonlight was filtering down, it was hard to pick our way by the dim light of the bicycle-lamp I'd brought with me.

'You could at least have put in a fresh battery,' said John. 'Look at the feeble way it's flickering. The thing is pathetic. We'd have been better off with a candle.'

What John said was true, so I ignored him. He hadn't brought anything along with him. At least I'd brought the light, weak as it was, together with the rope. John had been as ill-prepared as if he'd been going on a country walk. As we passed the windowless side of the house, I became more conscious of the inadequate preparations we'd made. Away from the moonlight, we were in almost complete darkness.

'Let's turn back,' said John. 'I won't say anything. We can tell the gang we walked right around the house. That'll impress the lot of them.'

'Don't start that nonsense again,' I said. 'We *are* going to walk right around the house.'

John's mention of the gang did it. If only he hadn't said anything about the others! Privately, I was all for turning back myself. None of the boys even knew we were coming tonight.

My friend had planted an irresistible image in my mind of the two us boasting in the middle of an admiring circle of boys. I wouldn't have wanted to brag at all, if there was nothing to brag about.

'Ow!' said John. 'My ankle hurts whenever I put weight on it.'

I ignored his complaints and he kept walking, or hobbling, all the way until we were around the back. Stronger moonlight filtered down to this part of the grounds, so it was a shade lighter. But all the time the fog was getting thicker and, around the back of the house with only trees and shrubs for company, it felt as if we were a million miles away from boring old Thexbury. Boring, but safe old Thexbury.

The bicycle-lamp was barely flickering. At the moment it died out altogether, we saw the thing in the moonlight.

It came from behind a row of bushes, shambling towards us at an ungainly run. It was clearly in pain. The beast, if that was what it was, was the most hideous thing I've seen, before or since. It looked something like a large man, wrapped in an assortment of stained bandages. In the gloom the stains were dark but they could only have come from blood. And, even at that distance, I could see a misshapen claw sticking out from one of the bandages.

The thing's head was not fully human. In my nightmares the thing looks more like a bulldog than it does anything else, though with a much larger head than I'd ever seen on any dog. A row of sharp but rotting teeth and a lolling tongue caught a stray shaft of light and were momentarily illuminated between two slavering, massive jaws.

The pale luminescence the thing emanated was the oddest thing about what I saw. Unless my memory has deceived me over all these years – don't forget, there wasn't much light around to properly see either shape or colour – I'd describe it as being of a faint transparent blue. Yet, in form, the creature looked all too solid as it lurched painfully toward us.

'What is it?' John managed to gasp.

Then it spoke. The bloody thing spoke.

'I am Guardian,' was what it seemed to be saying in an odd, growling voice.

'Run John! Run!'

John didn't need telling twice. We easily outpaced the creature at first. But John must have really hurt his ankle, because soon he was falling further and further behind.

I was mightily relieved when I rounded the corner of the house and saw the boundary wall.

'Wait for me! My ankle hurts like Hell!'

I did want to go back to help John, I swear to you, but my legs seemed to have a will of their own as they carried me towards safety. Besides, what could I have done against a thing like that?

'Keep running, John,' I called back.

Although John was limping, he was still covering the ground faster than the apparition. I really did think he'd be all right.

At last I reached the wall. It was only then I realised I must have dropped the rope behind the house somewhere. But what could I have done on my own with a rope, anyway? I tried to scramble up but could get no purchase and slithered down, terrified. Twice more I tried and failed. Then I heard it behind me.

'I am Guardian.' This time, the words were unmistakable.

Sheer panic, nothing more, somehow got me to the top of the wall. As I reached it, I could see John not ten yards behind, stumbling in my direction. And the abomination was right behind him.

'I am Guardian,' it growled for a third time.

Just before I slipped to the ground on the far side of the wall, I saw it, leaping the last several yards straight on to John's back. Its weight brought him to the ground as if he were a kitten. It was the last I, or anyone else, ever saw of him alive.

Safe on the other side, I could hear a ferocious snarling and snapping, like that of a mad dog. I was rooted to the spot, listening to the horrific sounds for what seemed a long time. At first, I heard a few terrified screams. After a while, I could hear nothing at all. Then I slunk home.

*

It was two days before they found John's mangled body. When he didn't return home that night, a wide-ranging search of the area was made by the police and villagers. I could have told them where to look, of course, but didn't want to admit I was with him when he died. I even joined one of the search parties, though made sure the one I picked wasn't going anywhere near The Manor.

When they told me they'd found John, I cried like a baby. It was the last time I shed a tear for anything or anybody. I didn't even cry when my grandmother died, not much more than a year after this night. It was a good thing I did cry, really. It removed any lingering suspicion the police may have nurtured that I'd had anything to do with John's death.

Not that they ever really suspected me. They put it down to "wilful murder by a person or persons unknown". The stories went around Thexbury about John being killed by either a wild animal or a madman. Both versions were true, I suppose. After a few months, the stories stopped altogether. Though I've never forgotten a thing. I never will.

The only one who suspected I might know more than I was letting on was my grandmother. She knew I'd been out and had come home with cut and grazed knees. She knew John and I were always together. But she never said anything; I just caught her looking at me a few times with a question in her eyes.

Good old Granny! I could always rely on her. It was she who'd taken me in after Mum didn't come back from a night out in 1943. A few weeks later Mum sent her own mother a letter "to explain". The letter didn't explain anything, but with it she enclosed her St Christopher medallion. Granny gave it to me and I've still got it. It was the only family thing I had, really. Dad never came back from the war.

I had a few nasty moments when I remembered I'd dropped the old rope in The Manor's grounds. But I needn't have worried: the police traced it back to Mr Rowland's allotment. They tried to give the old geezer a hard time but he could never have killed John. In the end they assumed the rope had been filched from the allotment. They were right about that: I was the one who filched it. The police were short of manpower because of the war and they never managed a proper investigation.

*

That's the whole story, I suppose. I'm glad to have got everything off my chest at last. It's been eating away at me for all these years. Hartlebury House was knocked down in the summer of 1946 to make way for a small industrial estate. Its grounds now lie under the concrete of one of the warehouse-jungles.

No-one saw or at least mentioned anything about 'Guardian' again, except I heard that a few odd rumours circulated around the builders of the estate. But those grounds left their mark on me on the night the short existence of John Bolton ended. I suppose I'll have nightmares about that thing for the rest of my life. Still, there can't be many years left to me.

If I was being honest, I'd have to say that what happened on that night is the reason why I haven't exactly been sweet reason and light for all these years. My son and his wife have had a lot to put up with, I know this. My daughter-in-law called me "an old curmudgeon" the other day. I was surprised she even knew the word. I can't blame her, I suppose. But if she only knew the truth, she'd call me worse. So would everyone, if only they knew.

Ellyllon

Rita was alone on the bench overlooking the sea when she struggled into full wakefulness. The last of the stalls of Morydd Market were being cleared up on the coast road, fifty yards behind her. Her daughter Ellyll had gone. She had gone with him.

Looking down at the sea below her, bejewelled by the setting sun, it was hard to imagine that the busy industrial town of Milford Haven lay not so many miles to the east. Although it was an unseasonably warm autumn day, a sudden rising in the breeze sent a chill through her. Rita knew she'd never see Ellyll again. She was due to go home to London tomorrow. How could she do it alone? What would Tim, her husband, say when she returned by herself?

To think it was only a few days ago they'd met the man...

*

'You have a fine daughter, Mrs Brown. I've just been talking to her. May I?'

He indicated the seat opposite hers.

'Oh... er yes, I suppose so.'

She thought this a bit forward of him, although he seemed harmless enough. The twinkle in his eye and his smiling face made her relax right away. His features were delicately fine and he was short in stature, though clearly robust and healthy. In appearance he was rather like Ellyll herself, in fact. But she was only sixteen; he must be seventy at least.

'You have been to Pembrokeshire before?'

'No. Well... yes, once,' said Rita. 'It was a long time ago.'

The conversation on that Sunday morning in the hotel lounge was their first of several. Rita found the man to be amusing company. He was always ready with an anecdote. She told him why they were here: Ellyll had insisted on Pembrokeshire for her sixteenth birthday treat, despite their efforts to persuade her to go further afield. Tim wanted to accompany them but his busy work schedule made it difficult. Ellyll hadn't helped by being adamant about the dates she wanted for her visit.

'Ah well,' Tim had said with his usual easy going smile. 'You and your Mum have a few days together. We'll have another celebration when you get back.'

She readily told the man of their life in London; she reminisced on Ellyll's happy childhood; she described at length the insistence of Tim that their daughter should go on to university. There was an excellent chance she'd get a place as early as next year, far earlier than normal. She'd even revealed that Ellyll seemed to spread a light of happiness wherever she went. Then she wondered why she was speaking so freely of her family life.

In return, she realised after he'd left, he'd told her practically nothing about himself. He was vague about how he spent his time and even as to where he lived. 'Not here, but near here,' was the most she could get out of him. He'd told her his name, and then she'd promptly forgotten it. It was something she'd never heard before. It didn't sound like a Welsh name.

Then Ellyll returned.

'You've been talking to –'

Ellyll had pronounced the name clearly enough but to Rita's embarrassment it had wafted from her mind as soon as she'd said it.

'He's a lovely man, isn't he?' her daughter said. 'We'll be seeing much more of him.' Ellyll stated this as a matter of indisputable fact.

*

Next morning, Rita sat in the hotel lounge. She caught herself casting anxious glances in the direction of the street door. With a start, she realised she was waiting for the elderly man to appear. After she'd waited for ten minutes, the door opened and he walked in.

Rita guiltily tried to understand her feelings. It wasn't any kind of physical attraction she was feeling. The man was graceful for one of his years. He looked fit but he was at the very least twenty years her senior. She simply wanted to talk to him again.

Their eyes met. He smiled in a friendly, open way and crossed the lounge to greet her.

'I am very pleased to find you here, Mrs Brown. May I speak with you again briefly? This morning, I'm afraid I have little time, although I do hope you will be able to spare me a few minutes before I have to go.'

Again he wanted to talk about Ellyll. He was full of even more questions about her girlhood.

'Did you notice anything unusual about Ellyll in infancy?' he suddenly asked, quite directly.

Rita was taken aback. For a moment she wondered whether she should answer this bold question at all. But he had such a kindly light in his eyes. The very silver of his hair seemed to be saying, 'you can trust me.'

'To tell you the truth, Tim and I were worried at first. She seemed so small and delicate. Our daughter gained weight only very slowly. At ten years old she weighed less than three stones. We took her to a number of doctors but none of them could find anything medically wrong. Despite her size, Ellyll was robust and healthy. In all her life she's had not a day's illness. Bright, too: she was always top of the class. That's why Tim insists she must go to university soon.' She stopped before adding, 'And she was very lovely. She still is.'

Rita smiled to think of her daughter. The old man nodded his head to show he was pleased, too.

'And yet you worry about her still.'

'Not exactly *worry*,' said Rita. She wished she could remember his name. Why was she telling him so much? He was a comparative stranger. She continued, nevertheless. It was as if she had no choice in the matter. 'Ellyll is a wonderful girl in every way. But somehow she's always been, well, somehow *different*. She has no interest in pop music, fashion or films. Although so many of our local boys are keen on her, she has no time for any of them.

'She simply laughs and says she'd rather talk to the plants and animals. These are not empty words. My daughter really does exactly that. I've seen her do it, often. The animals seem to understand what she says to them, too. Ellyll speaks to them a strange language, trying not to let me hear a word. It must be a language she made up. Children sometimes do that, I know, but she still uses it, all these years later.'

'No need to be concerned, I am sure. Not all of us want the same things from life.' He said this calmly, as if Rita had done nothing more than announce Ellyll preferred the colour red to the colour blue. 'And now I really do have to be somewhere else.'

'So soon?' she said. 'I wanted to ask you whether you thought a veterinary course would be best for her, given her empathy with animals.' Why was she going to ask him this? 'Ellyll will be back shortly. She's only in the hotel garden.'

'I have already spoken to her, on my way in.'

This annoyed Rita. Why did he always want to speak to Ellyll alone? She quickly formed a plan.

'This evening you must dine with us,' she said. 'Shall we say eight o'clock in the hotel restaurant?'

'But...'

'I insist. My idea. My treat.'

For a brief moment he looked perplexed. Then he rose smartly.

'I'll see you tonight,' he said. 'By the way, Ellyll's favourite colour is neither red nor blue. It is green.'

Rita was sure she hadn't expressed her thought about colours aloud.

*

At half-past-seven Rita was crossing the lounge floor on her way back to her room. She was surprised to see the old man at the bar. He was sipping a pale yellowish drink.

'Well, hello again,' she said. 'You're here early.'

'Oh, I was nearby so I thought I'd call in for a drink before our dinner.'

'What drink is it?'

'This is called pineapple juice. It is very good. I discovered its existence when I was last on the mainland.'

'On the mainland? The mainland to what?'

'I live on an island.'

There were no islands anywhere nearby, as far as Rita knew. She wanted to ask him – she still couldn't remember his name – how he knew Ellyll's favourite colour was indeed green. Rita was quite sure she hadn't given voice to the thought. Ellyll's colour preferences had been no more than a casual fancy passing through her mind when they were speaking earlier in the day. Something prevented her from asking him exactly where his island was.

'Do you speak Welsh on your island?' she asked instead.

'No. There is little Welsh spoken in southern Pembrokeshire. At home, we speak our own language. It is far older than Welsh. And, before you ask, our island has many names. The most popular is Ynyslas. This means "The Green Island."'

Rita knew Welsh was one of the oldest languages in Europe. She wanted to point this out. Again, something stopped her.

'I must get back to my room to change,' she said. 'Ellyll and I will see you in the restaurant at eight o'clock. A table for three has been booked in the name of Mrs Brown.'

*

Dinner that night passed as if it were part of a dream. Ellyll and the man – she still couldn't remember his name, even though Ellyll had used it several times – made pleasant company. They were both talkative but now Rita could recall almost nothing of what had been said.

Only the conclusion of the meal had stayed in her mind.

'You have been very kind,' the man had said. 'Now tomorrow afternoon will be my turn. I am going to take both of you to Morydd Market. It opens only three times a year. Do you know, it is the oldest market anywhere in this country? It's been going since pre-Roman times.'

'Where is it? I've never heard of it. It's not mentioned in any of the brochures.'

'It is on the old coast road. Not many people know of its existence. The market is never advertised.'

But Rita did now remember Morydd Market. The memories she'd kept suppressed for nearly sixteen years came flooding back.

*

In the middle of that night, she sat up in bed, sweating. Her mind had drifted back to the start of it all. She and Tim had stumbled upon the old coast road only by chance. This was purely because they'd lost their way. They were surprised to come across a market by the side of the quiet road. It was only natural for Rita at least to want to go back to have a look. It looked like it belonged to an earlier century.

'You have a walk back around the bend,' said Tim. 'I'll wait here for you. I'd like to take the opportunity to dictate a report while I've half-an-hour spare. Save me taking time tonight.' Tim whipped the recorder from his pocket.

'Are you sure?'

'Of course I'm sure. You go on.'

Tim was dictating before Rita had even closed the car door. In the last few years, Tim had been obsessed by his work. This saddened her. Once, he'd been a real family man. But their family had failed to grow. There were still only the two of them...

After she'd walked back to the fair, she saw that the stallholders seemed normal enough. They sold their wares from beneath canvas structures like market traders everywhere. The goods they sold were familiar, too: a mixture of clothes, foodstuffs and odd trinkets. Nor was there anything unusual about most of the customers wandering between stalls. A few, though, caught Rita's eye as she watched their progress through the market.

These people, about a dozen of them all told, were on average a foot or so shorter than their fellow customers. They were, without exception, slender of build and graceful in their movements. The odd thing about them she noticed was that none spoke a word to the traders, or even between themselves. They would walk up to a stall, examine their chosen purchase, and wordlessly put the money down on the counter. They must always have given the exact sum, because in no case did Rita see any change passing hands. The stallholders seemed to accept this odd kind of transaction as entirely normal. It was all very strange.

Then she saw it. Behind one of the stalls was a basket made from woven branches. Inside was a baby, quiet and content. Afterwards, Rita tried to understand what possessed her to do such a thing but, without a second's thought, she snatched up the basket surreptitiously and walked boldly from the market and back towards the car where Tim was waiting.

'I see you've bought one of these country baskets,' said Tim, as Rita carefully placed her burden in the rear of their estate car. 'It looks fine now but I bet in a few weeks it will fall apart. You mark my words.'

'Can we drive straight back to the hotel now, Tim? I need to rest. I don't want to go any further along this coast road.'

The baby didn't waken until they were nearing the end of their journey. Tim's eyes widened when he heard the gentle sound of its crying.

'What have you done? We must return this baby!' he said. At first he made no move and sat in stunned silence at the wheel. Twelve years of childless marriage had been hard for him, too. Then, with sudden resolve, he turned the ignition key, spun the car around and, despite Rita's pleading, drove back.

'I'm sure this was the place where the market was, just around the bend from where I'd parked,' he said. 'I remember the rock near the road and the green island close to shore.'

Rita stared at the rock but could see no island.

'Well,' she said. 'There's nothing we can do now. Let's take our baby home.'

*

They told friends and neighbours it was the baby of Tim's sister they were taking care of. For weeks, both of them lived in fear of a large-scale media outcry. It didn't come. There wasn't even a paragraph in the local Pembrokeshire press, which Tim took steps to monitor carefully. After a few months, people hardly asked. Then they moved away to Pimlico to avoid the fiction that the child had anything to do with Tim's sister. Ellyll was their daughter now.

The basket proved to be altogether sturdier than Tim had predicted. Rita was still using it, though not for its original purpose, long after Ellyll had left her primary school. Despite their early concerns about her stature, she grew up to be the ideal daughter.

*

There had always been something different about her. And, on this short trip, which was all Ellyll had wanted for her sixteenth birthday, Rita was finding out what that *something different* was.

The taxi driver had never heard of Morydd Market and the silver-haired man had to give him precise instructions at every turn. Rita couldn't help noticing Ellyll's rising excitement as they neared their destination. The market seemed exactly as it had nearly sixteen years before: it had a generally old-fashioned feel to it but there wasn't anything really unusual to be seen except for the small number of slender, graceful people moving silently from stall to stall.

The three joined the throng of customers and wandered around the market. They could have been three generations of a family anywhere. Rita would have relaxed if she hadn't noticed Ellyll giving friendly smiles to each one of the slender people. But no words were exchanged and there were few passing between the three of them, either. Soon, Rita's legs began to feel weary and her eyelids heavy.

'I think, Mrs Brown, that you could do with a short rest.'

'No, really, I'm fine.'

'Nonsense. There's a bench over there. All three of us will take a break for ten minutes. Ellyll and I will talk while you close your eyes.'

Rita looked in the direction the old man was pointing. She could see nothing until they walked around the bend. Then, not thirty yards ahead, overlooking the sea, was a green bench. It did seem very inviting and Rita was grateful when Ellyll led the way to it without a word.

As soon as they sat down, Rita felt an immediate need to close her eyes. The sound of the waves below and the warmth of the afternoon sunlight on her right shoulder gave an almost tactile pleasure. Ellyll sat next to her and the old man was to her daughter's left. The two were talking about inconsequential things: Ellyll's life in Pimlico; the fortunes of Morydd Market; this beautiful autumn weather. Very soon, Rita began to drowse.

After a time, she half-stirred but found she couldn't open her eyes properly. She listened. Her daughter and the old man were deep in conversation, but she couldn't now understand a single word being uttered. The voices of Ellyll and the man were intoned at an unnaturally high pitch and seemed to flow together to make a mellifluous whole. She listened more carefully. Still she could understand nothing, although noticed that two words were voiced frequently. The old man was saying "ellyllon" in every third sentence and her daughter was repeating what sounded like "avasa" often. What did those words mean?

Rita tried to listen for longer but the redness of the sun through her closed eyelids darkened to blackness and she slept again.

*

By the time she awoke fully the sun was much lower in the sky to the west. Her daughter and the man were now silent. It was Ellyll who spoke first.

'We've been waiting for you to wake up, Mother, Avasa Gwirol and I.'

She didn't answer her daughter but spoke instead to the man.

'What language were you speaking – "Avasa Gwirol"? And what does "Ellyllon "mean?'

He looked at her for a long moment. There was a kindly light in his eyes. He didn't answer Rita, but instead posed a question of his own.

'What is your daughter's name?'

'Ellyll. You know it is.'

'And where did you find that name?'

'It came to me in a dream.' Rita was telling the truth. The dream had come to her on the same night she and Tim had gone home with their new daughter from Pembrokeshire.

'What entered your dream were the tears of our people. We wanted the one who had stolen our baby daughter to give her a name which would speak of her real home.'

'And is this name a Welsh word?'

'The word is the same in the Welsh language. They borrowed it from our own. Ellyll is one of us, the Ellyllon. You would say "Elf" and "Elves". I am the avasa of the one you call your daughter. You would say "grandfather". My own name is Gwirol. Now Ellyll is all I have in this world.'

Rita could find no way to voice her shame. The guilt she had carried within her for sixteen years rose to the surface.

'How you must both hate me.'

'No, Mrs Brown. Ellyll is your daughter in many ways. A daughter's love does not change. And I, too, am grateful to you.'

'Grateful? Don't try to be kind. I did a terrible thing.'

'No. Wait!' His voice was gentle. 'Six months before you walked away from Morydd Market with her daughter, the

husband of my own Serenell was killed in a hunting accident.
An arrow had pierced him. My daughter became mad with grief
and was lost to us from that day. Her own mother – my wife –
had died soon after Ellyll was born. Our granddaughter became
cared for by another far away. You. I was afraid to move her
until she was old enough to understand but I have kept watch
quietly. She has grown into a fine young woman. You have
done well. Now it is time for her to return to her people, the
Ellyllon.'

Ellyll rose and, bending forward gracefully, placed two
kisses on each of Rita's eyelids. They lulled her back to sleep.

*

Now, awake, she found herself alone on the bench. She
looked below her to the sea and was surprised to see a small
green peninsula. It was shimmering at the edge of visibility.
Looking more carefully, she saw a couple walking across a
narrow causeway. For a moment, they stopped and waved back
to her. She could make out the slender form of Ellyll and the
silver-haired man, her true grandfather Gwirol, standing next to
her. As soon as she caught sight of them, they turned and
carried on walking. She watched until they disappeared into a
gap in the rocks at the end of the path.

Rita wanted at first to try to run after them. Instead, she
returned her gaze to the peninsula, rapidly becoming an island
and even fainter to her eyes now. She continued to stare at it
but all the time it grew fainter until it was quite gone from her
sight. The gap in the rocks at the end of the path leading to
where the causeway had been had also now disappeared. There
would be no point in going down to look for it.

She turned her head and saw the taxi coming towards
her. Gwirol had thought of everything. Tomorrow, she'd return
home to Pimlico. Then she'd have to do her best to explain it
all to Tim.

Ellyll had returned to the Ellyllon.

The First and Last Letter
to his wife from Thomas Griffith

In early 1800, one of the two keepers of the Smalls Lighthouse, Thomas Howell, died. Fearing he would be blamed for the death if he buried him at sea, his fellow-keeper, Thomas Griffith, put the cadaver in a box. He then suspended it from the lantern-rail so it could be seen by passing shipping. The result was as described below. Thomas Griffith was white-haired and insane when he was finally relieved. The incident directly gave rise to the Trinity House policy of manning all lighthouses with three instead of two men. This policy was maintained until remote control was installed in the last lighthouse early in the present century.

*

15 February, 1800

Beloved Wife,

Strange it may be to relate but this is the first letter I have penned to you in all the years of our marriage. Some might call it strange for me to be writing at all, when there can be no hope of you reading this letter until I am relieved one month from today. But it gives me a few crumbs of comfort to know you will see my words. I will surely need anything falling from the Good Lord's table before this month has passed.

Last night my friend Thomas Howell died. His passing was quick and I have not the medical knowledge to say what ailed him. I fear to be left alone on the Smalls Lighthouse for so long. The thing that took poor Thomas, be it sickness or Demon, may seek me out next.

Now, I must be about my duties in the lighthouse. There are all the more of them with myself alone to turn a hand to the tasks. But I shall return to this letter as soon as I may.

*

18 February, 1800

Three days and nights have passed since I last put pen to paper. As well as maintaining the light for shipping, I have engaged myself on the most gruesome of tasks. Fearing others may read too much into our past quarrels and say that Thomas Howell's death was by my own hand, I have constructed a box from old timbers and placed his corpse inside it. This I have hung from the lantern-beam of the lighthouse so it may be seen by passing vessels.

I would to God we had both kept to honest labour on our farms in Mathry Parish. Work on the lighthouse may have brought more reward in silver coin but here, twenty miles out to sea from St David's head, I fear my only companion is the very Devil who surely lurks in the shadows of this tower.

*

19 February, 1800

No passing vessel has set down a lighter to row near and investigate the reason why a timber construction should be hung from the lantern-beam. None has even approached the lighthouse by so much as half-a-league. Worse, the winds have buffeted the wooden box in a way that has loosened its lid. My relief is still more than three weeks away. I do not see how I can retain my sanity for that length of time. All that is left for me is to pray for my soul. And I hope that, safely abed in Mathry Parish, my beloved wife prays to the Lord, too.

*

21 February, 1800

Now I know this place is wicked beyond the power of the darkest dream. The lid of the wooden box has quite fallen away. Thomas Howell's dead right arm now hangs within inches of the lighthouse window.

And I swear it is beckoning me outside to face the harshness of the waves and the evil spirits that manifest themselves on the surface of the sea. Back and fore the arm swings like a dread pendulum. The forefinger of Thomas is extended as a pointer to the spirit-world only his dead eyes see.

*

23 February, 1800

I have taken to sleeping with The Good Book for my pillow, in the hope it will protect me from the darkness of the otherworld. Even so, I close my eyes in rest for barely an hour through the night.

Scarce after one o'clock last night, the Demon's knock interrupted my fearful dreams. Then I understood what I heard to be the sound of the dead hand of Thomas Howell tap-tapping against my night-window.

It was then I knew, as surely as grass may grow on land I fear I will never see again, that the finger was pointing out to the sea-goblins and wraiths the way in to the lighthouse and to this wretch shivering within. My very soul is imperilled.

*

24 February, 1800

This is something that I can no longer endure... O, Beloved wife! ... O, My Dearest Lord! ... All ... Save ...

[*The rest of the letter is indecipherable*]

Yellow Eyes

The chill wind raked in harshly from the east and Peter pulled his jacket more snugly around his chest. Spring was slow to come to this part of the world. Perhaps he'd been even more rash than usual to want to come here quite so early in the year. Or perhaps he was foolish to come here at any time.

His misgivings didn't last for long. It was hard to find real regrets about choosing such an unusual holiday; not when he could almost taste the freshness of the cold air rolling around the thickly wooded foothills of the Carpathian Mountains. On every side, all he could see were the sights of nature. This was a paradise that, for the moment at least, belonged solely to him.

His friends had considered him eccentric to think of such a place for a leisure trip. The Republic of Moldova: not really the sort of destination you'd expect to see in a holiday brochure. But, in a sense, it had been tourist literature that brought him here. Catherine, his partner of many years, had brought home a Spanish holiday glossy, happily informing him she'd put a deposit on a holiday for them.

'Not Benidorm again!' he'd shouted at her. 'We've been there for the past three years. Why can't we go somewhere different for a change? I'm sick of the Costas with their sangria-and-chips.'

Catherine's face had immediately fallen. One thing had led to another, and before long they were having another blazing row. This ended, as usual, with him walking out in a huff. As they always did, they'd patched things up a few weeks later, but in the meantime Peter had already made his own arrangements for this camping holiday.

They'd been back together for only two weeks before Peter had revealed his plans. Catherine's reaction was scornful:

'You only picked such an out-of-the-way place from sheer awkwardness. It's exactly like you.'

Perhaps she was right with the "exactly like you" taunt but this trip had only been possible after a long and trying correspondence with the government of the newly-independent Republic of Moldova. Peter wasn't going to give up so easily on what he thought was a bright idea. Anyway, there was a point to make, wasn't there?

The stand-off had almost given rise to another argument but Catherine was anxious to smooth things over and so he was able to come to Moldova with her agreement, if not her blessing. He'd made a half-hearted suggestion for her to accompany him, all the time knowing that a two-month trip wouldn't be practical for her to undertake at such short notice. So he was here, alone as originally intended.

Alone, but not lonely. Yes, he missed Catherine but it gave him a wonderful feeling of freedom to be here in this beautiful country with only the sights and sounds of the wild and his own thoughts for company.

It was over five miles from his camp to the sleepy village of Drakova. There was no way to reach the place other than by walking. He had to go there twice a week to get supplies of food and to report to the taciturn local policeman, under the terms of his visa. Apart from the policeman and Nicolae, who kept a tiny shop in the village, he rarely saw or spoke to another living soul.

And yet he could feel the presence of the creatures of the forest all around him. There were birds in plenty to be seen, some with a plumage he could not recognise, although it seemed that the weather was still too cold for many of the four-footed creatures to be active in the daytime.

But, on what was only his fourth night of camping, he'd been thrilled to his marrow to hear the distant howling of a wolf. Nicolae had told him that sometimes, in hard winters like the one from which they were only now emerging, hunger drove the wolves out of their fastnesses in the forests beneath the mountains. They often even ventured close to the village in their search for food, although they were seldom dangerous even then. They'd always prefer flight to attack, to scavenge rather than hunt, Nicolae told him.

It was towards the end of March, during Peter's third week in Moldova, when the old man came to his camp. The weather had turned sharply colder, and there'd even been a flurry of snow. Peter was breaking the ice on the surface of the brook he used for his water supply, when he became aware of the presence of another. He looked up, startled.

'Good day to you, your honour.' Peter was surprised to hear the man speak in perfect if rather strange English, with little trace of accent. 'My name is Va Rog.' He spoke the name slowly and emphatically, taking care to distinguish its two parts.

'Good morning. I'm Peter Roberts. I didn't hear you approach.'

The old man smiled. 'My people have learned it is wise to tread softly through the forest.'

Peter studied his visitor. He was tall and broad-shouldered, cutting a noble figure as he leaned on a heavy, rough-cut staff. The man was well advanced in years, although he looked strong and healthy, save for a certain gauntness around the cheekbones. But the thing Peter first noticed about the man was that he was blind, or appeared to be so, with his tightly closed eyes.

'Have you come from the village?'

'No, I come from afar,' said the old man, waving his staff in the general direction of the Carpathian Mountains behind him. 'And I am very hungry. I have walked for days. May I ask if you would be good enough to share a little of your meat with a stranger?'

'Yes, of course. I'll be pleased to. Take a seat. I should have asked you before.' Peter was glad to have a full pot of stew bubbling on his log fire. Va Rog's nose was visibly twitching at the smell of the food, and he licked his lips in a sensuous anticipation. Peter suddenly realised the reason for the old man's leanness: he was surely near to starving.

'I should think it's well enough cooked by now.' Peter ladled a generous helping of the stew on to an enamel plate. 'I'll get some bread for you.'

'Please do not concern yourself with bread. The meat will be sufficient for me. And I do not care for my food to be cooked for too long.'

Peter watched in fascination as the old man devoured the plate of stew in minutes, and then cleared another even more swiftly. He spurned the spoon proffered by Peter, preferring to use his bony, sharp-nailed fingers to thrust lumps of meat into his drooling mouth. After eating, he downed a pint of water in one steady draught, and then rose to his feet.

'I give you my thanks. It is many days since I had such a meal.'

'Wouldn't you like to sit by the fire to rest for a while?'

'No, no. I must return to my people. There is much to do. But you will see me again before you depart from our country.'

Peter did not take his eyes from the striding figure of Va Rog until it disappeared from view beyond the brow of a hill. The odd contrast between the man's gentlemanly speech and the almost beast-like way in which he had swallowed his food intrigued him.

But more disturbing was what he saw as his visitor set off on his homeward path. When Va Rog had walked twenty or so yards, he'd turned around towards Peter and lifted an arm in brief salute. As he did so, he opened his eyes for a single moment. Peter could not be totally sure of what he saw; it may have been a trick of the light or even of his imagination, although he did not think so. He was ready to swear he'd seen that the eyes of Va Rog were of a luminous yellow hue.

*

Spring at last truly came to Moldova. Warmth seeped into the air and in grateful response the trees and shrubs came into full blossom in a way that gladdened Peter's heart. He spent many a day simply walking through the forest, in the hope of catching a sight of the squirrels and other small animals only now beginning to stir from their long winter sleep. Sometimes, he'd fish for trout and grayling in his brook, now swollen by melting snows from the distant Carpathian peaks. There were hours together when it pleased him to do nothing but sit in his camp and enjoy the delicious smells of the greenery and his smoky log fire.

Neither the old man nor any other visitor came to his fireside and the weeks passed in this idyllic routine, broken only by his twice-weekly visits to Drakova. During these visits he always held long, halting conversations with Nicolae the shopkeeper, although never once did he feel the need to mention his encounter with Va Rog.

April passed into May, and so came the time for Peter to leave Moldova. Early on his last morning in the camp, he was lying awake in his sleeping bag, reflecting on his experiences of the last few months, when he heard the sound of light, quick footsteps outside the tent.

Emerging into the half-light of morning, he met with a sight that almost made his heart stop beating. Completely surrounding his camp was a circle of wolves, all steadily, silently regarding him. Save for an occasional twitch of nose or ear, none of the creatures made any movement.

Peter was rooted to the spot. Seconds passed, then minutes. He'd almost recovered his senses sufficiently to wonder whether he should dive back into the tent when a grey wolf, much larger than the others and with a grizzled muzzle betraying its age, moved purposefully forward from the pack.

Stopping no more than a few yards away from him, it suddenly threw back its head and let out a long, blood-chilling howl. The sound seemed to touch directly on some primeval chord within Peter himself, and he was filled with a fear he'd never before dreamed could exist.

At last the sound ceased. The wolf did not leap to the expected attack. Instead, the gleaming yellow eyes looked deep into Peter's own. They seemed to hold him rigid. He couldn't move even an eyelid. Slowly, Peter came to see there was no malice in those eyes: something in their gleam spoke of fellowship. They were not the eyes of a monster, but of a fellow creature. And Peter knew where he had seen them before.

'Va Rog?'

The wolf gave a short, excited yelp, and then suddenly wheeled around and trotted off, swishing its tail from side to side as it ran. The rest of the pack quickly followed. Before long, the easy, loping strides of the animals had carried them far from Peter's sight.

Within minutes, everything was still once more. The countryside was as peaceful as ever. Nothing had changed, except something within Peter himself.

*

Catherine was there to meet him in Victoria Station, even though he'd arrived a full two hours later than the time he'd given in his letter. It was some time before she saw him coming towards her from the throng. He studied her face, as if seeing her for the first time. She was a fine looking woman. She always had been.

When at last she saw him, she smiled quickly and brightly. But Peter could see, too, the shadow of something else flicker across her face, an expression he'd seen before but failed to appreciate. He'd been unable to see before the splinter of ice that had long lain buried deep in his heart. Now it had melted in the Moldovan spring. It was as if Catherine was trying to read something in Peter's own face, straining to understand the thing within him that had never been quite comprehensible to her.

Peter knew what he must do. He ran towards her. He'd wasted enough time already.

Memento

'Are you sure this was a good idea, Claire? I mean, you couldn't say it's in the best of taste, could you?'

'No,' thought Claire. '*And neither could you say it was in good taste for him to keep me awake for night after night with that awful hacking cough of his. Every single gasp was down to those dreadful cigarettes. And what would he do when the coughing got too bad even for him? He'd get up from bed and light another one.*'

But to her friend Polly she answered: 'Luke would have seen the funny side of it. He had a sense of humour, if little else. Even if he did like nothing better than to laugh at his own jokes in that wheezy chuckle of his.'

'That's a bit harsh, Claire. You will be all right if I go now, won't you? It's just... it's just that I feel so uncomfortable with that thing sitting on the dining table.'

'You run along, Polly. I'll be absolutely fine. I'll be making my lunch in half-an-hour. Are you sure you wouldn't like to share some with me?'

'I'd rather go home. There are so many things to do.'

'*And we all know exactly what those things are,*' thought Claire, as she waved goodbye at the front door. '*You'll be rushing home to cook a meal for that Tony of yours. Always at his beck and call you are. And if it's not your husband you're running around for it's your son and daughter or your grandchildren. Why don't you show some independence for a change? Think for yourself, Polly, why don't you?*'

*

Unlike Polly, whose partnership had been rock solid, Claire hadn't had much luck. Malcolm had walked out after twenty-four years. He'd muttered something about being disappointed when their marriage had proven to be childless. Claire knew this wasn't the real reason.

For a while she'd suspected there was another woman on the scene. It was a dark time for her. Meeting Luke, only six months later, had helped the healing process. Now, after five years, he had gone in his turn. Claire had vowed to remain strong. She would not become a single version of Polly.

She was determined to show everyone she was made of sterner stuff. The role of the-little-woman-left-behind wasn't for her. Yes, Luke had also left her. His reason for going had been entirely different. As far as Claire knew, Malcolm was still living a healthy, if selfish, life in the next town. Luke had died.

Or perhaps Luke's reason hadn't been so very different after all. Malcolm had waltzed out of Claire's life as the result of his infatuation with a bimbo half his age; Luke had left her because of infatuations of his own. His weakness came in packets of twenty and with cork tips, rather than tight red dresses and surgically-enhanced breasts. Make no mistake: they were an obsession in exactly the same way.

The doctors had told Luke that if he didn't leave cigarettes alone they'd kill him. Well, he didn't leave them alone and they had killed him. He couldn't do without his fix. The doctors' predictions had come true even sooner than she'd thought they would.

Claire had begged Luke to stop smoking. She'd even booked him in to see a hypnotist. Of course, he'd refused to go. At least now the air at home was fresher, though only after she'd opened every window in the house for a week after Luke's death and scrubbed all the carpets to rid the place of the stink of stale tobacco.

Probably it was all this activity that had given Claire the idea of sealing some of Luke's ashes into his favourite ashtray. This would be the perfect memento of their marriage. It was meant to be nothing more than a small joke. It wasn't really revenge.

In reality what Luke had called 'his special ashtray' had started life in a grander way. It had been a lovely glass-and-porcelain dish Luke had bought for Claire's collection soon after their wedding day, only to almost immediately purloin it and pile it high with his disgusting cigarette butts.

Having the ashes sealed in with Perspex might have removed any cash-value the piece had but surely she'd earned the right to this much? Polly couldn't or wouldn't see the funny side of it.

Claire retreated into the kitchen and began noisily to prepare her solitary lunch. She found some odd jobs to do and the best part of an hour had passed before she returned to the dining-room. Her mood hadn't improved in this time.

Now, what was wrong with the ashtray? Somehow, it had moved to the other side of the table. She picked it up and almost dropped the object in fright as she looked into it. Instead of the random layers of Luke's earthly remains she was used to seeing, these were now arranged into a crude image of Luke's face.

Claire nearly cried out, but managed to suppress her instincts. She knew she had to be tough. After all, she'd been successful in business for thirty years. Nothing had surprised her more than falling for Luke in her maturity.

She gripped the ashtray more firmly and shook it vigorously, then banged it hard against the side of her chair. Sure enough, when she looked again, the ashes had re-arranged into a normal random scatter. With a sigh, she replaced the ashtray in its proper place on the dining-room table. She told herself this incident must have been due to the combination of chance factors and her own over-active imagination.

*

In the lounge, e-mails were the next thing on her agenda. She picked up her old tablet reluctantly. Luke had been the main user of computer technology and was always nagging her about buying an up-to-date model. What for? Claire was inexperienced in the intricacies of all the fancy stuff Luke used to demonstrate. In working life, her secretary had looked after everything of a technical nature.

She had half-a-dozen or more e-mails to answer. None could be dealt with briefly. Relatives and friends were still offering their electronic condolences. Also, there was one of those really annoying circulars from the utility people who wanted to make you their unpaid meter reader. Her fingers were aching and she'd been looking at the screen for too long by the time she came to the end of the task.

The last e-mail she opened was from Polly. This she must have sent as soon as she'd arrived home. It was typical. Why didn't she say what she had to say earlier, in person? Now she was trying to express regret that she'd not been able to stay for lunch and at the same time saying if there was ever anything she could do... Well, she could have stayed and kept Claire company with her lunch for starters.

Claire stared at the screen, trying to find words to express her disappointment without scaring the super-sensitive Polly away. She stared for a long time, although couldn't think of the right thing to say. With a grunt, she reached for the off-switch, even though she knew this quick manoeuvre would mean the next time she turned on the tablet, another of those hectoring messages about closing down correctly would appear. Or was that with the old-style computers Luke used to prefer? Her hands were shaking as she lay the machine down.

*

Remembering she had an unread magazine on the coffee table, she reached out to pick it up. But, as she was about to put her hand on its cover, she realised there was something else next to it. It was the ashtray. Why should it be in this room at all? She forced herself to look at it carefully. Staring back at her, she saw Luke's features. Now there was nothing rough or random about the arrangement of the ashes. And the corners of Luke's mouth were turned up into the beginnings of a mocking smile.

*

'Polly? Is that you?'

Her friend had taken a long time to answer. Polly hadn't even bothered to pick up the phone the first time she rang. Her husband Tony's newest piece of domestic gimmickry was one of those fancy handsets displaying the name of the caller and giving an individual ringtone. Claire would be on the machine's index. She was hurt by the thought that Polly had tried to ignore her call.

'I'm glad I managed to catch you. I wanted to ask - '

Polly launched into one of her little-wife monologues without letting Clare complete her sentence. Tony had done this and was going to do that. He'd been able to come home early and they'd shared a mushroom omelette for lunch. Claire thought she was going to scream. She interrupted Polly in full flow.

'It's only that I'm having computer trouble again. I wondered if you and Tony could call around and...'

Claire had thought hard about this excuse. She knew that nothing would be more likely to bring Polly and Tony around than the mention of technology. Tony was almost as much of a digital wizard as Luke had been. As far as she knew, there was nothing wrong with her tablet, other than old age. But she needed some company this afternoon. She really didn't want to be alone.

'Next week? I was hoping that... Perhaps Tony could pop around without you?'

Immediately, Claire realised her error. Polly would never let Tony call around without herself acting as chaperone.

'Oh well. See you soon, then.'

*

Claire knew she had to get out of the house.

It was a cool day for early summer, even though the air was pleasant. The sensation of the gentle breeze on her skin quickly restored some sense of perspective to her thoughts. She'd done the right thing to get out in the open. Now she felt her worries to be ridiculous. The ashtray had probably been in the lounge because she'd unthinkingly carried it there herself.

The murmur of the crowd about her was reassuring. Along the busy pavement at low level, flying high above the heads of everyone, an off-course butterfly followed its graceful urban pathway. The creature was one of those attractive ones with large circular markings on its wings – a Peacock didn't they call it? – rather than yet another of the plain white ones which were all you seemed to see these days. The ordinariness, the sheer peacefulness of the scene, made her relax for the first time that day.

'*Big Issue*! *Big Issue*!'

Claire found herself flinching away from this everyday sound. Analysing her own reaction, she realised she'd been more than half expecting the vendor to have the features of Luke. She made herself look directly at him, and with relief saw the worn, unfamiliar face was framed by a straggling red beard. She smiled.

'*Big Issue*, Madam?'

Buying anything on the street was strictly against her principles but she could hardly avoid getting a copy now, having raised the man's expectations. She dropped the coins into his outstretched palm, forced a smile, and took the proffered copy.

What was in it, anyway? With a shudder, she realised the pages had fallen open at an article entitled *How to Stop Smoking*. Illustrating this was a line drawing of an ashtray piled high with cigarette ends. The feature opened with the words '*Luke desperately wanted to call a halt to his habit.*'

*

Her evening meal that night, although elaborately prepared, was as tasteless as had been her lone lunch. Claire was trying to force herself to clear the plate when she saw the ashtray, now sitting almost companionably on the sideboard. How often had she been picking it up and moving it, without thinking?

The TV programmes on offer were dreary – mostly soaps, repeats, and documentaries lacking any focus. At midnight she found herself staring blankly at a programme of outtakes featuring "celebrities" she'd never before seen. Claire knew she should get herself off to bed. She could always read for half-an-hour. The remote control was by her hand and it was with pleasure she picked it up and turned off the screen.

The TV had been silent for a full ten minutes before she reluctantly raised herself from the easy chair. Claire felt foolish as she progressed from lounge to hallway, from hallway to staircase and from staircase to bedroom, each time first making elaborately sure all the lights were turned on and off as she went. In the hallway, she quickened her pace as she flipped off the last switch to leave the darkened room behind her.

Upstairs, she remembered the weekly refuse and had to reverse the process. Tonight was the night to put out the rubbish. This had become something of a fetish with her since her husband's death. Luke had always seen to things of that nature. Acting on impulse, Claire snatched up the ashtray and rammed it into the black bag. She tied the top of the bag in a tight knot and carried it to the end of the drive.

'There. Done. That's you finished, Luke.' She said these words under her breath but they gave her deep satisfaction.

*

Even so, she resolved to fall asleep with the book in her hand and the bedside light glaring brightly at her side. This wasn't a book she'd been enjoying: it was an autobiography of someone currently in the news whose teenage years seemed to go on interminably.

She yawned. What did she have to fear now?

Her sleep that night was better than it had been since Luke had died. Next morning, the clock told her it was still only five o'clock when she first opened her eyes. This didn't matter; she'd rested well. Then she glanced again at the bedside table. The ashtray was on it, too.

'OK Luke; shall we call it quits? As soon as I get up I'm going bury you in the garden. I'll put you down good and deep. Then I'll plant a rose bush over the top. What colour would you like?'

Red would be good, she thought. Or, hadn't Luke liked the deep yellow variety they'd looked at together in the garden centre? Contentedly musing on the relative merits of flower colours, Claire almost dozed off again.

*

The ashtray on the table beside her was illuminated by the first beam of full sunlight entering the room through a chink she'd left in the curtains. She looked across to the other side of the eiderdown and gradually made out Luke's face in the shadows. He seemed to be staring across at her from the pillow next to hers.

She blinked her eyes and shook her head. When she looked again, Claire clearly saw the outline of his mouth, now shaped into a wide smile. The lips were mocking her; letting her know she wasn't nearly as strong as she pretended. The smile was telling her she was missing him more than she wanted to admit.

Then, from the vicinity of the ashtray behind her, she heard a wheezy laugh.

Before the Kettle Boils

1

Two years ago, I changed my life. Now, after Llanwonno, I need to change it again.

Two years ago it was through my own choice, although I couldn't now say exactly what brought this about. Should I say it was my grandmother's death? Was it the fact that life in London was slowly grinding me down?

Many people, I know, endure similar lifestyles, and for far longer than I managed to do it. The early rising and scurrying from my tiny flat simply to grab a few square feet on a crowded tube train, the acquaintances with whom I shared a few hurried drinks or a rushed, overpriced meal and the constant edginess of life in general are things I remember all too well. Together, they made the background music to one's whole existence.

Most people I knew in the business world would smile or laugh a lot when in reality all the time they were itching for the chance to boast about how much better than you they were doing in the material world. If they weren't doing that they were trying to say how much cleverer they were than you because they'd read this or that book, seen this or that stage play.

It would be wrong of me to try to pretend I had no real friends in London. I had many and even now miss their company. In one of the few concessions to their Welsh backgrounds, my parents had named me Morgan. This would have been fine but my family name was also Morgan.

In 2014, the year of the centenary of Dylan Thomas, his 'play for voices', *Under Milk Wood*, briefly found fame again, even in London. One of my friends gave me the mocking epithet of 'Organ Organ' in honour of one of the poet's characters. This was quickly shortened to 'Organ', and there it firmly stuck. Everyone outside of work, even some of my colleagues, knew me by this name. They weren't teasing me about anything to do with music, either. It was anatomy they were jesting about. Still, most of my relationships in the city were the grimmer ones associated with the workaday world.

In fact, according to the standards by which my work colleagues measured everything in life, I was doing well enough. I hadn't yet been out of university for four years and knew the days of a six-figure salary wouldn't be too far into the future for me. The fact that I had to work – or at least to be present in the office for long hours and oblige at constant social (antisocial, more like) functions for this privilege – was a simple hazard of the job, so those "in the know" kept telling me.

My new life didn't come about because of any carefully thought through decision or sudden attack of patriotism on my part. It happened very suddenly after a chance conversation. You could say everything started to happen when, on what was then only my second visit to Wales, I was staring idly into the fireplace in my dead grandmother's home.

*

Without at that time thinking about it too deeply or being especially troubled about the fact, I was conscious of finding myself in a different world from the one I was used to when I took my place with the others in my grandmother's lounge in Llwyncelyn. At least, that's what the room had been less than a fortnight before. If you don't know it, this is a small village just to the eastern side of Porth. My London friends would never have been able to pronounce or spell the name of Llwyncelyn, let alone have heard of the place.

Most of them wouldn't even have known where the town of Porth is. You'll find it where the two Rhondda Valleys, Fawr and Fach, meet. "The Rhondda" is one of those areas of which most have vaguely heard, even though few would be able to point to its location on a map with any accuracy, let alone realise there are in fact both large and small valleys.

Both of my parents were dead by this time. I'm sorry to have to admit that it was with portentous gravity I announced to the few relatives and numerous neighbours present that the reason I'd come to Llwyncelyn was from what I took delight in describing as "family duty". I was an only child and my father had been his mother's only child. Unless, that is, you counted, which no-one else did, his elder brother, my Uncle Geraint. This worthy had emigrated to Canada when I was less than two years old. He hadn't told a soul of his plans.

After his sudden flight overseas, the wayward brother had never been heard of again, by the wife and young daughter he left in his wake, by my father or by anyone else. All the grey heads smiled and nodded approvingly when I repeated my carefully-prepared speech. You could see all of them were thinking *'thank goodness there's someone in this family who's aware of his obligations'*.

The real reason I was in the small room with so many people I didn't know and with whom at that time I had little in common was somewhat different. When I heard my grandmother had died, I was unable to purge myself of the newly-descended memory of my one and only previous visit to Llwyncelyn, seventeen years before.

The vague idea that it might even be pleasant to repeat the experience grew within me until I decided, at the last moment, to catch the train to Cardiff and from there another northwards to Porth.

Standing in front of the vigorously stoked-up fire I was coming to realise exactly what a vainglorious thought this had been. My sole previous visit was when I was only eight years old. At that time I was a naïve and, although I say it myself, engaging child. My father and mother were with me and took delight in showing me off to their old friends during the week we spent in Llwyncelyn.

Now, my parents weren't present in the room with the slick metrocentric I'd been trying to become in the intervening years. More importantly on this occasion, my grandmother, whom I remembered as a neat, breathlessly enchanting woman, wasn't here either.

Her funeral was in late April, during the same season it had been on the occasion of my childhood visit. The first thing that struck me when I entered the house, as it had on my first time in Wales, was the huge banked fire roaring in the grate, despite the mildness of the day. In my childhood the fire I remembered had been in what they puzzlingly called "the back kitchen". This one was in what everyone called "the front parlour". It was the room my grandmother had preserved, almost as some kind of shrine. No one had been permitted to enter this exalted place during my earlier visit, except my grandmother herself.

My parents informed me she only did this one morning a week for cleaning purposes, though I could not reason how it could ever have become dirty if it remained unused. Certainly I, as an eight year old, was allowed nowhere near this "best room". Still, for the time I stood before its magical glow as an adult, the fire was the same one I'd stared into years before.

'You'll get dry eyes, staring into the flames like that.' This was my only cousin, Hedd, daughter of the feckless Geraint. Hedd was a cheery girl, only a year older than me. For some reason she hadn't been here on the occasion of my first visit to Llwyncelyn and I'd only that day met her. Still, already I liked her vivacious company.

'It's all central heating where I live. We only see open fires in those olde worlde pubs where they charge five or six quid for a pint of lager.'

Hedd laughed.

'You'd be unlucky to pay much more than two pounds here.'

'Where do you live, Hedd?'

'Oh, I rent a flat in Taff's Well, not far north of Cardiff. It's a bit more expensive than around here, but that's life I suppose. We were hoping to get a place near to where we work, in Whitchurch when Stu and I set up together next month, but it'd be too pricey for us. Looks like we'll have to get used to living up here in the valley for a few more years now. Mamgu left this house to me.'

She looked at me questioningly, as if I might challenge her right to this inheritance. As if I would! No doubt Hedd had performed numerous services for our grandmother over the years to earn her privilege; all I'd ever done was spend a week in her company as a child.

'Why don't you sell this house and put the proceeds as a deposit on one in Whitchurch?'

Hedd laughed again, although this time with less mirth.

'Stu and I have done the sums. We'd be lucky to raise ninety thousand for a house like this. The place we've got our eye on in Whitchurch is priced at three times that. We've worked it out that we'd need to put a deposit down of at least £140,000 if we were to have any chance of meeting the mortgage payments, even if we could borrow enough.'

She paused and looked down at the floor, a little sadly. Suddenly she decided to share her innermost wishes with me.

'No; it'll be Llwyncelyn and a daily commute to Whitchurch for us for a few years yet. We did think of getting somewhere in Taff's Well as a sort of stepping stone but that might make it all too complicated. We might never move from there. So, we've decided to go for it. We'll just have to be patient for a bit longer.'

'I see,' I said. I didn't really see at all. I'd had many similar conversations with London friends, although always with larger property price figures in them. My eyes had always glazed over. Now my determination never to set foot on what they charmingly referred to as the "property ladder" had once again been reinforced.

'Well.' She smiled. 'I'd better go and have a word with Mamgu's friend, Mrs Siân Price, from Ynyshir. She was very close to Mamgu. They did help each other a lot when they lost their husbands. First our grandfather Sior and then Siân's Bleddyn. Would you like me to introduce you to her?'

'No, thanks,' I said. I had visions of having to repeat my "family duty" speech. I'd had enough of it.

'Well, the poor old thing is missing Mamgu terribly. Excuse me for a moment.'

I watched Hedd as she walked over to one of the elderly women in the room. She, a bright looking lady, smiled cheerfully, if wistfully, when she saw me looking in her direction. Perhaps I'd spoken too quickly and she'd have been more interesting to talk to than I'd blithely assumed. Odd as it might be to say about someone I hadn't seen for so many years and couldn't really claim as a major part of my childhood. I was missing my grandmother at this moment, too. I missed her more than I'd ever done in life.

*

'You'll dry your eyes out, looking into that fire,' had also been my grandmother's words to me on my childhood visit to Llwyncelyn. It had been the first thing she said directly to me after the ritual greetings and hugs from people I'd considered to be strangers.

As soon as we'd been ushered into the "back kitchen", the fire had exercised a fascination over me as an eight-year-old. It was hard to wrench my eyes from the sight of the gentle spirals of flame, so it seemed of every possible colour and of a few impossible ones. I was bewitched by the sight of the hollows and caverns, beyond which surely dwelt who knew what dragons and other fantastic beasts.

Most mysterious of all was their setting of shiny black lumps. I'd been told, although couldn't reason why, that every day my grandfather had burrowed into the earth to retrieve black lumps like these, armed only with a lamp and what were mysteriously called his "butties". In some mysterious way the lumps had blackened his face and in the end they'd killed him. At that tender age I believed every word I'd been told, although I didn't wholly understand what they meant.

'You know,' my grandmother had whispered. 'Nearly three hundred years ago a very famous man used to live on a farm close to this village. His name was Gruffudd Morgan in English; some sort of ancestor of your grandfather Sior, he was. Very proud was your grandfather to be from the old farming stock. Most families in the Rhondda didn't come until much later, when the valleys were opened up to the coal. Fat lot of good it did Sior, mind. He went underground like the rest of them. Killed him it did, when he was still a young man.'

I feared that my grandmother was going to go off into a long personal reminiscence. My father had warned me I was bound to hear many of these. He'd told me to always be polite and listen attentively. But no, she continued with the story of Gruffudd Morgan. She had my full attention.

'Guto Nyth Brân they called him. This means "Gruffudd Crow's Nest" in English. He was the finest athlete there's ever been, they say. Young Guto could run to Pontypridd and back before his mother had boiled the kettle. They used to heat kettles on fires like this, only bigger, in the old days. Back then, they burned wood, not coal. The coal was still under the ground. They should have left it there.'

I had no idea where Pontypridd was. My grandmother made it sound like it was on the other side of the world. The idea crossed my mind of asking my grandmother to take her whistling kettle down from the gas stove. If she did that, I'd be able to see how long it took to boil a kettle on the fire. In those days, I was a shy boy and didn't dare to do it. Still, it surely couldn't have taken so very long. Was this Guto some sort of magician?

Over the ensuing week my grandmother told me more about Guto's achievements. His father, a shepherd on a nearby farm, was the first to notice his talents. One day the young man ran after a hare, caught up with the creature and seized it with his bare hands. Soon he was regularly catching birds, hares and other small animals. In those poor days trophies like these were welcome additions to the cooking pot.

He could outrun the fastest horse, so they said. Several times he caught the foxes that troubled his father's sheep. On one famous occasion, he even chased away a large grey wolf. Until that day, everyone believed the last wolf in Wales had been seen in Coed Bleiddiaid – Wolves' Wood – many years before. Nor were his achievements limited to the countryside about him. One remarkable deed was that, at night, he could blow on a candle and then hop into bed before the flame went out. This only reaffirmed my belief that he really must have been a wizard, rather than an athlete.

Every morning, so I was told, he would run to Llanwonno, "high on the mountain above this valley" as my grandmother described it with a backward tilt of her head. I had no idea where this was, either, but was told it was no fewer than seven miles each way. To me, at that age, this seemed an extraordinary distance.

Soon he started to take part in prize contests against other men in places like Mountain Ash and Hirwaun Common. The very names sounded impossibly romantic to me. His last race, when he was only thirty or so, was from Newport to Bedwas. It was against someone with the exotic name of "The Prince of Bedwas". With a last-minute sprint, he claimed the prize of one thousand guineas, an enormous sum in those far-off days. It still sounded huge to me at the age of eight.

However, after the race someone slapped him on the back in congratulations for his win and he collapsed and died.

He was buried, so my grandmother told me, in Llanwonno. This was said to be his favourite place in the whole of Wales.

Apart from the ending of this last, these stories all held immense appeal for me, although the one I liked best was the first I heard, that of running to Pontypridd and back before the kettle had boiled. My grandmother must have had a special liking for this one too; at least she delighted in repeating it as often as I dared to ask. This was at least three times a day.

Our week came to an end and before long we were heading back to Surrey. At school, I threw myself into the trials of competitive education at the urging of my parents, devoting all my attention to the quest for a "good" school in later years. Before very much more time had passed, all my effort was directed towards finding a place at what was called a desirable university, then the next target was building a strong career.

All thoughts of Guto Nyth Brân and my grandmother's stories about him were submerged by these demands. But they were never quite forgotten.

*

At the funeral, whilst gazing into a fire in my grandmother's house and thinking about the stories I'd heard about Guto Nyth Brân as a child, I made the decision to change my life. I say 'made the decision' but in reality it was nothing so deliberate or conscious. Such are the brief moments upon which a life turns. When Hedd came back to my side I announced, apropos of nothing:

'I'll buy this house from you for a hundred and fifty.'

'A hundred and fifty *thousand?*' She was startled and looked at me incredulously.

'Of course I mean a hundred and fifty thousand pounds. Do you think I'm some kind of joker?'

'No; I couldn't allow it. You could get bigger houses in Llwyncelyn for far less. There's a nice one a few doors up going for seventy-five.'

Now it was my turn to laugh.

'Not much of a salesman, are you? Those other houses wouldn't be *this* house. They wouldn't be our grandmother's house.'

'You're mad. Give me a hundred and twenty, then.'

'A hundred and fifty thousand. That's my final offer. Take it or leave it.'

'You'll never get a mortgage for that much.'

'Who said anything about a mortgage? I'm going to pay you cash.'

And this led to me living in Llwyncelyn.

2

The locals were friendly. The fact that everyone – not only those who'd attended my grandmother's funeral – seemed to know everything about my family connections helped a lot. Life became very simple. Soon I started to run again, something I hadn't had time to do since my university days. At first I didn't try anything more ambitious than gentle jogging but, before many weeks had passed, I found myself maintaining a respectable pace.

My favourite route was the long one from Llwyncelyn to Llanwonno and back. This could involve road running as far as Stanleytown and then up to Llanwonno via sheep paths and worn tracks. This route was perfectly OK, if I left early enough in the morning before the streets became busier. Or, if I chose, it was easy to find my way to the mountain behind Stanleytown, using the low hill tracks. Either way, the path was wonderfully varied.

There might have been not much to Llanwonno beyond an inn called the Brynffynon Hotel and St Gwynno's Church but, early in the morning before the walkers started to arrive, it had a peaceful quality of its own. When the tip above Tylorstown came prominently into view about halfway through the outward leg, my heart always lifted. I couldn't help but feel I was about to enter another world.

The route itself was blessed with these perfect charms but my knowledge that this had also been Guto's favourite morning outing added a special dimension. Moreover, it wasn't long before I came to notice that the one-way distance was the same as that of the now-urban route to Pontypridd and back. The houses and scars of industry, somehow more prominent than they were near my new home, made this prospect less prepossessing in the twenty-first century than it would have been in Guto's time.

On my very first day when I reached Llanwonno I was thrilled to discover the tomb of Guto in St Gwynno's churchyard. It was wonderful to have this tangible confirmation of what my grandmother had told me. If only she were still here so I could share my discovery with her.

Mind you, if she were still among us, I wouldn't have found anything myself. I started to think of it as a private memorial to my grandmother as well as a public one to the man from the eighteenth century who was fast becoming the cornerstone of my life.

On the very next morning after discovering the stone I saw a flock – I think the fancy name is 'murder' – of crows cawing down from trees near the Brynffynon Hotel. I'd been told that the name of "Nyth Brân" had come from Guto's parents' farm but now doubted if this were true. In his time the trees I saw wouldn't have been fir trees. Surely the native deciduous trees would have provided better homes for crows' nests?

Not all of my running was made to Llanwonno. The route I used more often than any other was the comparatively short distance – only a mile-and-a-half each way – by road to nearby Ynyshir.

After I'd been living in Llwyncelyn for two months I had the fancy of putting a kettle on the gas stove in my kitchen as I left the house and seeing if I could make it back before it had started to boil. Naturally enough, I suppose, the kettle I thought of was the one I'd seen in my grandmother's house as a child, but there didn't seem to be one in the kitchen. I hadn't brought one with me from London, since I never drank tea or coffee, so had to buy a new utilitarian one especially for this purpose.

I was always disappointed to find the water had been bubbling merrily for some while by the time I returned home.

3

My time trials started to become something of an obsession with me; I have to admit this. Even the longer distance to Llanwonno gave me less pleasure than it should because of my anxiety to cover it at a fast pace. One morning, after a fruitless fortnight of racing against the steaming kettle, I sprained my ankle at the farthest point of the shorter run, in Ynyshir itself.

I knew the joint wasn't seriously hurt but I was still relieved to limp into the general store run by 'Siân the Shop' in the middle of the village. People told me hers was one of the last of the old style shops in the Rhondda Fach, operated independently by its owner.

Siân Price was an elderly, pleasant woman. I'd first seen her at my grandmother's funeral some months before. I hadn't spoken to her then but she'd been very friendly when we'd chatted a few weeks ago. She'd been happy to listen to all my tales of Guto. It was only afterwards I came to realise she must have discussed them all with her friend, my grandmother, perhaps many times.

On this morning, since my time was shot to pieces by my tumble anyway, I thought I might as well buy a loaf of bread while I was here to save going out again to the local mini-supermarket later. Anyway, I knew I needed the short rest and I looked forward to talking again to this interesting woman.

'Why, Mr Morgan, it's good to see you again. You've got your running gear on this time. Very dashing, I must say.'

Was the old lady teasing me, with her "*dashing*"? But her smile of welcome was entirely genuine. She was probably simply paying me a compliment and had chosen the wrong word. Besides, she couldn't have known about my accident.

'It's just "Morgan" if you wouldn't mind, Mrs Price.' At least she hadn't called me "Organ" like my London friends. 'Otherwise I'll have to start calling you "Mrs Price the Rice", won't I? Would you mind if I called you "Siân"? That'd keep it simple for us.'

Her eyes widened. Had I overstepped the mark with my clumsy jest? Fortunately, her features soon creased into a smile.

'You cheeky devil. You're exactly like your grandfather when he was a boy. Anyway, how are you today – Morgan?'

'Well, I can see you're fine yourself, Siân. I am, too, really, but like a clown I tripped over the kerb back there and hurt my ankle.'

'Would you like me to take a look?'

'No need at all. Thanks for offering, but it will be OK after a few hours' rest at home.'

She looked at me as if she couldn't quite bring herself to believe what I was saying when I said I was fine. I had been pushing myself extra hard on this particular morning and was now clumsily trying to mop my brow with the back end of my tee-shirt.

'Here, use this,' she said, passing me a clean white rag she pulled from under the counter. 'You make sure you don't overdo it, my boy. I know you want to make the most of your leisure time before you start that job in Cardiff, but still. You have to think of what's good for you.'

'What job in Cardiff?' I was genuinely surprised.

Now it was Siân's turn to be puzzled.

'Well, they're all saying it won't be long before you start working in Cardiff, doing the same sort of thing you did in London. Most of them are saying this, anyway. There are some who are saying… something else.'

'What else? What do you mean?'

She looked guiltily down at the counter.

'I've said too much again. Ignore me.'

'Come on, Siân. You can't leave me up in the air.'

'I'm not saying any names, mind.' She looked me in the eye. 'There are a few of them who say you made so much money in London that you don't need to work ever again.'

I laughed out loud, startling her.

'Neither thing is true! There's no job in Cardiff lined up for me and I certainly don't have pots of money. Very soon I'll have to start looking for a job.'

She looked at me doubtfully. She, like everyone else, must have heard I paid cash to Hedd for my house.

'Well, it's a fact you won't find anything to suit you around here. You'll have to go to Cardiff to find something in your line.'

'Exactly in my line, Siân, would be a job around here. Anything would do, as long as it helps me to keep body and soul together. Do you know of something like that?'

She looked at me again, hesitant to answer. Then, reluctantly, she spoke again.

'Well... I hardly like to mention it, but I've been thinking of getting someone in to help me. It's all been getting a bit much for me lately. Having someone in the shop would be good for the people around here, too. Otherwise, I'd have to shut up the business or at least shorten my opening hours. Perhaps it would do you for a week or two, just until you find something to suit you better?'

'Working here sounds like it would suit me perfectly. What did you have in mind?'

It didn't take us long to come to an arrangement. I'd start next morning at seven o'clock and would be here until six in the evening. My wage, although parsimonious, wouldn't be as low as I'd feared. Even my ankle was throbbing far less by the time we'd finished our discussion.

I couldn't think of my progress home as being even a semi-hobble. I actually ran, albeit at a slower pace than usual. But, when I stepped inside, my kitchen was full of steam. Worse, the dribble of water left in the kettle was seeping out through the overheated base.

After only a fortnight of a life spent not for the purpose for which it had been designed, my eccentric timing device was dead.

Still, I reasoned as I opened the back door to let out the steam, life wasn't so bad. I would now be a real member of the Llwyncelyn community with a proper job, one that would suit me down to the ground.

The truth was I'd left my job-hunting a bit late. By this time, I had only a tiny amount of cash to my name. Although my earnings in London had been good I'd always spent freely, too. Most of my savings had been used up buying this house. I didn't have much left over for "improving my property". Not that I had the slightest wish to alter my grandmother's home.

Everyone, certainly including my old business acquaintances in London, would have said I'd paid far too much to Hedd to become its owner. Still, when I thought of her happy face when my cousin realised she'd after all be able to afford her dream house in Whitchurch, it didn't seem that way to me.

*

'You're an early bird this morning, young Morgan. I see you've got your running gear on. You're sweating a bit hard, mind. Not the way to impress the girls, you know.'

For a moment, it seemed as if Siân were taking her turn to tease me. I studied her features. No, she was simply pleased to see me. And I was certainly sweating.

'I like to be early for everything. Especially on the first day in my new job; I've got to show the boss I'm willing, haven't I?'

'It'll be no use you trying to make an impression on the boss. No promotion for you here, my lad.' She looked happy to be saying this, and more so at my calm acceptance of what she said. 'Anyway, it's not even twenty to seven yet. We've got plenty of time for a cup of tea before we open the shop.'

'No tea for me. I only drink beer or wine. Or water. Water will do.'

She wrinkled her nose.

'No tea? Everybody drinks tea. If you drink beer or those sorts of things you might as well sup with the Devil. You'll find no wicked things of that nature in my house or my shop. Plenty of water in the tap for you. You look like you could do with some on your face, too. You've been running too hard for your own good again, by the looks of things. Through here you'll find the sink.'

She pushed the back door of the shop open and soon we were both standing in the tiny kitchen. She looked on approvingly as I went through my ablutions. For a moment I couldn't help feeling she was going to urge me to wash behind my ears. Fortunately, she didn't.

'I've brought proper working clothes to change in this rucksack. I hope you don't mind if…'

'Through there,' she said. 'You can change in my front kitchen every morning and evening. You don't think I'd let you serve my customers dressed in those shorts, do you? This is a respectable shop. No, you can leave your working clothes here every day. I'll be pleased to give them a rinse through at the end of the week.'

'But I'd prefer to…'

'I won't hear of it. Now, get yourself along. We haven't got all morning. I want a cup of tea before opening time, even if you don't.'

Obediently, I did as I was told. It might not be so diplomatic to mention my desire to change my running gear more frequently than once in a six-day working week. This could wait until later. So, here I was standing in the mysterious front kitchen, then. With its table, chairs and a single rocking chair, it seemed to serve the function of a dining-room and a lounge as well. There was even a small television set and a larger radiogram, as they used to call them years ago, in one corner.

Set in the back wall was yet another door. Perhaps behind this lay that holy of holies, the "front parlour". This would be the never-used "best room", exactly like that of my grandmother. I did not dare to ask. It was a funny thing that, although I'd now owned the house in Llwyncelyn for a few months, I never felt comfortable in what had been my grandmother's "best room".

As I emerged into the back kitchen, Siân's kettle was beginning to sing on the stove.

'Gosh, that kettle takes me back. It's exactly like my grandmother's old one.'

'You can't have it. Your cousin Hedd took the new electric one belonging to your grandmother. You'll have to go to Whitchurch for it.'

'No, no. It's all right, really.' I chuckled at the thought of knocking on Hedd's front door and demanding she hand over her kettle. 'I didn't mean that. It's only that this kettle looks so much like the one I remember from the time I was eight years old. It's even got the same brown stains on the front. They'd be from the gas ring, I suppose.'

Siân looked wistful.

'This kettle is the one that used to belong to Angharad until five years ago. I bought a new one – a fancy electric one, mind – for her birthday. Angharad was my good friend. So was Sior, before he was taken from us at such a young age.

They'd both be pleased to know I'm keeping an eye on their grandson. Loved that electric thing she did but I always preferred a proper one like this, with a whistle. This kettle was newer than my old one, so she gave it to me. I've still got my old one somewhere, if you'd like it.'

'No thanks. I'd have no real use for it.' For a moment I thought it could replace my ruined one but my running arrangements would now have to change. I had a job.

Just at that moment the whistle began to shrill.

'Siân, that sound has given me an idea.'

'Full of ideas you are. Most of them are a bit daft.'

'No, really. How would you like me to make you a cup of tea every morning?'

She put her hands on her hips.

'Do you think I can't make a cup of tea for myself now? I'm not that far past it, not yet at least.'

'It'd be a kind of exchange. Every morning, the moment I'm leaving the house, I'd ring you and ask you to put the kettle on; not a moment before or after, please. Then I'd run to your shop and try to get here before the kettle boils.'

She looked puzzled.

'Why should you want to do that? Why don't you use one of those stopwatch things?'

'It's one of my daft ideas. Will you do it please, Siân?'

'Of course I will, you daft hap'orth.'

4

The next two years flew by. I was readily accepted by the regular customers and Siân turned out to be even sparkier than I thought she'd be. Before long, a real affection grew up between us. I was sure this wasn't purely because I was her old friend's grandson.

The six day working week didn't leave me with too much time for running but I never missed a morning's 'time trial' or the evening's home run. Every Sunday I took the longer trail to Llanwonno, normally using the road route but sometimes choosing the unofficial low mountain tracks to reach the steep ascent behind Stanleytown.

My Sunday mornings began well before it was light through most of the year. This was the special time for me, even though the run itself, especially on the incline, was physically demanding.

After my first year Siân began to happily assume I'd take over the running of the shop in the near future. She started to talk seriously about getting someone in to help me for our only busy hour or two on Fridays and Saturdays. I'm sure she nursed vague dreams of seeing herself spending her last days, or years, in her 'front kitchen', feet up, while the tiny profits from the shop rolled in. She rarely read and didn't care to knit so quite how she'd spend her time wasn't clear to me. I'm sure a life of idleness wouldn't be for her, either.

This didn't matter much in practice because she kept on postponing the date of her retirement. The 'in a few months' time' she spoke of were always somewhere over the horizon. The truth was, I think, that she enjoyed the gentle rhythms of shop life too much to want to put them behind her.

She insisted she was the one who'd taught me to make "a lovely cup of tea" and, at intervals through the day, I took to despatching her into the "front kitchen" with one of my brews, together with instructions to put her feet up for at least half-an-hour. Often she would doze off for a full hour or even more.

On one occasion, much to a regret accompanied by profuse apologies, she slept for a solid two hours.

The only fly in the ointment for me was the lack of any real progress with my running. At first the kettle was already whistling away merrily when I made it to the shop. Then I arrived at the moment it started to boil, to Siân's applause and encouraging noises.

Finally, I managed to arrive even before this happened. But I could always tell from its impatient spluttering that the kettle wasn't so far off the boil; if I tried it I'd never be able to have run anything the mile-and-a-half home before it began whistling in triumph.

Siân's happy greeting and congratulations soon made way for a more discouraging repertoire: '*I don't know why you bother*', '*you'll be making yourself ill*' and '*it's only an old story*' were her words of greeting to me on most mornings. What I really dreaded to hear was '*you'll be running yourself into an early grave like that*'.

5

This morning, the Sunday before Midsummer's Day, I was due to run the longer distance to Llanwonno. Although Guto's favourite run was now itself becoming hard going for me, I was starting to see Sundays as something of a relief from the grim slog my dashes to Ynyshir had become. Not that I took it easy on the way to Llanwonno, you understand, even on the final ascent. I frequently looked at my watch and was always anxious to achieve a good time.

These June mornings were always my favourite time of year. Setting out very early, I'd be sure to reach the top before the weekend walkers began to crowd the place. The streets in the valley were always deserted at this time and I knew I wouldn't have to think of taking the mountain track route as far as Stanleytown. At this early hour the June light took on an incredible, fresh yellowish quality. I felt I was running toward a world that belonged to me and no other.

Ynyshir was my first important marker. I was happy to see my wristwatch was telling me I was making good time as I passed the village road sign, even though my legs were starting to ache earlier than usual. Siân's shop was firmly locked and shuttered as I loped past.

Fondly, I thought of her still asleep upstairs. Chapel wouldn't be calling her for a few hours yet – she prided herself in attending whatever the weather and her state of health. I thought warmly of her sleeping softly. No-one deserved their Sunday rest more. I saw not a soul in the streets of Pontygwaith or Wattstown, their streets and houses spreading up the mountain peacefully. This was the way I liked the first part of my Sundays to be.

As my more arduous ascent began on the sheep paths above Stanleytown, I was dismayed to become aware of a knotting of my calf muscles. This could be a prelude to a painful cramp, something from which I didn't suffer to begin with but now had to watch for. I tried to ignore the discomfort. Thankfully, it didn't get any worse.

But, as I passed Cefn-Llechau-Uchaf and Ty Mynydd farms, my chest began to feel tight and my limbs were moving far less smoothly. These were sensations new in their intensity. Again, I tried to ignore the worst effects of these. I knew the forestry tracks I always saw as a kind of gateway to Llanwonno weren't too far ahead. These would take me to my goal – to its halfway point at least.

It seemed to take forever to reach the final track. My chest was becoming tighter and my breathing felt laboured in the extreme. Suddenly, I became aware that another athlete was running alongside me. He was matching me stride for stride. His movements, in contrast to my own, were natural and lithe.

'Good morning to you,' he said.

I wasn't used to company at this hour and particularly didn't welcome it during my struggles of this morning.

'H-' was all I could manage to splutter out. I tried to look toward my unwanted companion but found I was quite unable to turn my head.

'You need to relax your body more. Find your natural pace. Don't push yourself so much all the time. You need to keep something in reserve.'

Who did he think he was? My coach? But, involuntarily I slowed and lengthened my stride a fraction.

'I'm trying... to... Guto –' I managed to gasp out. I wasn't sure why I was sharing my thoughts with this stranger.

'You don't want to take too much notice of all those old stories.' His breathing was as easy and regular as if he'd been talking to me across the bar in the pub. 'Things get changed and exaggerated over time. The last wolf in Wales was shot hundreds of years ago, well before I was born. As for that tale about being able to jump into bed before the candle flame blew out…' He laughed easily. 'Nobody could do that. It's a fairy story.'

Now I was angry with him, but couldn't get my words of protest out.

'Kettle…' was all I did splutter.

'Ah, but the kettles in my day were huge pots; not like the little things you have now. You'd probably be able to run to Pontypridd and back yourself before one of our kettles boiled. You're a good runner. If you were more sensible about it, you would be, anyway. Go with your body; don't work against it.'

These were the last words I heard from my companion. He sprinted past me; or at least I felt a light touch of wind on my cheek and thought for a moment I saw a change in the light on the path ahead of me.

Then there was nothing to be seen. I found I could now move my head easily and looked up and down the track. There was definitely no-one in sight. I was alone with the light of the morning once again. With a lengthening stride, soon I found myself running easily.

Before long I was passing the Brynffynon Inn. St Gwynno's Church was just ahead of me. Now I was moving entirely comfortably. It seemed I was almost flying over the forest track, although I thought it would be sensible to take a minute's rest at the halfway point of my run in view of my earlier scare. Reaching the church, the sight of Guto's headstone was a reassuring sight.

'No,' I thought. '*I'm going to take more than a minute to rest here if that's I want to do.*'

The peace and stillness of the morning, the happy solitude I was feeling, the branches of the fir trees being gently lifted by the light breeze passing through them, all made me want to almost shout my words, although there was no-one within miles to hear me.

'I'm going to enjoy my running from now on! Never mind all this kettle nonsense!'

'Yes,' came the answer from the empty churchyard. 'You enjoy your running.'

A spiral of dust swirled around Guto's headstone. Then everything became still.

Clairvoyant

Clairvoyant n. a person claiming to be able to
predict the future or communicate with the dead.

That's the dictionary definition, as given in the *Compact Oxford Dictionary*, no less. I had to look it up to see if I could better understand what's happened. I don't know anything about 'communicating with the dead'.

Still, I have to try to write this... well, *confessional* I'd have to call it... to say I've had to change my mind from what I once believed. There are definitely people out there who are able to predict the future. I met one, late last year. And now I can do it myself.

Some people think of clairvoyance as a gift. Not me. I know it's the exact opposite. It's a curse. In my case, traditionally enough, you could say it was a gypsy's curse.

*

Endish-by-sea – I couldn't believe it when I saw the name – is one of those British seaside resorts that perhaps might have seen better days in the 'fifties and 'sixties, before the opportunities for cheap foreign alternatives came along. But it was hard to imagine any such golden era in the case of Endish.

And I had to spend a night there last October. My car broke down on the country road. While the unreliable machine – OK, so it had seen better days – was in the local garage being repaired I found myself wandering around something grandly called "The Endish Autumn Carnival".

After half-an-hour of such delights as "pin the tail on the donkey", "fish for a prize", and "the Endish darts' super-challenge", I suppose I ought to forgive myself for allowing my eye to be caught by the colourful sign outside a tent even grubbier than its canvas neighbours: "*Let Gypsy Rose Tell Your Fortune. Rose is a Genuine Clairvoyant. Only £10 per reading.*"

From my childhood, I could remember my parents talking about someone called "Gypsy Rose Lee" – some singer or stripper or something – but I suppose it was the word "genuine" that persuaded me to lift the dirty tent flap. "Genuine" and "clairvoyant" seemed to be contradictions in terms. Probably it was this that made me overcome my reluctance to shell out the inflated fee.

*

Actually, I didn't part with £10. The first thing I saw inside the tent was a discoloured brass bowl on a small table. It held a few forlorn-looking £10 notes. There was no sign. *"Throw your money away in here"* would have been perfect, I remember thinking.

I calculated that Gypsy Rose, who was seated in semi-darkness at the back of the tent, wouldn't be able to see what I was doing, so dropped in a £5 note and advanced upon her. For a moment I even thought of taking £10 out of the bowl. That might have been pushing things a bit too far.

No wonder she'd chosen to hide away in the shadows. She was ferociously ugly. More than anything else she resembled a giant frog. Unless, perhaps, it was a giant toad. I would have made a bet with myself she'd have warts all over her body but the last thing I wanted to do was call this bet in. She had a prominent moustache. My eyes kept being drawn to this luxuriant growth, especially during the latter part of our interview when she became agitated and a thin film of sweat formed on her upper lip.

Her thin red hair straggled about her drooping shoulders and she wore nothing more exotic than a faded green overall. As I noticed the red hair I realised what was most unsettling about this woman.

It wasn't the bulging eyes or general lack of feminine, or even human, appeal. After all, she was supposed to be a clairvoyant gypsy, not a Carnival Queen. No, there was something missing: how could she claim to be a gypsy without some sort of scarf on her head? I nearly left the tent then and there; now I regret I didn't.

'Have you finished staring, young man?'

Young man: I was in the last few months of my thirties. I'd have put her at a decade or more older. Something about the way she spat out that "*young man*" made me realise I'd done precious little with my dull, very ordinary, life. I felt sure she knew this. I tried to ignore my thought, though I'd have to admit to being chastened.

'That's better,' she said, allowing herself something approximating a smile. 'Now, sit down and make yourself comfortable. I'm going to tell you about your future.'

I'll say this for her: she may not have had a gypsy scarf but she had all the other props. The opaque glass globe upon which she fixed her bulbous grey eyes was perfect. It was bigger than anything I'd been expecting.

'I see discontent,' she said, staring into its smoky centre. 'You have not made full use of the gifts life has bestowed upon you.'

A discontented existence was exactly what I could see in myself. I'd had encouragement and the opportunity to do well but had chosen otherwise. The bit about "gifts" was smart. The old witch knew her trade.

'Now your life is going to change. Today will mark the beginning of that change.'

This was easy for her to say. I reasoned that she probably said the same thing to everyone who was stupid enough to come to this tent. Which of the tricks of her trade would she employ next? She continued to stare into the globe.

'*Come on*,' I muttered under my breath. '*Get on with it. I've paid good money for this.*'

Still she said nothing. Her eyes grew rounder and rounder.

'I can say no more,' she said at last. 'This reading has to end. I don't want to tell of what I see.'

It was her misuse of the word "reading" that most irritated me. She hadn't read anything. She'd told me next to nothing.

'I haven't come in here and paid a small fortune simply to be told you don't feel like doing your job,' I said. I tried to sound even more indignant than I felt.

'The money isn't important,' she said. 'I'll give you your five pounds back.'

'Your fee is ten pounds,' I said.

'Yes it is. But you put only five pounds into the bowl when you came in.'

How could she have known this? I could have sworn the brass money-pot wasn't in her line of vision. If only I'd taken my five pounds and gone quietly at that point... But I persisted.

'I'm not going without my ten pounds,' I said. 'I'm going to call the police.' This was the last thing I'd have done but I wanted to put the wind up her.

For a long time she didn't answer. When she did there was the hint of a sob in her gravelly voice.

'You think it's easy for us, don't you? Well, it's not, believe me. It's a trial to be able to look into the future.'

"A snort" is the nearest description I can find for the noise I emitted involuntarily from my throat and nasal passages.

'You can look into the future, can you?' I said, mockingly. 'Well, you haven't done a very good job of looking into mine.'

'From some things even we clairvoyants should avert our eyes.' I barely heard. She said these words almost to herself.

'You can stop calling yourself that. What am I going to do next, Mrs Clairvoyant? Tell me if you know so much. You're an old fraud.'

Something about what I said, or the way I'd said it, seemed to hit a nerve. She went very quiet and then said, 'Very well. I will speak of your future. But you must not expect to hear good things.'

Then she reverted to silence. My inclination was to taunt her again, but I thought better of it. At last she spoke.

'You will be involved in a terrible road accident. You will be in hospital. You will be in hospital for a long time.' She shuddered. 'The doctors will give you no chance of living. But wait – against all the odds, you will survive.' Her voice lifted almost in triumph. 'They will think you are heading for a miraculous recovery.'

'Doesn't sound so bad,' I said. 'I hear hospital food is better than it used to be. And I won't have to work for it.'

'Things will change for you,' she continued, ignoring my interruption. 'Oh, this is bad. I don't want to say more.'

'Go on,' I urged. 'You can't stop there.'

'Quite suddenly, when everyone thinks you are making good progress, you will suffer a relapse.' She fell silent again. Then she spoke again, in low but distinct tones. 'You will die at the end of the coming summer.'

The way she made her pronouncement took the wind out of my sails. I searched her ugly face, but there didn't seem to be any real malice in her expression. She could have been reading a news bulletin. Still, I at last managed to reason, anyone could spin a tale of this nature. I tried to fight back.

'It's easy to make up a cock-and-bull story like that,' I said. 'You still haven't told me what I'm going to do as much as a minute from now.'

I didn't even know what I was going to do next myself. Of one thing I was sure: I wouldn't be going anywhere near the police. They knew me too well for all the wrong reasons.

'You're going to accept my gift before you leave here.' Her voice was almost inaudible.

'What? What do you plan to give me? You'll need a lot more than ten pounds to buy me off.'

'My gift to you is my clairvoyance,' she said. 'It is mine to pass on to you if you wish to take it from me. The choice is yours.'

'*What a crazy old woman*,' I whispered beneath my breath. But I thought it safer to humour her.

'Of course I'd want it,' I said. 'That is, if you even had it in the first place.'

'Do you really want me to pass it to you?' she murmured. 'Your decision now is irrevocable.'

'Of course I do. Don't keep asking the same question. Who wouldn't want it? It'd be great.'

For a moment I allowed a picture to form in my mind of me at a racetrack, going from bookie to bookie and stuffing my pockets with tens, twenties and – why not? – fifties.

'Well, now it's yours.' She sighed. 'You can't give it back to me.'

'I don't feel any different,' I said.

'You won't,' she said. 'Clairvoyance takes time to set seed and grow. It will take an especially long time to take root in someone as cynical and bad-minded as you. You won't be able to control how your visions come to you at first, either.'

'I've had enough of this!' I pushed back my chair and made to leave.

'Use your clairvoyance wisely,' she called.

'Huh!' I said. 'Five pounds this nonsense has cost me! And you couldn't even be bothered to put a scarf on your head!'

I could hear her low tones outside the tent as she moaned to herself, though couldn't make out any of her words. Then, quite distinctly, came a single loud sob.

*

Naturally, I didn't believe a word of what she'd said. But, back in my hotel room that evening, I have to admit I did out take out the pack of playing-cards I always carried with me. *Jack of Spades*, I thought. The Queen of Hearts turned out to be the top card. *Three of Clubs*. Seven of Diamonds.

I soon forgot all about clairvoyance. If it hadn't been for my five pounds I'd have forgotten all about Endish and its Autumn Carnival as well.

*

Then, what seems like a short time ago, although the calendar and radio tell me was nearly six months back, in February, some whim prompted me to get out my pack of cards again. *Jack of Spades*, I thought – the same card as last time. Jack of Spades. *Five of Diamonds*. Five of Diamonds.

Oh, you five beauties. Come to Daddy. This went on for several more turns. Seven cards in a row matched my prediction exactly. Perhaps my vision of the racetrack was going to be more than an idle fancy, after all. There was to be a meeting at Wolverhampton next week. This one would be perfect. I'd lost spectacularly at Wolverhampton only three weeks before, with borrowed money I still hadn't been able to pay back.

*

But then, four nights later, I had this terrible dream.

I'm walking briskly along a busy road. I'm not taking the slightest notice of my surroundings. It could be somewhere like

Wolverhampton, or it could even be outside the front door of my flat.

Suddenly, I hear a squealing sound. On the street, there's a big red car, a Ford. It's seen better days. And it's well out of control. Everybody else has the sense to get out of the way, but I'm fascinated and don't move a muscle. Too late, I realise the car is going to mount the pavement and come straight for me. I start running. I don't run across the pavement to get out of the car's way. Instead, like a clown, I lope straight along it. It feels as if I'm running ridiculously slowly.

The car is bound to hit me. And it does. I feel a searing pain in my legs and across my back. Are you supposed to feel pain in a dream? I know I did: a hot exploding sensation I'm sure is going to end in my death.

Then, in the dream, everything becomes black for a moment. I wake up in my bed at home, shaking and lathered in sweat. I don't dare to go back to sleep. I can't anyway; I'm trying to think not of the dream but of all that lovely money waiting for me at the racetrack.

I had exactly the same dream on the next night: the busy street I was unable to quite recognise; the red Ford mounting the pavement; the pain; the moment of darkness before waking up in a sweat and panic.

On the Wednesday night, two days before the race meeting, I had the dream once more. Only this time there was a subtle difference. As I swung around to see the out-of-control car, I recognised a person scuttling along on the other side of the road. She was an ugly woman with thin red hair, looking like a giant frog in a faded green overall. She used to be a clairvoyant…

On the Thursday night, I had no dream at all. I'm sure of this, even though I can remember nothing else for a long time after. Until now…

*

'You look even chirpier today. The doctors are very pleased with you. You'll soon be up and about.'

The speaker was a cheerful blonde girl in a smartly-pressed nurse's uniform.

'How do you know that?'

'All the doctors are saying it. You've even been claiming yourself you'll be out of here soon.'

'I ...I don't remember. How long have I been in this bed?'

'You came in last February. We don't know what you were doing in Wolverhampton. Perhaps you'd been to the races. It was a race-day and you had a lot of money in your wallet. And I mean a *lot* of money.' She grinned. 'Don't worry: it's in one of the hospital safes. You'll have it all back when you leave.

'Anyway, you should count yourself lucky. The doctors almost gave up on you. But you showed them. Boy, did you show them. It's the end of July now. I shouldn't be surprised to see you out of here before we're too far into August.'

Proof Positive

'Matt, you used to be in love with the place when we were boys. Now you've got the chance to see it again I don't know why you won't take it,' said Luc.

'The Mountain Centre still had novelty value when we used to go there, back in the 'seventies and 'eighties. It used to be an adventure for us. Now it's all four-by-fours parked by families who sip coffee and never move ten yards from the building. That sort of thing isn't for me. I get more than enough of it in Brum.'

Luc was persistent.

'The Centre was never what you and I used to go for,' he said. 'We used to pedal the eighteen miles on our bikes to go walking on Mynydd Illtud common. Then we'd make the return journey the same way. We couldn't afford headlamps in those days so we'd have to get back before sunset.

The Common isn't over-used even now. Probably because all the young families stick around the centre, like you say. Anyway, it was the Common I was trying to get you to, not for a coffee in the Centre. Nothing wrong with the coffee you're drinking now, eh?'

Matt was on the verge of telling Luc what had happened to him on the Common six weeks before. His nerve failed him. He couldn't tell his old friend anything about that evening without admitting he'd been down this way and not called in to his house.

The guilty feeling this omission had left him was the reason he'd made a detour from a business trip to call in to see Luc today. He probably wouldn't have done so if he knew Mynydd Illtud was going to be their subject of conversation. Certainly he wouldn't if he knew Luc was going to try to get him to go there.

'I've got to get back to Birmingham, Luc. There'll be no end of people in the camera shop on a Friday afternoon.

They'll all be after one of these new digital cameras. At first I doubted those things would ever really catch on. Seemed to me they were no more than gimmicks. You can't beat the artistry of a photographer really on his game making a good positive under a safety light. I'm not complaining about the business these digital cameras bring in, mind. They've been fattening my wallet over these last few months. Saturday always has been our busiest day, but Friday evenings get the punters out in droves as well. It's late already but, if I hit the road now, I can be back in harness for a while at least. The hour before shutting up shop is always the best for trade.'

'Digital cameras, digital cameras. You hear nothing but these days. Well, I'm sure the tide is going to be unstoppable now. You and I were brought up on the old darkroom, negative and positive stuff. You even went on to make a career out of selling photographic stuff when you moved to Birmingham. You're going to miss the art of the old days. I know I will and I don't do it for a living.'

'Maybe I will regret it at that, but I know I've developed my last positive print in a darkroom, Luc.'

Matt couldn't go as far as admitting one of his final batch of black-and-white prints lay in his wallet at this moment. It had been there since he'd developed it, a month ago. He hadn't been tempted to take it out even so much as to glance at again. The truth was he was afraid of what he'd see. Luc would insist on having a look at the photograph if he told him what it was.

He was the last person Matt wanted to see it. Nor did he want to say anything about the small silver penknife that still lay in the pocket of the overcoat he was wearing for the first time since that winter's evening. Earlier this afternoon, his hand had felt its hard outlines through the lining and a shiver had passed through him.

'You must have time for another coffee before you have to make tracks for Birmingham at least? I've got something I want to tell you. It's about Mynydd Illtud Common, funnily enough.'

While Luc was in the kitchen, Matt sat on the sofa in silent regret. He wished he was already on his way back to the shop. But his friend would have been offended if his offer of a second coffee had been refused. The worst thing was that he knew exactly what Luc was going to say about Mynydd Illtud when he came back with the coffee cups.

*

'Coffee as you like it, Butty,' said Luc. 'Strong and black. This'll see you back to Brummie-land.'

At first they sipped their coffees in silence but before long Luc started talking again.

'You remember how you always used to say the Common could have had little to do with St Illtud, despite the name? You liked to remind me that Llantwit Major, or Llanilltud Fawr to give the proper name you always insisted on, was where the saint built his monastery? Well, one of those old academics has done some research blowing all that out of the water. It's all in this article I read in the December *New Silurian*. I still take it every quarter. Pity you don't, Matt.'

In fact Matt still did subscribe to the journal. It was his only real way of keeping in touch with one of the passions of his youth. Gethin Ifans' research hadn't exactly "blown it all out of the water", as Luc colourfully put it, although it had certainly been thought provoking.

The monastery in the Vale of Glamorgan remained central to St Illtud's story. All Ifans had really done was add to the limited knowledge about the Celtic saint's life. But Matt had to sit there in silence and feign ignorance, even though it had been Ifans' words that led him back to Mynydd Illtud six weeks ago. He did not trust himself to speak, so confined himself to nodding at Luc to continue.

'This professor, a bloke called Ifans it was, says Illtud was originally from Brittany. He's got some definite proof of it, apparently. The first place he made a mark for himself was in Pembrokeshire, though. He was a contemporary of St David and knew him well.

'Although Illtud was later renowned as one of the early Celtic Christian saints, you'd have to think of him as more of a Dark Ages magician at the beginning. His magic was too strong for St David and he put one over on the big boy once or twice, so the article claims.

Matt noticed Luc looking carefully at him as if to make sure he still had the attention of his friend before he continued. Luc certainly had Matt's attention, even though he knew exactly what was going to be said.

'Anyway,' said Luc. 'Something or other – Ifans doesn't know what – eventually persuaded Illtud to take up Christianity. The trouble was, almost as soon as he did, some weird plague hit his followers and they all fled to Brittany to escape it. This wasn't really a part of France in those days. It was another corner of the Celtic world, exactly like what we now call Wales and Cornwall.'

'*I know all about that*,' Matt wanted to say. '*I've read the research, too*.' But he held his counsel, took a sip of his coffee, and indicated that Luc should keep talking.

'Anyway,' said Luc. 'When the disease had died down, Illtud and his followers came back to Pembrokeshire. But they didn't stay there, did they? No, they moved eastward. You can trace their route on a map by looking at the dedications. There are St Illtud's churches at Pembrey, Ilston, Oxwich, Llantwit-Juxta-Neath and Bridgend. Then, finally, they established the monastery we now call Llanilltud Fawr.'

Luc fixed Mat with another enquiring look. He clearly did want to make sure he was holding his visitor's attention.

'Here's the really interesting bit. The experts had always thought the saint would have been buried somewhere in the vicinity of the monastery and the exact whereabouts of the grave had been lost in the mists of time. But Gethin Ifans has now proved conclusively that his body was taken further north and east. It's in a place you and I know very well: Mynydd Illtud, just to the south of here.'

Matt could see Luc expected him to say something. He obliged.

'But that can't be, because...'

'Ah,' Luc helpfully interrupted. 'I know what you're going to say. You used to insist on the same thing when we were kids. Bedd Illtud is no more than an odd earth formation, or maybe a grave pre-dating the Celts by centuries. That's what you used to insist. And you used to like to point out that the old church of St Illtud was nothing more than a Victorian church built in 1856.

'All of this may be true but the church was built on the site of a Celtic chapel dating back to the Fifth Century. It was in the old chapel the saint was buried. In centuries past, the local people used to keep watch for Illtud to make his appearance at night. He did it sometimes, too, going by some of the stories Gethin Ifans uncovered. What do you think of that, then?'

'Interesting. But now I've got to head back to Birmingham.'

'Interesting?' echoed Luc incredulously. 'Is that all you've got to say? I thought you'd have wanted to get down to Mynydd Illtud like a shot. In fact, since you told me last week you were coming this way, I've been postponing my own visit so we could go together. It'd be like the old days. Only now we'd travel in a flash car or two instead of by push-bike.'

'Sorry, Luc; I've got to get back to Birmingham. Business, like I told you.'

'You've changed a lot in these last twenty years.'

Of course Matt knew he'd changed in the last twenty years. But not as much as he had in the last six weeks.

*

Good friends though they still were, he was glad to get away from Luc's house.

When he reached the A470 at Erwood, Matt pulled up the car and sat irresolutely at the wheel. From here he had the choice. He could drive north-eastwards towards Birmingham and his shop. They could do with a hand for the last hour or so, though if he was being honest, not as much as he'd pretended to Luc a short while before.

Owais and Jackie would manage well enough without him, even on a Friday afternoon like this one. So, if he could dredge up the courage, he could drive the short distance south to Mynydd Illtud to see if he could find some way of purging himself of his recent experience.

He'd sworn never to go anywhere near the place again after his experience. But, on this springlike March day, the sun was shining. Now that winter evening six weeks before seemed so unreal. Had any of it really happened? He felt again for the outlines of the penknife in his pocket. They were solid enough.

Then he drew out his wallet and looked down at it for several minutes. He wanted so much to remove the photograph to take a look. Then maybe to throw the print away. But he was afraid to do it... That February evening was too vivid in his mind...

*

Mynydd Illtud had been far from his mind since the days of his youth. Now, the research he'd read by Gethin Ifans in the *New Silurian* last month had brought it all back. These days he rarely visited this part of the world.

On impulse on his way back from a run to Merthyr Tydfil, he'd decided to turn off the A470 northward to call in to see his friend and neighbour from youth, Luc Jones. But the piece he'd read was nagging at his mind. Instead of continuing northwards to the village they'd shared as boys and where Luc still lived, he turned off towards the Mountain Centre.

Already it was getting late but he should have enough time for a quick look at the Common. There might still be sufficient light in the darkening February sky. He hadn't travelled more than a mile when something ahead in the road caused him to brake sharply. It was a young man, smartly but inadequately dressed for such a cold day.

'Sorry,' the youth said in a casual tone. 'I shouldn't have wandered out in the road.'

'You might have got yourself killed!'

'I said I'm sorry, didn't I? It would have been my own fault if I'd bought it. Any chance of a lift?'

'I'm only driving another fifteen or so miles. I turn off not far ahead.'

'Anything would help. I'm only going as far as Libanus myself. A lift would beat walking.'

Matt looked properly at the young man for the first time. He was wearing a dark suit. This was not as smart as it had first appeared. Where was his top coat? It was a bitterly cold afternoon. Why should he be walking? His expression was keen and eager. The boy could have been himself thirty years ago. Near Libanus would be where he'd have to turn off for the Mountain Centre himself.

'Get in,' he said.

'I'm dead grateful. What time is it?'

Matt looked at his wrist, conscious of its burden of an expensive watch.

'After ten past three.'

'Great. I should make it in time.'

'Do you live in Libanus?'

'No. I'm on my way to a funeral nearby. It's later this afternoon. My grandmother. I spent all my benefit money in a charity shop on this outfit. This meant I had no choice but to walk. I'd been walking for six miles before you stopped to give me a lift.'

Matt was thinking he hadn't exactly planned to pick up a passenger. But he was very conscious he could have run the youth down. It would have been partly his own fault if he had, no matter what the young man said. His mind hadn't been on his driving. He'd been thinking of Gethin Ifans and his theories. And he'd been barely polite since picking his passenger up.

'I used to live down this way years ago,' said Matt, trying to adopt a friendlier tone. 'My friend and I were on the A470 all the time. There weren't so many cars on the road then. We were forever going to and from the Mynydd Illtud Common on our bikes. It used to be our favourite place.'

'Is that where you're going now? It's not the day for it. It'll soon be dark at this time of year.'

'I haven't been there for ages. This time it'll be no more than a quick call in. I'm going to...' Matt didn't want say exactly why he was really going. '...check a few things out. Libanus is coming up soon. Where would you like me to drop you off?'

'Put me down where you turn off for the Mountain Centre.'

'Are you sure?'

'Suits me.'

Matt eased the car to a halt. He regretted his earlier coolness. Maybe he should give the boy a tenner. On impulse he pulled out his stuffed wallet and peeled off a twenty-pound note.

'Here you are. I'm not sure you'll be able to get a bus home at this hour but it might help.'

The young man took the proffered money, slammed the car door and was swiftly out of sight. He hadn't even said 'thank you'.

*

Matt remembered the way to the old church from the car park. It wasn't far; a short step past the tourist building and then roughly northwards past a line of trees. But first he wanted to see again the two standing stones and then walk on to the large formation called "Bedd Illtud", Illtud's Grave.

As far as he knew, no-one had for years seriously claimed any part of this formation had anything to do with the Saint. The standing stones had been there since the Bronze Age, centuries before Illtud came over from Brittany, assuming he ever did.

When he reached the site of Bedd Illtud, Matt couldn't understand how people could ever have believed Illtud was buried here, even in the Dark Ages. Back in those days its appearance must already have been ancient. The large stones in their sunken pit were almost overgrown with moss and bracken.

All in all, there was hardly anything to see. This was a pity, because he had with him his favourite Yashica camera, loaded with fresh 800 ASA film. The camera must be all of twenty years old by now but Matt still swore by the results it produced.

Pen-y-fan and Corn Du were only four miles distant, but he knew they wouldn't make good photographic subjects under the threateningly low, brooding sky. Besides, he had many far better pictures of the twin peaks at home in

Birmingham. With a sigh, he shouldered the camera and made for the old church.

It was no more than a short walk eastward but already the sky was getting appreciably darker. The funeral the boy was attending must be late indeed.

The path was wet and the mud sucked at his shoes. He knew he'd have to pass the farm gate and braved himself for snarls of unwelcome from the farm dogs. The final obstacle was a broken stile, consisting more of rusty binding wire than wood. This was the same wire that had held the stile together since the days of his youth, probably well before. The repair still looked temporary, as if it had been carelessly lashed together by some unknown hand. He remembered enough to be careful not to snag his clothes or his skin.

At last he faced the church. This had been closed for as long as he could remember. Cracked and splintering wooden shutters sealed off all the windows. It was an unremarkable building, even though its setting was something special.

For the first time in his life, Matt properly looked at the circle on the ground around the church. It was clearly marked by the lack of vegetation throughout its circumference. This must be the old 'Llan' the church was named for. He remembered reading somewhere that 'Llan' didn't really mean church, as it is usually loosely rendered, but 'holy enclosure of a saint'. Gethin Ifans' argument was essentially that this circle marked the holy enclosure of Illtud.

Matt scoffed quietly to himself. The circle had probably been carefully designed and laid out by the nineteenth-century builders of the church. All the same, he couldn't help wondering once again why a church should have been built here in the first place. The congregation must have been pitifully small in such a remote site, even later on in the glory days of the early twentieth century. By then it would probably have been drawn from farms over a wide area. He walked slowly around the building, wondering if light ever penetrated into its interior.

Suddenly, he felt a bony hand brush his shoulder.

Terrified, he whipped around, just in time to see a clutch of dead twigs from last autumn whipped away on a gust of wind. He resolved to get away from this gloomy place as soon as he could; his imagination was already starting to play tricks on him. Besides, now he was actually here he had no more the vaguest idea of what he wanted to do.

When he reached the back outside wall of the church, he found the thing he'd half-remembered. It was still there, exactly the same, all these years later. One of the wooden shutters was more broken than the others. Stretching up on tip-toe for a few moments, he was barely able to catch a glimpse of a few pews in the interior gloom.

The few shreds of daylight left to the late afternoon were fast receding; before long the light would be so bad he'd be able to see nothing inside. His diversion would have been a complete waste of time. Then he remembered his camera was loaded with fast film and he had a flashgun. Triumphantly, he hoisted it with both hands, levelled with the opening, and took a single shot.

Breathing hard more through nerves than physical exertion, he leaned against the church wall, watching the final descent of the winter night. Soon, the only light was that provided by the nearly-full moon. Matt's original intention had been to take more pictures but now, as true darkness rapidly descended, he felt the need to get away, deciding this time to take the direct route when walking back to the car park. He'd only gone a few yards when he was startled by a figure jumping out in front of him from the gloom.

'Give me your wallet. Hand it over. I have a knife and I'm ready to use it.'

Matt recognised the voice. It was the boy to whom he'd given a lift earlier.

'Have you come here from your grandmother's funeral?'

'She died before I was born. You didn't believe that crap, did you? Look, I've got a knife and now I want your big fat wallet. I know you've got one. You showed it to me in the car. Stupid of you to do a thing like that.'

The knife glinted silver, catching a few beams of moonlight. It wasn't a large one but the boy's voice sounded high-pitched and desperate.

'Wait a minute. I'll....' Matt didn't know what he was going to say. He knew it would be unwise to say anything at all.

Suddenly, the boy looked over Matt's shoulder. His eyes widened. He gave a gasp of fear, dropped the penknife, then turned and ran.

Matt glanced behind himself but could see nothing. Then he saw the knife on the ground and bent to pick it up. It was even smaller than it had appeared in the boy's hand. The youth himself could now be seen only as a shadow, haring off toward the Centre. He caught a last sight of the receding figure before it merged with the rapidly falling darkness.

For safety, he thought he should wait here for a little longer. But, after only a few minutes, he found he couldn't bear to stay and shakily trudged off toward the car park. His BMW was the only car there, as it had been when he arrived. Gratefully, he climbed in and turned the ignition key. His mind was a tumble of emotions all the way back to Birmingham. He didn't make it in time to help with the late evening trade in the shop. Not that he'd have been much help in his nervous state.

*

For the next few weeks after that February evening there was a prolonged rush on in the shop. Everyone in the world, so it seemed, wanted to talk about digital cameras. It was as well Owais knew a great deal about them. Matt realised he could no longer delay bringing himself up to speed and resolved to spend every spare moment he was able to find reading everything he could on the subject. Another week had passed before he had the chance to finish the roll of black-and-white film, mostly on street scenes in Birmingham.

At last he found time to develop the negatives under his trusty red safety-light.

The first picture on the roll was the one he'd taken through the broken shuttering. Inside the church it was dark but Matt could see that beside the pew, looking up at the camera, was the outline of a cowled figure. It had lowered the cowl to partly cover its features. Matt knew he should be grateful he couldn't see the whole face.

He rushed into the lavatory at the back of the shop. There he was violently sick.

*

Now, parked at Erwood six weeks later, Matt so much wanted to examine that photograph once more. It had lain in his wallet since the day he'd developed it, but never once had he been able to steel himself to look at it again. Nor had the found the courage to take the silver knife from the pocket where it had lain since that February evening. He'd forced himself to wear the coat today but knew he'd be unlikely ever to put it on again. And he was absolutely sure he'd never revisit the Church of Llan Illtud.

He started the car and began his journey north-eastwards to Birmingham.

The Eve of St Eligius

At last you can hear me! Now I can tell you why you're here. It's been hard work trying to explain things to someone who has a bucket of drugs in them.

I'm sure the place is still there. I read something about it in one of the newspapers. It gives me hope I'll be able to put things right after all these years. Soon, I'll be going back to St Mark's for the first time in more than half a century. And you'll be coming with me. You'll have an extra special part to play. Don't look at me in that miserable way. This is your big chance to do something with your life. You should be grateful.

I hope the graveyard will be exactly the same as it was back then. My fear is now it'll be all prettified. You know the sort of thing: the best of the stones cleaned up and cemented around the edge; a well-kept bench in the centre; coloured paving slabs; tasteful little flowers in the borders. Someone like you would be sure to love it. You'll get the chance to see whether they've ruined the place before long. Shame if they have, but we'll do our best.

If they have ballsed it up, that would fit in with the gentrification that's been smothering old Wandsworth these days, from what I hear about the things they've done to it. There's probably even a glossy brochure somewhere: 'come and see a genuine Huguenot burial ground'.

Things were different then, back in 1962. That was when I was last there. Yes, I know it was a long time ago. Yes, I'm well aware that fifty – alright, nearer sixty – years have passed since then. I've already said so, haven't I?

Me, I'd only recently turned fifteen on the night it all happened. You wouldn't even have been born then. You haven't a clue what the world was like in those days.

People wouldn't go past the burial ground then unless they had good reason to do it. Or at least they wouldn't unless they were too stupid to realise this wasn't the sort of place anyone should go anywhere near. Even with my special gifts, I used to avoid the place. Oh yes, I did say 'special gifts'. By now I've had them so long they don't seem anything out of the ordinary to me.

Earthbounds, they call those things. I can see them. Don't ask me how or why. It may be nothing more than all those bumps on the head I had when I was a kid. These lost spirits are normally harmless enough. They're confused most of the time, to tell you the truth. 'Lost' is usually the right word for them, too. Most of them are wondering what they're supposed to do next. Some of them don't even realise they're dead. Can you imagine?

It isn't usually more than a few days before they're drawn away to the light or wherever it is they're supposed to go. But not all of them are so harmless. Some you should stay as far away from as possible. That's why I always made sure I avoided St. Mark's Churchyard whenever I could. It has more than its fair share of horrors. On that night I didn't stay away.

*

Look, it's probably best if I tell you the whole story in the way it happened. We've got nearly an hour before the car comes. At least if I'm talking we won't have to listen to your whimpering all the time. So, be good and shut up for a while. SHUT UP!

St. Mark's Churchyard was – still is according to what I read in that newspaper – in between Huguenot Place and East Hill. It's only about five miles from here, so we won't have much of a journey ahead of us. I've arranged everything with the driver. Marvellous what a bung of fifty quid can do. There'll be no questions. Look, I've told him you're off your head so it won't make a blind bit of difference if you insist on shouting and screaming.

Back then, more than half a century ago, there used to be a sort of narrow passage down the side. There still is, as far as I can make out. This was a short cut between the two roads.

To the left of the passage or path, going towards East Hill, there was a high barred fence and beyond this was the churchyard.

It was fine to take the short cut in the daylight. You could even have some fun if you stopped and tried to read the lettering on the gravestones. These were blackened through centuries of London dirt and soot: Roger Montpelier died 1688; Bernard Duplace died 1710; Charles Leon died 1691. They're some of the names I still remember to this day.

In the night the passageway definitely wasn't the place to go. There was no proper lighting to read the stones by, anyway.

Dozens of people told me they became aware of things moving behind the fence, or even that they saw them dimly. Some went so far as to say they were sure they heard steps on the path behind them, though they could see nothing when they turned around. A few were even brave enough to admit that they heard whispered voices or felt something cold near to them.

I didn't say too much, because I knew those people were telling the truth. I told you I'd often seen Earthbounds myself. There was a lot worse in the Churchyard than ever they realised. There were shadowy figures drifting over the ground behind the fence right enough. That's an understatement.

If people could have seen the things padding after them down the pathway, they'd have moved a bloody sight quicker. Some of the phantoms even tried to get in touch with passers-by: that's what the whispers and sudden drops in temperature were all about.

Yes, I know I've told you that Earthbounds usually stay around for no more than a few days; a week at the most. And most of these poor wraiths had been in the churchyard for a couple of hundred years or more. Such a long period of being in an earthbound state only happens when there's something to prevent the spirits from leaving. I always wondered what it was.

Before I'd got halfway along the passageway on that November night, I'd found out more than I'd wanted about what it was.

Running like an idiot I was that night, and all because I thought I was going to miss my bus back to Hammersmith. I'd puffed like a clown all the way along Trefoil Road and right down Acris Street. It wasn't so much further from there on to the bus stop near St Mark's if I took the shortcut.

It wasn't because I needed to draw breath that I had to stop. It was the last place I'd have chosen to rest, even if I'd had hardly a breath left in my body.

I've had plenty of years since that night to think what it was that made me stop exactly where I did. The only thing I can come up with was that it was pure will, a dark malevolent malice, bringing me to a halt exactly there. This, now I know, was the same force that had been holding all the rest of the lesser wraiths in the Huguenot ceremony for all those years.

There was nothing I could see. No disembodied head or putrefying organs this time. There were none of the theatrics you sometimes see from the more exhibitionist variety of Earthbound. But there was something there, right behind the wrought iron fence. I was afraid to go another step further. At the same time I feared to turn back. I'd seen plenty of horrible-looking things before in St. Mark's Churchyard. None of them had scared me a fraction as much as this thing I couldn't even see.

This invisible being had what I can only describe as a kind of aura of evil about it. And it possessed unbelievable strength of will. I couldn't move a muscle. I really couldn't. As I said, most of the spirits you see are lost, pathetic things. Not this one. It seemed to know exactly what it wanted.

'You're James Emmar. I knew you'd come.' It hadn't really spoken, you understand. I still couldn't see it, but the words formed in my head exactly as if I'd been talking to someone standing in front of me.

'Who – who are you?'

'Call me Gaston. I've been waiting a long time for you. I'm only allowed to ask this bounty when the centenary of my birth comes. That's tonight – Friday the last day of November, the Eve of the Festival of St. Eligius. In 1762 and 1862 no one who might have been able to hear me came within half-a-mile of my grave. But tonight is different. You've come. I knew you would.'

'You're a Huguenot? St. Eligius is a Huguenot saint?'

'No, of course I'm not a Huguenot. My family was and for most of my lifetime I lived among the Community. Huguenots don't hold with saints and idolatry. Don't you even know that much? I have no idea who St. Eligius was supposed to have been. Nor do I care. I know tomorrow is the Saint's Day, nothing more.'

I knew he – I already knew it was a he – was waiting to plant an idea in my head. I couldn't bear the suspense of waiting to find out what this idea was.

'You're going to ask me for something?' I realised as I spoke that this ghastly presence was actually making an effort to be friendly. For goodness' sake, it was trying to be nice to me. I'd have laughed if I hadn't been so frightened.

'Yes. I'm going to ask you to do something for me. It's a thing that's going to take every last scrap of your courage. But I know you can do it, James. I have a real belief in you, young man, even if nobody else ever has. And you don't have to do this thing on your own. You can bring a friend with a strong back for digging and a sharp spade. He should have a keen mind as well. Both of you will need to keep your wits about you.'

'You mean you want me to…?' Suddenly, I realised what it was it wanted me to do.

'That's what I want. That grave over there is mine. That'll be the one to dig.'

He didn't indicate it in any physical way, but I knew he meant the grave marked by the smallest stone. The pathetic thing was all but crumbling away and was so much less grand than the others. What was left of the stone was almost completely sunken into the ground. It was as if the other stones were keeping their distance from it, although the graveyard was otherwise crowded. The small tombstone was about fifteen feet in from the fence and looked oddly out of place. It was odd I hadn't noticed it before.

'No, I don't think I -'

'PROMISE ME!'

'I promise.' I don't know what made me say it. It was as if I'd had no choice.

'Don't forget. And bring the sharpest blade you can lay your hands on as well as your friend and the spade. You'll need that. Make sure you're back within a week. It will be no use if you come after that. Remember, you promised!'

With that, he was gone. There seemed, for the first time since I'd known it, something like peace in that place. And I found I could move again. So I didn't wait around: I ran as fast as my legs would carry me. Not only because I was so frightened but because I was still hoping to catch that last bus.

*

As it happened the bus was late and I did make it in plenty of time after all. On the top deck, away from St. Mark's Churchyard, in the bright light, I saw it all so differently.

There was this bloke sitting on the front seat. Well, I say "sitting on the front seat", but most of the time he was comically slipping off it. He was three sheets to the wind. Blotto. Stewed. *You* know. The way he kept sliding down made me laugh I can tell you, exhausted as I was after my frightening encounter.

St. Mark's Churchyard seemed a world away. Before I'd

even got to Hammersmith – I'd been sleeping there for the last few weeks in a lock-up tool shed – I'd decided that not only would I not go back to St. Mark's but I'd make damned sure I wouldn't even go anywhere near Wandsworth ever again.

*

'Where are we going then? I've never been to Wandsworth before.'

'Look, Keithie, don't you worry about a thing. We're not far away now. You make sure you keep the cloth wrapped around the spade. We don't want people asking awkward questions now, do we?'

Keithie Hartson wasn't exactly my friend, but then there was nobody who you could give that name. And if he was carrying a sharp new spade and had a strong back to use it with, he didn't have anything like a sharp mind. In fact even his father, if anyone knew who this mysterious paternal figure was, would have been forced to admit he had an achingly dull one. All the bouncing around his mother dished out when he was a little kid had a different effect on Keithie than the treatment I'd been meted out when I was younger. Still, two out of three would do. The steel and the muscle should be enough. That's what I was thinking.

You could say it was because of his mother I was able to count on Keithie's help that night. A few days after she'd died I mentioned casually to Keithie I'd seen her as an Earthbound.

And I had seen her, too. She was floating about, wondering where she was. At the same time you could see her wondering how she could turn this new situation to her advantage. In life, everyone had always been able tell exactly what the old witch was thinking. Nasty bit of work, was Mrs Hartson.

She saw me and tried to communicate with me. I didn't want to know. As I said, I only mentioned it to Keithie in passing. What surprised me was Keithie's reaction:

'You've *seen* her! Was she well?'

'No, Keithie. She was dead.'

'I mean, was she happy? Did she ask about me?'

Here I cottoned on. You'd think Keithie wouldn't have given a monkey's jump about his mother after the way she'd treated him. But, no, his sunken eyes were shining as if I'd told him I'd been having a conversation with a saint.

'Yes, Keithie. She's fine. She'll soon be going on to a better place. But first of all she wanted to make sure you're OK. You were her only child, after all.'

I'd seen her spirit only the once. Mrs Hartson wouldn't have thought of asking about Keithie if I'd talked to her for a week. Do you think people suddenly become angels and sprout wings simply because they're dead? But this was exactly what Keithie seemed to believe so naturally I played along with him.

After that I was always telling him I'd seen her here, seen her there; that she'd said he was to do this, do that for me. I thought there might be something in it for me somewhere along the line. It was a pity Keithie never had any money to speak of.

Never mind, he would make up for it on this night. Otherwise I might have had to do the digging myself.

Yes, I know I'd said I was never coming back to St. Mark's or going anywhere near Wandsworth. I'd meant every word. That was before I'd had the dream. In fact, I had it more than once. The first time I had the dream was during the night after I'd met Gaston. Neither on that night nor on any of those that followed, could I remember any of the details but everything about it was bloody terrifying. I always woke up in a sweat, with the words 'PROMISE ME' ringing in my ears. I had the same dream every time I closed my eyes over the next few days. It was driving me mad.

Those dreams were the reason I borrowed the spades

and stuff from the lock-up. They were why I went to see Keithie to ask him for a special favour. It was the dreams that brought Keithie and me to St. Mark's Churchyard at two o'clock in the morning.

*

'You want me to keep digging? I don't like it here, Jamie.'

'I've told you, Keithie. Your Mum wants you to dig all the way down.'

'But my Mum has never even been to Wandsworth. I don't get it.'

'You keep digging, Keithie. It's what your mother wants.'

Keithie kept digging. Good old Keithie. The ground must have been hard because, although he was slogging away with the sharp spade, he was making slow progress. For a moment I even wondered whether I should start digging with the other spade, but I decided against it. Keithie could do all the digging.

So I had plenty of time to look around me. Everything was still: this was in the early hours, so there were no people and hardly any cars about. The crook in the pathway at this point only accentuated our feeling of isolation. There was a crescent moon, and the juniper and hawthorn were thrown into silhouette.

It wasn't "creepy" in the sense someone like you would use the word. The churchyard was as peaceful as ever I'd known it. You couldn't even say it was as dark and lonely as it had always seemed to be before. There was – how can I describe it? – an air of expectation about everything. Keithie must have felt the same way, too, because the further he dug down, the faster he worked, and the more excited he became.

When he had dug down all of six feet, I suddenly

realised what it was I'd really brought him to the churchyard for...

*

I didn't see or hear the policemen as they crept up on the pair of us. Even when the Rozzers shone their torches I was no more than half aware of them. I was so intent on what I was doing.

'Ugh, I think I'm going to be sick, Ron.'

*

It was the evidence of that copper, the geezer with the weak stomach, that really made the newspaper reporters so excited. I thought he was going to throw up again right there in the courtroom as he spoke:

'As Constable Smith and I approached we could see a figure bent over and scrabbling in the hole. It was dark, so we couldn't see very well what was going on. We got right up to him before we switched on our torches. Even then he didn't stop what he was doing. That was when we saw it. He ... He...'

'Go on, Officer.' The old judge knew exactly what the copper was going to say. He'd heard it before. Who did they think they were kidding?

'It ... it was as if this young man was trying to squash the object he was holding in his hands into the earth. All bloody, his hands and arms were. So was this thing he was holding. We couldn't make out what it could be at first. Then at last we realised exactly what the boy was holding in his hands...

'Lying next to him on the ground was another young man, or the body of a young man, I should say. This other poor boy had the top of his head sliced clean off, exactly as if he'd been a boiled egg at breakfast-time. And this one, the accused, he... he ... It was the other boy's brain he was holding and trying somehow to squash it into the earth. He... he...'

I don't remember what happened after that. They

cleared the courtroom or something dramatic. I don't remember anything else of the trial. Perhaps there wasn't any more for me to remember.

There were lots of cosy and not-so-cosy chats with intense-looking men in white coats for me over the next few weeks. Their answer to everything seemed to be to drug me up to the eyeballs. The bastards even did the same trick with their pills when I wasn't making a fuss. I admit I did quite a lot of screaming and shouting in the beginning. So would you have done. At least you would've done, going by the way you're whimpering now. You shout if you have to. Nobody can hear you.

Anyway, the next thing I properly remember is I'm in this special place in Middlesex. I was only turned fifteen at the time, remember?

Not many of the other boys in Feltham would talk to me, but they liked to talk about me. Bastards. My little adventure had caused quite a splash in all the newspapers. One of the Sundays even ran a serial of my life. I ask you! It wasn't only because of the way that bloody copper had given his evidence, I know, even though that had a lot to do with it.

No, some bright reporter somewhere had worked it out that old Gaston was Gaston Emmar, my Great-by-something-or-other Grandfather. It was the first time I even knew such a thing myself. Of course, the newspapers didn't half go to town after that. They wouldn't be allowed to do such things nowadays. Some committee would put a stop to it. I didn't mind really; it kept the other boys off my back.

I didn't stay in this Middlesex place for all that long. They moved me as soon as I was old enough to go to Broadmoor. After a year or two there I worked out that all my ranting and raving about Keithie's weak brain not being good enough for old Gaston wasn't getting me anywhere at all.

If I was ever going to get out of the place I reasoned I'd have to do a lot of smiling and talking sweetly to the doctors.

So, naturally, this was what I learned to do. Before long, some of the doctors almost liked me. None of the other patients ever did, though. Suited me.

It took all those years of smiling and nodding like an idiot before they'd let me out. Towards the end they were labelling me with things like "institutionalised". That's justice for you, eh? Well, I wasn't "institutionalised".

All I ever really wanted to do was to get back to Wandsworth to correct the mistake I'd made all those years ago. Gaston deserves a better brain than Keithie's.

*

Well, it's ten minutes to midnight now. Ten minutes before the Eve of St. Eligius. We'll wait for an hour or two to make sure no-one's around the graveyard after we've been dropped off in the car. I'll be doing all the digging this time. No problem. I may be old but I'm fit. Don't worry too much about your pain. I know the effect of the extra dose of drugs I'll soon be giving you will be starting to wear off before we go. I'll be giving you some more a while after we reach St Mark's. I wanted to tell you this story first, so you'd understand what this is all about.

Anyway, you can be sure it will be a quick operation. This blade is very sharp.

Waxlow and Lilac

1

Seeing the bright red telephone box with its graceless outlines at the side of the pond had almost prevented her from making an offer.

'What on Earth is this thing doing here in the garden?'

Veronique's sudden question seemed to unsettle Mrs Brown, the owner of the bungalow. Up to that point, she'd displayed at least outward poise and confidence when showing her prospective buyer around the premises. You'd swear she was in the estate agency business herself.

'It's a telephone box. A GPO one going back to the early nineteen-fifties, so I've been told.'

'*Yes, I can see it's a bloody telephone box,*' was what Veronique wanted to say. She didn't. This would have been grossly impolite especially when, unannounced, she'd knocked on the front door. After all, the woman had been good enough to let her see the house and garden. The agent's sign had said '*Viewing Strictly by Appointment*' clearly enough.

'Wh-what I mean,' said Mrs Brown, when she saw Veronique's look of disbelief. 'Is that I wasn't the one to put the box there. It was the previous owner. I know hardly anything about her; she died a year or more before I moved in. The house had been empty in between times. People have told me this used to be the payphone for Northolme Village. When Telecoms decommissioned the box, she snapped it up, apparently. There's quite a demand for them as a feature these days, I believe. Can't think why, myself. They're ugly things to have in a garden. And this big garden needed a lot of work after a year of neglect while the house had been empty, let me tell you.'

Veronique looked more appraisingly at the other. Mrs Brown looked to be a woman of about her own age – fast approaching her half-century – and she could now see that the air of cool confidence was no more than a veneer. She was distinctly unhappy about something. What could this be? Oh well; it was none of her business.

'I can understand that,' said Veronique. 'Still, it's a wonder you didn't decide to have the box removed while you were at it in the garden. There must have been an enormous amount of work to get a garden like this into trim.'

Mrs Brown cast down her gaze and was thoughtful for a moment.

'Never got around to it, really,' she said, a little too quickly to sound convincing. 'I'd only been living here for less than a year before I made the decision to sell up and move back to The Midlands. The previous owner had some sort of sentimental attachment to the box, so I heard. I was reluctant to have it torn from its foundations after I'd discovered that. All I've been able to find out is that it was important to her in her teenage courting years. No-one would tell me any more. They're an incredibly secretive lot, the villagers here.'

'Yes, but what has this sentimental attachment got to do with you? You never even met the woman.' Veronique wanted to ask this, but held her tongue. 'Can I have a quick look inside the box?' she asked instead.

She could see Mrs Brown was going to object in some way, so she swung the door open and stepped inside before she could speak. What could she have said, anyway? Mrs Brown stood resolutely on the outside, holding the door open at arm's length. The interior of the booth was clean enough. All the window-panes were intact and had even been recently polished. She reached up and pulled the switch above her head. A dull click was the only response.

'It doesn't work,' said Mrs Brown. 'The previous owner must have added the pull-switch for some reason. I don't know why: the box isn't connected to any kind of electricity supply or telephone system. I made sure of that when I moved in last year.'

Then Veronique noticed that, instead of the expected push buttons, the telephone was fitted with an old-fashioned dial. On its face, in bold lettering, was the number 'WAXlow 7901'.

'Well, that's most odd...'

'Oh, I should think the owner had the dial specially fixed on when she bought the phone box. In the old days they used to use letters instead of some of the numbers. I expect this was the original dialling code under the system used in the days of her youth. It would have been changed to all numbers during the sixties. Something like 919-7901. I think that's the way it worked back then, if I remember rightly from my own girlhood. They've changed the pattern a few times since.'

'Phew! Must get out of here. It's overpowering.'

Following a sudden impulse, Veronique stepped out of the box. She did so more hastily than intended, almost barging into the surprised Mrs Brown.

'Sorry,' she said. 'But the smell suddenly became too much for me. It seemed to become stronger while I was inside.'

'I've scrubbed every inch of the box,' said Mrs Brown. 'I was born with no sense of smell myself but others have noticed and pointed it out to me. It wasn't a nasty smell, I hope?'

'Far from it. Sort of flowery, I'd describe it as. Pleasant in its way, but far too overpowering for me to be able to endure for long. It was something like Lilac, I'd say.'

'There is no *Syringa Vulgaris* planted in this garden. There wasn't even when I moved in. Anyway, this is still early May. Lilac doesn't flower until later in the summer.'

'Whatever you say,' said Veronique. 'I'm no expert. Let's get away from here, shall we? Time to have a proper look at the rest, I think.'

Mrs Brown visibly relaxed as they stepped away from that corner.

The garden was a horticultural delight. It was even bigger than it had first appeared and its charms revealed themselves bit by bit. Already many flowers were in bloom. Veronique recognised a lot of them: despite her earlier declaration of floral ignorance she could identify Pansies, Yellow Trillium and Hyacinth. A wonderful blue Iris was already coming into bloom. What must this garden be like under the full summer sun? But Mrs Brown was right: there was no sign of anything remotely resembling Lilac.

'This garden is so astonishingly beautiful,' said Veronique. 'You must spend a lot of time with it.'

'This was my intention when I moved in. But I have to confess,' said Mrs Brown. 'In the end I needed a lot of paid help. Before I decided to put the property on the market I realised I'd neglected the garden over the autumn. So, I had the professionals in to do a purge for me. I had to use an out of town firm, too. The locals didn't seem interested.'

It was while the two of them were weaving a pleasant way through a small group of cherry and redcurrant bushes to the side of the bungalow that Veronique made up her mind.

'Where did you say that Estate Agent was?'

'In Greenbury. Thorpe and Thorpe they're called. Their place is just four miles straight down the old Sudlip road ahead of you after the local village. You can't miss them; they're the only agents in town and it's hardly a metropolis.'

'You can guess what I'm going to say next. I'm going straight from here to put in my offer.'

Mrs Brown looked at her as if dumbstruck. Then, slowly, a smile broke across her features, which before that moment had never been quite free of the shadow of worry.

'You make your mind up quickly, I must say. You've only had a quick look around inside the bungalow itself.'

'It looked like a fine interior to me. Of course, I'll be getting a surveyor to check things out. I don't see the point in hesitating if you like what you see.'

'I'm so glad you do like what you see.' Mrs Brown beamed happily

'When I go to the agent, I'll make only one offer, mind, but it'll be a fair one. I don't hold with all this shilly-shallying for a few hundred more or less.' Veronique thought she'd better add this, in case she'd appeared too enthusiastic. But how could she not be enthusiastic about the prospect of living here? Once she'd removed that pond with its geometric lines and the monstrosity of a telephone booth, she'd be very happy.

2

She was in the bungalow by mid-June. Mrs Brown had accepted her offer immediately and there'd been no difficulty about the building survey. Nor was finance a problem, after the funds she had from selling her flat in the city back in March. Mrs Brown was eager to please with dates; indeed, she was the one who was the more anxious to conclude the deal. There must be some great attraction in The Midlands, Veronique thought.

On her second evening in her new home the weather was balmy. It had been a difficult day in work so, after dinner, she was pleased to relax among the flowers. She contentedly watched the erratic flight path of a Comma butterfly in its ragged-winged dance across the breadth of the lawn. Finally, it settled on the tallest Hyacinth behind her. She turned to watch its purposeful rest on the flower as it sipped at the nectar. Then, as it took wing again, she rose and followed its weaving flight over the tall Laburnum hedge and into the lane at the back.

On impulse, she'd decided to follow the insect. But it had already flown out of sight when, for the first time as the new owner, she unlatched the wicker gate leading to the lane behind the house. Instead, she chose to follow the course it had probably taken away from the busier Sudlip road. Everything looked so inviting.

This was the life! How could she have anaesthetised herself into living in London for all those years? True, living here meant a drive of nearly forty miles to and from her workplace but, after all that time in the city, working in the busy insurance office and then trudging through the crowds for over a mile back to a cramped flat which had never truly felt like home, this place was heaven.

She followed the course of the lane, firstly through a long, curving incline and then fairly straight and level for another two miles or so. After this, the way became less defined and the track underfoot gave way to grass and open fields.

For a moment she dared herself to walk across the field nearest her but, fearing she might become foolishly lost, decided it would be better to retrace her steps. She strolled, rather than walking purposefully, back down the lane. What was the rush? She was a country girl again. Tonight, she'd sleep well. What was called for was a relaxing cup of hot chocolate and then early to bed. That would be the thing for her. Tomorrow, she could face all the mountains of work in the office more happily. She wouldn't even bother to take her novel into the bedroom with her.

It was a quarter-past-ten when the bungalow and garden came into sight. She stopped suddenly. Strange; from this point a little above her home, she could have sworn a light was shining brightly in the telephone box. This couldn't be; it must be a trick of the Midsummer evening. The lane entered a wide arc shortly afterward and the bungalow vanished from her line of sight. Sure enough, when the garden came back into view, all was in darkness. When she let herself in through the front door – the front door of her dream cottage, she thought happily – she no longer felt the need for the cup of hot chocolate. It had been a busy day, ending perfectly with the longish walk. Tonight, she knew she'd sleep without trouble. Veronique decided to leave the bedroom window ajar to allow the warm night air to circulate and settled herself contentedly on the pillow.

*

The radio alarm on the bedside table told her that it was shortly before three o'clock in the morning. The now cool breeze coming through the window must have woken her. No … it was the sound of a telephone ringing. How could this be? Her mobile was always switched off at night. The telephone company hadn't yet connected the landline telephone service to the bungalow. Mrs Brown had never got around to having one installed when she lived here; like so many people she relied on her mobile. Veronique would probably have done the same herself but she needed broadband for her tablet.

Then, following the direction of the sound, she realised the sound was drifting through the window from the red booth in the garden. It was partly concealed by the large Camellia shrub outside the window but, unmistakeably, the box was illuminated. As she looked at the shrub a strong flower perfume wafted through the window. Wait a minute… she remembered Camellia had little scent. She could smell Lilac.

The bell shrilled insistently for a full minute. It seemed longer, but Veronique was watching the figures change on the face of the radio alarm. As the sound finally ceased, so the light in the telephone box went out. The sensible thing, she knew, would be to go outside to investigate. But she wasn't so brave; all she could find the courage to do was turn on her mobile and ring what she thought was the modern equivalent of the number she'd seen on the dial six weeks before.

Carefully, she picked out 0207-0919-7901. Nothing. Was that the number she should be calling? Was her memory of the old number even correct? She tried again, varying one of the digits. Still nothing. After the fourth fruitless attempt, she collapsed on the bed, near to tears. It was only the powerful smell of Lilac that forced her to stand up to close the window.

She slept no more that night.

3

Somehow, she managed to force herself into work the next morning, a Thursday. Before she left, she even found it within herself to step inside the box to lift the now-silent receiver. But, on the Friday, she had to call in sick for the first time in twenty-three years.

Veronique chose not to stay at home that afternoon or on the weekend following. Instead, she went out to try to get to know the villagers in order to learn something about the earlier occupant of the bungalow. Mrs Brown had been right in what she told her. It was indeed hard work to get much out of the locals; most of those to whom she spoke were tight-lipped about almost everything. The nearest she came to finding out anything at all was at the village fête on the Saturday, where she contrived to fall into conversation with two local women. After fielding their own barrage of questions, she dared to try some gentler probing on her own account:

'I know very little about the people who lived in my bungalow before me. Can you tell me anything about them?'

'Mrs Brown, you mean?' said the sterner faced of the two women, who carried the unlikely name of Mrs Sweet. 'We don't know much about her. Kept herself to herself, she did.'

The look she shot at Veronique suggested that she thought the questioner would be wise to do the same.

'The lady wasn't living here for long,' said the woman by her side, a Mrs Smith. 'Went back to The Midlands, didn't she? That's where she was from. Warwick or somewhere near there, I think.'

'No, I mean before Mrs Brown,' said Veronique.

'The house was empty for a long time,' said Mrs Sweet, in a tone that announced this conversation was coming to its conclusion.

'I was talking about the time before it became unoccupied,' Veronique persisted.

'Oh, she must mean the *bad* woman,' said Mrs Smith, casting a nervous glance in her companion's direction.

'We don't talk about her,' said Mrs Sweet bluntly. 'Come on, Ann. It's time we were going.'

And that was it.

*

The telephone in the garden rang and the light in the box came on Friday, Saturday and Sunday nights. But it came to life only once on each, shortly before three o'clock. After a minute or so everything became still again. Veronique kept all windows closed after the Friday and somehow she was able to get some rest each night, although her sleep was far from undisturbed.

Monday she'd booked as a day's leave for the purpose of having her telephone line and broadband installed. Before the engineer arrived, she'd already resolved to return to the office on Tuesday. She thought the man might be able to offer some technical advice on the odd goings-on but he was a taciturn type who'd only grunt that the call box was 'off system' and so nothing to do with him.

She was disappointed but vowed to keep to her resolve. There was far too much work waiting for her to skulk here at home. The strangely alive telephone box might be inexplicable, even frightening, but she wasn't about to let it dominate her life.

That night, she almost changed her mind. At a few minutes before three o'clock, the opening bars of *Lilac Wine* shattered her sleep. On a whim, this was the chime she'd selected for the new phone by her bedside table. She struggled up in bed to look at the small screen, wondering who could be calling her at this hour. It read 'WAXlow 7901'. How could this be?

She didn't dare to pick up the receiver. Instead, she got out of bed, pulled aside the curtain, seeing through the branches of the Camellia shrub the illuminated call box in the garden. When the unmusical tones of *Lilac Wine* ceased from her bedside table, the light outside went out. Silence returned, although for only a short while. The sound of a ringing bell drifted through the closed window. It was almost as if a missed call were being returned.

The next weeks were almost unbearable. The sunny promise of early summer was washed away in daily torrents of rain. Despite her best efforts, her work in the insurance office continued to pile up. She was almost forced to admit to herself that the new computer system was beyond her, even though the younger staff had taken to it with ease.

Even the daily drive to the city somehow became more arduous. She struggled through the restless nights with the aid of a sleep-mask, ear plugs and by means of disconnecting the telephone by her bedside at ten o'clock every night. She'd changed the tone to an innocuous ring, but knew this wouldn't be sufficient. The red box in the garden still rang unfailingly at three o'clock.

4

July was ebbing away before she was able to sit outside again and even then there was still a cool dampness in the air. Despairingly, she looked about her. Weeds flourished in the flower beds and the grass was already growing long again. All she'd found time to do this month was give the lawn a quick run over on a few evenings after work. She'd tried to telephone the two gardeners listed in the local directory but neither of them had been willing to help once she'd given her address.

On one occasion she'd been into Northholme in a fruitless search for advertising postcards. She'd even ventured into the general store to see if they could tell her of anyone who might be able to help. At the moment when it looked as if the cheerful shopkeeper was going to try to help her, who should walk in but Mrs Sweet.

Her stony glance in their direction changed everything in an instant. The conversation ended with the shopkeeper giving a non-committal 'I'll let you know' and Veronique withdrawing from the store with nothing, not even the loaf of bread she'd intended to pick up.

It was no good. Much as she didn't want to, she'd have to follow Mrs Brown's example and get a company in from further afield. Precisely at the moment she came to this conclusion, she heard a loud 'plop' behind her. The hyacinth plant she had so admired in June was flowerless. Veronique realised she should have cut it back long since as she watched a second large raindrop drip down from the bedraggled topmost leaf to a broad, cupped one at the bottom of the plant.

'Hello? Excuse me.' The speaker was a man standing in the lane running past the bottom of her garden.

'Yes?' she said.

'Clive Simkin. From the village. I'm looking for Mrs Pearce.'

'Ms Pearce,' she corrected. 'But I dislike that even more than "Miss". I prefer to be addressed by my first name, Veronique. My mother was French.' Talking about herself as 'Ms' and 'Miss' made her feel so old.

'Sorry. Syd Vincent in the village store was telling me you were looking for some help in the garden.'

Veronique looked more closely at the man when he said this. So, the shopkeeper had done something for her, after all. Clive Simkin, standing nervously in the lane, was younger than her and had friendly, open features.

'Yes, I am. You can call me Veronique. Most people do. Come in. Sit down and we'll talk about it.'

Veronique watched as her prospective gardener carefully leaned his bicycle against the hedge. Then, he opened the wicker-gate, smiling nervously. He walked over to her chair and stood before her, clasping his hands, as if awaiting her approval. He didn't take the seat opposite until she gestured toward it.

'So, you're an experienced gardener, are you?'

'Not really. I work in one of the Sudlip shops for five full days a week and have only a small garden to look after at home. I used to do more gardening some years back, though.'

'*I'd be grateful for anyone's help,*' thought Veronique. 'We'd better talk terms, then,' she said.

'No terms now, please,' said Clive. 'I'll do a couple of days for nothing and then we can discuss that sort of thing if you're OK with what you see. What time on Saturday would you like me to start? Ten o'clock not too early for you?'

'Come when you like after nine o'clock. Can't you start tomorrow? The weather forecast is good for the next week.'

'Sorry; I have my job in Sudlip in the week but I don't work weekends. I'll be here at nine-thirty on Saturday morning. Is that OK?' He looked around the garden. 'I don't think it will turn into a jungle by the weekend.' He laughed briefly, almost relaxing for the first time. 'Anyway, the place could do with drying out for a few days.'

*

That summer Clive Simkin became Veronique's weekend gardener. He was incredibly industrious, working solidly from nine-thirty every Saturday and Sunday, taking no more than thirty minutes to eat his sandwiches and have a cup of tea from the flask in the knapsack. It would never be earlier than six-thirty when he'd mount his pushbike and pedal off with a cheery wave.

He worked through all but the heaviest rain; in the fiercest downpours, he retreated into the tiny potting shed for the minimum possible time. The pay negotiations on the second weekend worked in reverse: Clive suggested a ridiculously low rate and she had to bargain hard to get him to accept more. Veronique considered herself to be very lucky except in one respect: Clive's shyness made him stumbling and awkward in conversation. She'd made no friends locally, despite her best efforts, and she'd have liked to share more than the occasional word that wasn't connected with gardening or the weather.

*

On the first Sunday afternoon in October, Veronique found Clive Simkin not working with his usual impressive industry for the first time. Instead, he was standing in the corner of the garden near the telephone box and the angular pond. He was deep in thought and didn't hear her approach.

'Idling the afternoon away, Clive? I don't pay such high rates for this, you know.'

He gave a start.

'Oh, I'm so sorry, Mrs... I mean... I'll get back to work straight away.'

'Don't be silly, Clive. You work so very hard. You should take a breather sometimes. Tell me, what were you thinking?'

'Nothing much. Only about the garden.

'You were indeed thinking deeply about the garden, I could see that. I'm so sorry I interrupted your thoughts. Tell me.'

Clive looked at the pond and rockery for a long time before answering.

'This is my favourite part of the garden, even though I don't care much for the pond and rockery.'

'Well, it has potential. But I do think it feels incomplete, somehow. Almost as if there's something missing.'

'Perhaps there is,' said Clive. 'Anyway, I've got some serious work to do over on the other side. You don't pay me for gossiping, so I'd better get back on the job.'

Almost before he'd finished speaking, Clive was striding across the lawn. Veronique was tempted to walk over and ask him what he meant. She managed to resist the temptation.

*

There was incessant rain on the following Saturday. Disappointed, she had to agree with Clive to give it a miss for that week. The rain pattered against her bedroom window through the night and she awoke to see leaden skies above her on the Sunday.

Through the week, she left for work to the accompaniment of intermittent rain and it was the same when she returned home. It was a different story on Friday. The sky was lighter when she left for London and a brilliant blue when she returned in the evening.

Clive arrived promptly at nine-thirty next morning but was taciturn in the extreme for the rest of the day and on the

Sunday morning. Veronique regretted her light remark of a fortnight before, fearing that Clive had taken what she'd said to heart. She need not have worried. In the afternoon, standing in what he'd called his favourite part of the garden he became, by his standards, positively talkative.

'Well, what do you think? I've done most of what there is to do. One more full weekend and then I'll have a few odd bits and pieces to finish off the weekend after. That'll just about do it for the year. If it's OK with you I'll come once more for the last time in the middle of next month, weather permitting, for a final tidy-up and to give the lawn a final mowing. There'll be plenty of time before then for me to plant the bulbs you mentioned as well. Of course, I'll be pleased to come back in the spring, if you want me to, that is. You might prefer to hire a professional, I realise that, Mrs – Ms Pearce.'

Veronique looked around her. The garden was a delight, far better than when Mrs Brown had first shown it to her. A professional? What for? No-one could have done a better job. But there was more to it than that. Despite his quietness, she'd sorely miss having Clive around.

With a start, she realised he was the reason she'd passed up the chance to go to Guernsey for two weeks with her friend Avril from work. It was Avril's last year and she'd just bought a retirement cottage on the island. She'd told her, and convinced herself, that the reason she couldn't go was that she was too busy in the office. This was at best partly true.

'But I want the pond filled in and some adjustments to the rockery.'

'You'd be better getting in a builder to do jobs of that kind.'

'I want you to do it for me please, Clive.'

Clive looked uncomfortable and scratched his chin, thoughtfully.

'Well, we'd have to buy some boulders and soil for the infill. And I suppose we could hire one of those mini-excavators for all the earth-shifting there'd be. You can get a machine of less than half a tonne size. I know a firm in Sudlip that hires them out. Reckon I could handle one of those and then do the tidying up with a spade afterwards. It's a big pond, mind. The work would take me a weekend, maybe a weekend and a half. It'd push up the cost if we had to go into a second weekend – the hire price, I mean.'

'Good. Never mind about a few pounds extra,' said Veronique. 'Then there's the telephone-box to be removed.'

'I couldn't touch the telephone box.' Veronique thought Clive said this a little sadly. 'It used to be the one serving our village. It's got sentimental value, you might say.'

Sentimental value. She'd heard that description before. Veronique looked again at the call-box. Despite the fact that it had disturbed her sleep nightly throughout the summer, she, too, had grown used to it. Unaccountably, she'd even started to like it. She made a sudden decision.

'The telephone box stays. Can we talk a bit about what you'd need to do with the pond?'

'I'll find out some costs for you and jot them down on a piece of paper so I can drop it through your door the week after next. We can have a chat about it next weekend.'

As he pedalled away at his usual six-thirty Clive gave a smile and wave, as he always did. This time, the smile was broad and happy, instead of being quick and nervous. Had something changed?

*

Veronique could see that the garden work was indeed coming to an end. The promised 'chat' about Clive's planned construction tasks turned out to very brief. She found herself looking forward to Clive's note but when she returned home on the Monday there was nothing on her doormat. On Tuesday evening there was a pile of paper. On inspection, all of it proved to be junk mail. But on Wednesday there was an envelope addressed *Ms Pearce – Estimate.* Veronique didn't even close the front door before she read the small, neat handwriting:

'Dear Ms Pearce.

Sorry this is later than I'd hoped. I've been waiting for some figures from people in Sudlip…'

There followed, in incredible detail, Clive's plans for the filling-in of the pond. The cost of hiring the excavator seemed quite reasonable, but he'd carefully noted the extra costs there'd be for the work to continue into the following weekend, which he now thought to be necessary.

There were precise measurements everywhere and several competent and neat sketches. Two of these had even been shaded with coloured pencils. On several parts of the largest sketch, he'd indicated by means of arrows where he thought new plants were needed. Three were indicated anonymously as 'plants', but the fourth as 'Lilac shrub'. He'd even gone to the trouble of colouring in the flowers. Veronique noticed that, on the drawing, some things had shrunk in dimensions whilst the Lilac bushes Clive was clearly so keen on had grown in prominence.

She studied the note carefully, re-reading it three times. Her disappointment grew as she read. Great care had been taken in its preparation but there was absolutely nothing personal about it.

Had she been foolishly won over by Clive's modest personality? What had she been thinking? He must be at least ten years her junior and from a very different background. What would people in the village like Mrs Sweet say?

5

There was another downpour lasting all the next weekend. Clive telephoned on the Friday with a long story about the hire firm – it seemed the manager had been fussy about some paperwork and he wouldn't be able to get the digger until his friend, the assistant manager, was on duty. He said the rain didn't much matter because the mechanical digger wouldn't be available and there wasn't much he could do without it.

But the digger arrived on the following Friday evening as rearranged. The sun was already low in the western sky by the time Veronique had eaten and put things away but an Indian Summer was now beginning to chase away the cool dampness of early autumn. This was her favourite kind of weather and, although she had no interest in machinery, she went out to inspect the excavator. It was small, although seemed to exude power and purpose. Its yellow paint glistened in the setting sun. It was clearly a new machine; this might even be its first time out.

'*Clive will love this thing tomorrow,*' she thought.

And he did. He didn't actually say 'wow' but he might as well have done. His eyes widened when he saw it and, after the bare minimum of morning pleasantries, he climbed into the seat and started the engine.

Veronique went indoors, feeling foolish again. There was no denying it: she was jealous of a pile of painted metal. All morning she tried to concentrate on her novel but the constant mechanical whirr outside distracted her. She was grateful for thirty minutes of peace when Clive stopped for his break but the noise started again at precisely one o'clock. Then, shortly before three, it stopped. Ten minutes of silence followed and, with a sudden chill, a question formed in her mind.

'*Has he had an accident?*'

She dashed into the garden. No, Clive was standing by the machine, looking at it wonderingly. He glanced around when he saw her.

'I'm sorry,' he said.

'Sorry? Why on Earth should you be sorry? You're doing a grand job.'

'That's the trouble. I thought I'd need the digger for at least two, more likely three, days. So I had you pay for two whole weekends. Now I find the work didn't take much more than a half day. I'm sorry I've wasted your money. You can deduct the cost of the extra weekend from my own pay.'

Veronique laughed, gently at first, though soon she was doubled up with laughter.

'It's not funny,' said Clive. But her laughter was so infectious that soon he was laughing himself, without knowing what he was laughing at.

'It doesn't matter, Clive,' said Veronique, struggling to speak. 'It really doesn't matter. What's your plan now?'

'Well, it won't take me more than a few hours to tidy things up with the spade. Tomorrow, I could put the bulbs in and do the other final planting. But, if it's all the same to you, I'd rather come back next Saturday to do it. It'll only take me an hour or two. Did you get the Lilac for me to plant?'

'Next Saturday would be fine,' said Veronique. 'Tell me, why did you ask for the Lilac?'

Clive's expression became serious.

'Oh, I thought the garden could do with some more scent. There isn't much else here. And the spot I suggested gets lots of sun.'

Veronique knew she wouldn't see any Lilac in flower until next summer.

'We've had enough of Lilac, don't you think? There's a strong scent of…' As she spoke, Veronique realised that the perfume which had so dominated the garden had quite gone. It had not been present for some weeks, although she hadn't noticed its absence.

She looked at Clive's downcast features.

'There's more to this, isn't there? Please tell me about it.'

'This garden used to be full of Lilac! It was so beautiful!'

'How on Earth would you know a thing like that?'

'I used to do the gardening here.' Clive spoke quietly and assumed a guilty look, as if he were confessing to a crime.

'You used to work here? When?' said Veronique incredulously. 'You never told me a thing about it!'

'It was a few years ago. When… when…'

A sudden thought came to her.

'When the one they call *the bad woman* lived here?'

Clive's eyes met hers directly. They flashed with anger. She'd never seen such strong emotion in him before.

'Angela was *not* a bad woman. They were always good to me, both of them. Ever since I was a child they were the only ones in the village who treated me with respect.'

'They? Both of them?'

'Angela and her friend Pauline lived here for many years. Angela was from the big house on the other side of Northolme. Pauline was…was her lady friend. She was just a poor girl from the village. The two of them were inseparable as teenagers. Goodness knows – Angela's parents tried hard enough to keep the two of them apart. Pauline used to phone her from the village every day they couldn't find a way to meet. This was the telephone box she used. Then, when she was twenty-one – it used to be twenty-one in those days, not eighteen – and came into some money of her own, Angela moved out.

'Well, Angela bought this bungalow for them to share. There was such a fuss in the village and they were saying such wicked things. As if it was anything to do with them! Anyway, Angela and Pauline did their best to ignore them. I was only a kid at the time – I didn't really know what all the gossip was about.

'One day I knocked on the door to ask if there was any work I could do for them. They gave me something to do in the garden – although I was too young to really be of much help then – and it started from there for me. They even helped me with my schoolwork. All I know is that there were many days I'd have gone without breakfast if not for them. Not all of us were born with a silver spoon in our mouths, you know.'

'Clive!'

'I'm sorry, Miss Pearce. I didn't mean to say that. It was the heat of the moment.'

'Why don't you ever call me Veronique? You never call me by name.'

'I'm sorry, Veronique.'

'Don't worry about it, Clive. I'd like to have met Angela and Pauline. They sound like wonderful people. Not like some of the others around here.'

'You can't do that,' he said. 'But I can show you their picture. A delivery man took it on my mobile for us about eight years ago and I've moved it every time I bought a new phone since. It's precious to me.'

Clive felt in his pocket and extracted a shiny new phone. This he manipulated with a nimble dexterity that reminded Veronique of the difference in their ages.

'Here.'

Veronique took the proffered phone, which displayed a group photograph of three people. In the middle was a younger version of Clive. He had his arms draped casually around the shoulders of two women, both of about the same as age as Veronique was now. All three were smiling happily. They stood in front of a sturdy bush of Lilac flowers. Both women wore dresses of a bold Lilac colour, almost of the same shade as the plants.

'What a lovely photograph!' she said.

'It was taken in this part of the garden. It was our favourite corner. The favourite part of all three of us.'

'But where are Angela and Pauline these days?'

'Gone. Both of them. Gone.'

'Where? Where have they gone?'

'If you don't mind, Veronique, I'd prefer not to talk about it.'

She noticed the 'Veronique'.

'I think it would be better if you told me the whole story.'

Clive looked down at the ground, clearly distressed. Had she overplayed her hand? For a long time, Clive said nothing. Then he spoke, haltingly at first but gradually more fluently. He told her of his difficult childhood and once more of the way Angela and Pauline had helped him when he most needed help. He told her again of the gossip in Northolme and the way the two women had done their best to laugh at it.

It was only natural, he said, that his childish attempts to help them with this large garden should have developed into something more purposeful. He even smiled when he recounted Pauline's suggestion that they should name the bungalow 'Lilac Cottage'. Angela wouldn't have it, saying that it wasn't really a cottage. Then his face darkened and he stopped speaking.

'There's more to this, isn't there, Clive.'

He looked at her and blinked hard. When he resumed speaking, his voice had dropped in volume.

'One day, a few years ago,' he said, 'they had some men in to install the new potting shed. I could have done it – I only wish I had – but Angela said the manufacturer would put it up for next to nothing. Next to nothing? Huh!'

'One of the men flirted outrageously with Pauline. I didn't see this myself. Angela told me about it before she threw me out.'

'Threw you out?'

'She told me to get out of the garden and wouldn't speak to me or anyone else for another eighteen months. You see this man – Beano, they used to call him – had persuaded Pauline to come and live with him in the village. His wife had just left him, so the story goes. Myself, I think all the talk in the village had been getting to Pauline. You wouldn't believe how old-fashioned and wicked some of them were. Pauline was never as strong minded as Angela.'

Clive's voice was now barely above a whisper.

'It didn't last. After only a few months Beano went off to London with a girl from Sudlip young enough to be his daughter. He hadn't been keeping up with his repayments and before long the house was repossessed. Pauline would have been out on the street but luckily she had an old aunt in the village and she went to live with her. I used to see her afterwards, moping about the place, hardly talking to anyone. She even treated me like someone she hardly knew.'

Clive stopped speaking once more. Hoping to prompt him to resume his story rather than anything else, Veronique asked him:

'Couldn't Pauline could have gone back to Angela? Surely she would have taken her back after a friendship lasting so many years?'

'You don't know Angela. If she had a fault…she did have a fault… it was that she was unbelievably stiff-necked. The week after Pauline moved out, she had every one of the Lilac bushes in the garden ripped out. That's why the pond was put there in a hurry, to fill the biggest gap. Someone told me she made a bonfire of every one of their lilac dresses in the garden – in the garden, mind you, the garden they'd kept so beautifully for all those years. Every photograph of Pauline in the house – and there was hardly a wall without one, let me tell you – she destroyed. And yet she was going to unbend at the end, I'm sure of it.'

Without even knowing she was doing it, Veronique looked down to see that her fingers were gripping Clive's elbow. She grasped his other arm firmly and gave it a squeeze.

'The end?' she said, as gently as she could.

'About eighteen months after Pauline had left, Angela came up to me in the village. I was surprised because she hadn't spoken to me at all for such a long time. She said, "This has gone on too long. I've been a stubborn old fool. Tomorrow I'm going around to see Pauline. I want to ask her to please come home. I wanted you to be the first to know. And, if she does decide to come back, Clive, I want you to come to us for tea on Saturday, in the way you used to do". Then she smiled, gave me a quick peck on the cheek – something she'd never done before – and was off down the street before I knew it. There was a spring in her step I hadn't seen for a long time.

'I was surprised – happy but surprised – and she was a few paces away before I came to my senses. When I did, I called after her: "Why wait until tomorrow? Don't hesitate. Do it today." I do believe she heard me. At least, she seemed to stop in her tracks for a split second.'

'Oh, Good for you, Clive. What happened then?'

'Nothing. Angela didn't call around to see Pauline. She must have decided to keep to her original plan to go next day. That night Pauline went out in her dressing gown to the village telephone box at the end of her aunt's road – this telephone box, the one in your garden – and tried to make a call. A neighbour who was coming home around three o'clock – as luck would have it he was a shift worker who had to leave his factory in Sudlip early because he was unwell – found her crumpled at the bottom of the phone booth, the receiver dangling above her head. She died soon after he found her.'

'How terrible. What did she die of?'

'The inquest returned a verdict of "*Death Through Causes Unknown*". Pauline was only in her mid-fifties and her heart was strong. There was a police enquiry. They followed up on the only clue they had. Before Pauline died, she'd whispered to the neighbour, "*She wouldn't answer my call*". That was all. They checked with the telephone exchange. They were able to supply them with the only number called from the box between midnight and eight o'clock. It was Angela's number.'

'But why didn't Angela answer?'

'Since Pauline left, she'd been in the habit of disconnecting the phone at night. Angela was doing nothing wrong with this, of course, but she was devastated when she found out. Soon after that, the box in the village was decommissioned – I think the death speeded up the decision – and Angela snapped it up to have it fitted where it is now, in this garden. Two weeks after it was put in, next to the pond she'd recently installed, Angela died herself.'

Veronique didn't dare to ask what was the cause of death. Anyway, it was clear from Clive's expression what he thought the reason was.

'Now, if you don't mind, I'll be on my way,' he said. 'I'll do what I planned to do today next Saturday. It won't take me long; there are no more than a few hours' work left in all.'

'Of course, Clive. You can come back tomorrow if it's better for you.'

'I couldn't,' he said. 'Tomorrow is the anniversary of Angela's death.'

That night, Veronique was going to unplug the phone as she usually did. She stopped herself: even the phone in the garden had been silent for the last few weeks. She went to bed at eleven o'clock, intending to read a chapter or two of her novel before settling down for the night. Settling down was the last thing she was able to do. It was after one o'clock before she drifted into a fitful sleep.

*

'We'll gather lilacs in the spring again…'

At three o'clock in the morning she sat bolt upright in bed as strains of the old song – words as well as music – came from the telephone by her bedside. She was sure this song was not on the instrument's menu of call tones. None of the others included lyrics. She looked at the small screen: *Waxlow 7901*. She snatched up the receiver.

'What do you WANT?'

There was silence but she was sure someone was on the line. Eventually, a female voice spoke. Only two words were said:

'Don't hesitate.'

It was Angela's voice. Although she'd never heard her speak before, she was as certain of this as she'd been of anything in her life.

*

The following Saturday couldn't come quickly enough for Veronique. She opened the front door as soon as he knocked it, at precisely nine-thirty. She smiled when she saw him.

'Good morning, Clive, It's good to see you.'

'I won't keep you long today,' he said. 'A couple of hours and I'll be finished.'

'What time would that be, would you say?'

'I should think half past eleven at the very latest. I'll be all done by then.'

'Perfect,' she smiled. 'Then you must stay to have lunch with me.'

'Oh, I don't… do you really mean that?' He smiled shyly but warmly.

'Of course I do. You'll find I don't hesitate.'

Both of them laughed together.

Pumlumon

Hypothermia. That was one of the words echoing around his mind. He knew with an icy certainty it was creeping upon him, dulling his senses, slowing his movements, all the time urging him to lie down quietly on this dome of a mountain and be done with it all.

If. That was the other word. If he had worn warmer clothes. If he had turned back at the first sign of mist. If he hadn't fallen and cracked his head on that boulder. If he hadn't left the warmth of the Dyffryn Castell Hotel for what should have been not much more than a stroll to the top of Pen Pumlumon Fawr[1] on a fine December morning…

He had no clue as to whether he'd been on the mountain for hours or days. The only thing he knew was that it had become dark and the fog had now given way to a sheeting rain, raking through his thin sweater and gnawing away at what was left of his consciousness.

Nor did he know when he had first seen the light. In truth, he hadn't seen it at all, but rather became half-aware of a glow from below. He'd been drawn to it by the last frail moth of hope fluttering within him. As he came nearer, he could make out that the light, a poor trembling thing, was coming from behind the window of the stone-built farmhouse he could now see below.

He thought of what he could see as a window, although in reality it was no more than a cracked wooden shutter, rattling in a roughly-made frame as the wind and rain pounded the building. It seemed to take him hours to reach the house, his whole being fixed upon its blurring image and the thought that no matter what, he must go on putting one slow-motion foot in front of the other.

Now something else touched the fringe of his dimming senses which, for so long, had known only darkness, cold and the dull pain lying heavily on his chest. It was, he slowly realised, the reek of animals. As at last he found himself clinging to the end-wall of the house, he could hear them, too: a shuffling of heavy feet in straw and a muted lowing.

Even in his half-alive state, it seemed odd to him that there were animals in the house but he knew he must reach the far end, where he had seen the feeble light and from where, he could now see, a thin waft of smoke ascended, telling surely of human help and safety.

Step by agonising step he made it to the splintered wooden door, and flapped weakly against it with the last of his strength. There was no answer. He tasted a bitterness rising in his throat as the fate awaiting him became clear. He lost consciousness and drifted into oblivion.

*

At first there was a flickering redness, nothing more. Then, slowly, he became aware of his own person: still, cold and tightly bound by something. With an effort he forced his eyes open. The redness was replaced by the wavering image of a tiny flame a few feet from his face. His eyes started to come into focus.

Gradually he could make out that the flame belonged to something akin to a candle, a reed held in place by a metal contraption. The binding he'd felt about him turned out to be layer upon layer of coarse blankets, all wrapped firmly around his body. For some reason, he was in an old iron bed. The feeble flame barely illuminated the low-ceilinged room, but he could see that it contained another, smaller bed, and two heaps of ragged clothes that might have served the same function.

Then, while he was taking in his strange surroundings, something else loomed out of the darkness toward him. It was the face of a woman. She was young and delicately fine in appearance, but worn-looking. Her fair skin was drawn too tightly across her high cheekbones for her face, oddly framed in a white bonnet, to be called pretty. Her eyes were an intense blue, lit by an infinite kindness as they searched his own.

'*Popeth yn iawn nawr, bach?*'[2]

'I-I don't... *Dw i ddim...*'

He had little enough Welsh at the best of times; now his memory baulked at the task of finding the words. He tried again: '*Dw i ddim yn siarad Cymraeg*'[3], he managed to stutter, hoping he was saying he didn't speak Welsh.

'*Sais?*'[4]

'No, I'm from Swansea. *Dw i'n...dw i'n dod o* Swansea...*o Abertawe.*' [5] The effort was too much for him. His eyelids drooped, almost closing, and he sighed deeply.

'*Peidiwch a phoeni; peidiwch a phoeni.*'[6]

She smiled at him, put a finger to her lips, and noiselessly left the room.

When she'd gone, he tried to gather his thoughts. In fact, considering his recent ordeal, his thoughts now seemed oddly lucid. Before long they were full of questions. Where was he? Who was the woman, and why was she dressed as if she belonged to a different era? What on earth were cattle and horses doing inside the house?

Before many minutes had passed, the woman was back in the room. He heard no step on the stair, and again she seemed to appear before him without warning. In her hands was a carved wooden tray, upon which she carried a steaming pottery bowl.

She sat down beside him on the bed and, without a word, started to feed him broth from a wooden spoon. She fed him patiently, easing tiny drops of the semi-liquid through his numbed lips. It was watery stuff, but hot and salty. It seemed to work directly on his system. Before long he began to feel stirrings of life within his aching frame.

When the bowl was half-empty, he tried again to speak to her. This time he abandoned his attempt to speak in Welsh, letting out a tumble of questions in English. The woman seemed not to understand, waiting quietly as he spoke, as if his words had little to do with her. Then, when he'd exhausted himself, she smiled her deep warm smile, and allowed those blue eyes to look steadily into his for a long moment.

She offered him her hand, but when he tried to reach out for it, he felt nothing. He told himself he was still suffering from exposure or worse and was very tired. He closed his eyes and slept.

*

When he awoke, sunlight was streaming into the room. He was still beneath his heavy load of blankets. Now he could feel the warmth they gave. The room seemed much larger in the light of day, and he was surprised to see someone must have removed the other bed whilst he slept. Nor were there now piles of clothes on the floor. Altogether, the room seemed tidier and newer, belonging to this century rather than some distant one.

He felt a gentle pressure on his hand, and realised that the woman was still holding it. He looked up at her, and saw again the kindly light of the eyes that had, he knew, kept him from sliding into the abyss.

'We thought we were losing you last night, young man. *Duw*[7], but you were just a breath away from the end when we found you.'

'You do speak English!'

'Of course I do. *Dych chi'n hoffi siarad Cymraeg?*'[8]

'No, English is fine. But last night we were speaking in Welsh, or at least I was trying to.'

'Last night? Last night you wouldn't be speaking anything to anyone. Now then, you still need your rest this morning. Doctor's coming back to look at you in a minute.'

Her tone was chiding, but she held his hand tightly. Strength and vigour seemed to be flowing directly into him from the plump firmness of her own. Strange, that hand had looked so different, frailer, last night, when she had held it out to him.

Then he realised other things were different about her, too. This morning she seemed older, but comely and with a fine glow to her cheeks. Her dress, too, was different; still dark, but now the material seemed richer, and the odd little bonnet had gone.

He looked more closely at her face. Yes, those blue eyes were unmistakable. All the rest must have been a trick of the light, or the spawn of a fevered brain. But still he *had* spoken to her last night. He wanted to speak to her now, didn't want her to go away yet.

'It was lucky I managed to get as far as your house last night.'

'But you didn't. My husband found you.'

'I reached the house. I'm sure I did. I remember getting to the door and...'

'Well, you reached *a* house, that you did, if you can still call it a house now it's all but fallen down. My husband found you by *Pwll Uchaf.* [9] It's nearly a mile from here. This is *Pwll Isaf*[10]. Nobody's lived at the old place since my great-grandmother's day. Now, no more talking; I'll get you something to warm the cockles of your heart.'

He waited, a thousand unanswered questions crowding in on him. After a few minutes, he heard a weighty tread on the staircase and the woman returned. She was carrying a steaming white bowl on an elaborately carved tray.

'Where did you get that tray?'

'Well, funny you should ask. It's after my great-grandmother. The last one of our family who lived at *Pwll Uchaf. Duw*, you're full of questions, you are.'[7]

But all the questions had been answered. He looked up. Now it was no surprise to see another woman standing behind his benefactor. She was thinner, younger, a little pinched from the hard life she'd led. In the sunlight, she was faded, frail and but a pale shadow of the other. Yet there could be no mistaking the likeness, the wonderful blue eyes.

He smiled. And both women smiled back at him.

NOTES

[1] Pen Pumlumon Fawr is the name of the largest of a group of five peaks in Mid Wales. At one time this was thought to be the highest point in the whole of Wales, but now accurate measurements are possible it is known that a number of others exceed it. The name is usually rendered in English as "Plynlimon".

[2] 'Everything's all right now, little one' – "bach" or "little one" is used as a term of endearment here.

[3] I don't [speak Welsh].

[4] An Englishman?

[5] I come from [Swansea].

[6] Don't worry; don't worry.

[7] God.

[8] Do you like to speak Welsh?

[9] A house or farm name: "The Highest Pool".

[10] A house or farm name: "The Lowest Pool".

Carnival Street

Carnaby Street? Doesn't mean a thing to me. Carnival Street, on the other hand, looms all too large in my life. Rock 'n' Roll? Rollers on the sea are the only ones to have ever made me excited. A year or two back I read in one of those smart newspaper features, '*if you can remember the sixties, you weren't there*'. Well, you could say I wasn't there. Not in the 'Swinging Sixties' sense, I wasn't, anyway.

*

All I'd wanted to be ever since I was three feet high was a merchant seaman. Some of the other boys in school had ideas to join the Royal Navy, serve the colours, that sort of thing. It wasn't my sort of thing. What had the colours ever done for me?

I was glad to be able to leave school a week after my fifteenth birthday in late October 1960 so I could start to make my dream a reality. The headmaster, a miserable old leftover from the nineteenth century, tried to tell me I was supposed to see out the Christmas term before I left. Was I going to wait for a thing like that? No chance.

Finding a boat wasn't anything like as easy as I'd expected. I ended up joining what they used to call 'the Norwegian Merchant Navy'. This wasn't really a navy of any kind. It was no more than a loose collection of commercial operations. Still, they had some kind of central recruitment office in Harrington Street, around the corner from where I lived in Camden, North London. The Norwegians weren't nearly as fussy as the British merchants. They spared me all the awkward questions about my juvenile police record. Their way of doing things was 'get yourself down for a medical, and get yourself on board the boat'. This suited me.

Early in the following January, I found myself sailing from Liverpool docks on the *MV Trondheim*. You can guess what I felt like. I was a real seaman at last.

My first voyage was a terrific one, to Madagascar. I'd never even realised there was a place called Madagascar. It's somewhere off the coast of Africa. In all, I spent slightly less than two years at sea but in that time I docked at Hong Kong, Tomé in Chile, New York Harbour and all the Scandinavian countries. Brilliant, it was. Everything I'd ever wanted and more. I'd still like to be at sea now, a veteran sailor with years of experience behind me. I might be, too, if it hadn't been for that night in Liverpool. Liverpool! After all the exotic places I'd visited, my time as a seafarer had to end in bloody Liverpool.

*

You'd have to say I did have a tiny sip of the Swinging Sixties. The last night I could call myself a sailor, in November, 1962, was the very same one The Beatles made their first appearance on national TV. It was on an early evening programme. I saw it in *The Black Lion*, a pub right there in Penny Lane. Would you believe a thing like that?

I didn't stay long in the *Lion*; I only had one pint, and I didn't even drink it all the way down. All the Scousers in the pub were shouting and screaming about their boys. It made me sick. So I left the *Lion* behind me and off I went to find a room for the night. The other drinkers were so excited about seeing their band on the little black-and-white screen that I didn't even bother to ask their advice on where I should look.

Anyway, anything would have done me for the one night. I wasn't going to be fussy. In the morning I was picking up a new boat – funnily enough, the *MV Trondheim* sailing for Madagascar again – and would have to get up early. But do you think I could find anywhere to take me in? No. Everywhere was full, except for the posh hotels. I wasn't going to pay through the nose for one of them. Couldn't have done, anyway.

The time was getting on for eleven o'clock when I stumbled across Carnival Street. It's a fair step from Penny Lane to Seaforth. Carnival Street was a dead end off Gladstone

Road in the Mersey Docks. Dead end? It was all of that in more ways than one.

*

Not to put it too kindly, Carnival Street was a dirty slum. Well, I knew that as soon as I turned the corner, and I'd seen more than a few rough places in my time. My old place in Camden Town wasn't exactly swish. There wasn't even a working street light in Carnival Street. Nor was there the faintest glimmer coming from any of the houses. Every one of them looked to be on the verge of falling down. The sea-mist you often saw in that part of town was mixing with the thickening November fog and the first bite of winter was in the air. I shivered and gripped the collar of my duffel-coat.

It didn't take me long to realise that I'd blundered into the wrong place. I wasn't so stupid, even then. And then I saw it: the greasy cardboard sign stuck in the front window of one of the houses: '*Rooms to let*'. It was what I'd been trailing around the streets looking for all those hours. Even so, I hesitated. The whole street was unwelcoming. This house was in the worst repair of all them. I can still see the peeling brown paint on its front door in my darkest dreams. Once upon a time, maybe fifty years before, it might have been a smart gloss. Now there was precious little paint left.

By this time I'd been tramping the streets for three hours. I was dog tired and had to be up early in the morning to get my boat. So I knocked. Every day for the last fifty years I've wished I'd turned tail and walked away into the fog.

No-one answered at first. Slowly, I began to hear muffled movements from within. Somehow, it made me think the house was stirring after a long slumber. Eventually, after a long series of noises sounding like creaking doors and groaning floorboards, the door was peeped opened a few inches and a tall woman in her middle years stared down at me.

She had the most expressionless face I'd ever seen. The woman said not a word to me. The most noticeable thing about her was the broad red sash tied around her neck. This contrasted oddly with the grey-blue garment, not quite like a dressing-gown, she wore.

'I'm looking for a room,' I managed to say to break the awkward silence.

Still she said nothing, but opened the door briefly to admit me, then turned her back to walk slowly down a long passage-way. The woman didn't even glance back to see if I was following. The only dim light came from a bare electric bulb hanging at an awkward angle from the ceiling. There was a tangle of cobwebs dangling between flex and ceiling. At the sight of this, I had the renewed urge to turn and get away from Carnival Street as fast as I could. But I didn't do it. Instead I followed the woman.

About half-way along the long passage-way, she stopped and opened a door. She held her arm forward, indicating for me to enter.

'*Speak, damn you,*' I thought, though said nothing.

At exactly the same moment, as if she could hear what was in my mind, she turned around stiffly – she didn't just turn her head like any normal person would have done – and fixed me with a look I couldn't read. It wasn't baleful, exactly, though it was far from friendly. It seemed to be asking '*what was I doing here?*' Still she said nothing.

While I was still wondering whether or not to enter, a small man emerged from behind the door. He was about the same age as the woman and was dressed in a smart grey check suit. The first things I noticed about him, though, were his polished black shoes and, of all things, the old-fashioned pair of spats he wore. His appearance, which otherwise I would have to describe as dapper, was spoilt by two red-brown stains on his otherwise shiny blue bow-tie.

'All right, Martha,' he said when he saw me. 'Don't you worry about a thing. I'll look after everything here.'

He creased his features into a wholly insincere smile and looked at me.

'Looking for a room, are we? Come this way.'

He took fussy little steps towards the end of the passage-way. I followed him. Nothing else was said.

'But we haven't even talked about the price,' I protested, almost running to catch up with him.

'It's free for the first night,' he called across his shoulder.

That settled the matter. I was only looking for a room for one night. I wouldn't have stayed in this dump for longer than a night, even if it was free for a whole week.

What I'd assumed in the semi-darkness to be the end of the passage wasn't that at all. It was a sharp corner, beyond which there was one more doorway. Fixed crudely to the door was, of all things, a pair of spats like those the man wore. I thought this odd, but said nothing.

'Here it is,' said the man. 'This is our best room. I am sure you will be comfortable here. May I wish a very good night to you.'

Comfortable was the wildest kind of exaggeration. There wasn't even a window. The only lighting was provided by a feeble candle flickering on a table in the corner. The eiderdown looked as if it hadn't seen the wash in decades. If this were their best room, what must the others be like? At least it didn't look quite as grubby as some of the other parts of the house I'd seen. Without even taking off my shoes I flopped across the big bed and was asleep in minutes.

*

Something made me wake up a few hours later. At first, I hardly knew where I was. Then, I became aware of somebody edging the bedroom door open from the outside. They were trying to do it quietly. It was so dark I couldn't see who it might be.

I sensed, rather than saw, someone coming into the room. This person lay gently down on the other side of the bed. Something told me to lie still and say nothing. I kept my eyelids half-shuttered and strained my ears. There came from next to me a faint hissing sound. You couldn't exactly describe it as breathing.

The candle on the corner table had burned right down by this time and there was no more than a tiny, guttering flame. As my eyes gradually got used to the near-darkness I half-turned and could make out in the shadows next to me a form that could only be that of the tall woman I'd seen earlier. She was quite naked, save for a narrow black ribbon around her throat. It made me think of some sort of undergarment to the broad red ribbon I'd seen before.

She started to raise herself on the bed. '*Oh, no you don't,*' I thought. 'I have to get up early in the morning.' She turned towards me, reaching out. Her figure was full and shapely. Then I saw...

The narrow ribbon hardly covered anything. Now I could make out the stark whiteness of her neck and throat and the way these were disfigured by a network of ugly, silverish scar-tissue. It looked for all the world as if she was in the early stages of recovery after the crudest kind of major surgery.

*

'Slow down, Teararse. Our boat won't be leaving the dock for another four hours yet.'

The speaker who'd fallen into stride with me was Fat Jimmy. He was due to sail on the *MV Trondheim* with me. Fat Jimmy was what we all called him, but he didn't much care for that name. To his face we called him 'Scouser'. Well, I didn't like being called 'Teararse' much either but Fat Jimmy was a lot bigger than me.

Had I done no more than run away from a horrible dream? It seemed like that in the fresh coldness of the early-morning air. Seeing my panting breath pluming in the air before me made everything seem so normal. I felt such a fool.

When I'd recovered my breathing sufficiently I tried to answer.

'Sorry. Must have read my watch wrong. Could have had another hour or two in bed, me. Should have done after all the performance I had in finding a lodging last night.'

'You're telling me,' said Fat Jimmy. 'Where'd you find in the end?'

'A place called Carnival Street, here in Seaforth,' I said. 'Bit of a dive, but beggars can't be choosers. Anyway, it was free.'

'Carnival Street? You couldn't have been there. The whole street was pulled down soon after the war. There are warehouses there now. The place was almost falling down when they demolished it. And there was another reason why they knocked it down. I read about it in the papers when I wasn't much above a nipper. Bloody gruesome it was.'

He must have seen my eyes widen but kept on with his story.

'Everybody around here knows about it. It's only ignorant Cockneys like you who haven't heard anything. An old bloke was living there in the nineteen-forties. He was as barmy as a bat's arse. The old geezer took in some poor homeless woman and then sawed the head off her. He did it in some room hidden away in the middle of the house. The police might never have found her if the old loony hadn't taken it into his head to tack a pair of his spats on the door. Spats! I ask you. No-one's been wearing those for years'.

*

I didn't wait to hear the rest of Fat Jimmy's story. I didn't go back to the docks. And I didn't want to stay another hour in Liverpool, so I scarpered back to The Smoke. Eventually, I found a couple of rooms over in Ladbroke Grove. Seems no-one else wanted them. Can't think why. They weren't *that* bad. Cheap, that was the main thing.

Yesterday was the first day I'd travelled beyond the few streets around my flat. It's taken me all these years to screw up the courage to do it. It was quite some time before I'd even leave the flat, let me tell you.

I went to visit my old haunts in Camden Town. Funnily enough, I ran into an old school mate of mine. He asked me where I was living now.

'Ruston Close?' he said when I told him. 'You know that used to be Rillington Place, don't you?'

Now, there's a funny thing to say. If he'd said it was once called Carnival Street, I'd have been out of there like a shot. But Rillington Place? Never even heard of it.

The Contract of One Thousand

1

These days, I can remember every detail of the time I last sat in more or less this spot except, oddly enough, the exact date. It was autumn, as it is today, but in my memory it feels as if it may have been later in the season on the previous occasion. Or perhaps this could be no more than faulty recollection seen through a prism of grey skies and misty dampness. It was so long ago.

Over the last few months, I have been replaying over and over in my mind every word spoken at my meeting with the man, and the strange path down which it took my life. It was inevitable, I know, that I'd find myself back in the place where it all started. This village – what once was the village – has changed beyond recognition with all the new houses and people. There's even a new church built alongside the old small one I remember from my younger days. Even so, it's still possible to imagine the churchyard as it then was.

How I wish I could turn the clock back, despite what that would mean.

2

I'm sure there were more leaves stripped from the trees by the wind and the first hint of winter was already in the air the last time I was here. Wintry would be the word to sum up the state of my own life, too. I, John Mitchell, bachelor of this parish, was then 39 years old, and the possessor of gambling debts to the alarming total of almost four hundred sovereigns.

Ned Whitehouse had already given me several unpleasantly graphic reminders of what those who chose not to settle their debts could expect. Mine was a large sum by the standards of the day, so he'd taken the trouble to nudge me with almost daily descriptions of what others before me had received and what I should expect if I should prove to be a defaulter.

Great Uncle Silas was my last hope. He was the reason that autumn day found me back in my home village of Greenford. Silas had always liked me. The old man had more than enough money in his bank, if only I could persuade him to part with a small portion of it. I thought I'd have a good chance of doing this, too. But, curse my luck: Silas had surprised everyone by dying on the very day I arrived.

His funeral service was why I was sitting on the solitary bench close to the grandly-named 'Church of the Exultation of the Holy Cross'. This was the Parish Church of what then used to be called Greenford Magna. It was my misfortune to be on the churchyard bench instead of warming myself by the fireside in the cosy parlour of Uncle Silas.

His only son, Herbert, had made the journey from Ealing to ensure all the money from the old man's estate settled in its rightful place in Herbert's bank account. Herbert was in Greenford at least as much for monetary gain as from any sense of filial piety. All right, this might be uncharitable to my cousin, or the man who I considered to be first cousin once removed if you will. He'd actually been, or so I thought, my father's first cousin. Still, I never had many charitable feelings in the direction of Herbert. I knew there'd be no chance of extracting as much as a farthing from his tight purse.

I sat alone in the churchyard for a full hour after the funeral service was over. My fob-watch told me two o'clock wasn't far off. All the other mourners had long since dispersed to pick up the threads of their dull lives.

The moment when the Rector, whose face had seemed oddly familiar to me, had droned the usual 'Ashes to Ashes; Dust to Dust' had chilled me. I'd heard these words a score of times before, like everyone else. They'd meant little to me but now I realised that, if Ned Whitehouse had his way, some Rector would soon be droning them over my cadaver, or at least the bits of it they might recover after Ned's men had done their work. Or, more likely, a few anonymous body-parts would be tossed uncared for into a pauper's grave somewhere in the Black Country, Ned's domain.

To say this was the lowest point of my life, up to that day, would be an understatement.

3

'Ashes to Ashes; Dust to Dust,' I muttered, in low, despairing tones.

'Yes; the burial service does have its own special music, doesn't it?'

The voice belonged to a man of distinguished appearance sitting alongside me. So wrapped up in my troubling thoughts had I been that I wasn't aware he'd taken the place beside mine, nor even of his approach. The sudden sight of this stranger made me start up and some seconds passed before I could collect my wits sufficiently to answer.

'Do you mind? This is a private moment.'

'Of course; I respect your wishes. Silas was a man of quality. Naturally you'll want to say your own prayer for his soul.'

I looked at his face more closely. He was supremely placid in his manner, and his quiet way of speaking suggested a genuine reverence for the old man. Yet I'd never seen him before.

'You're not a relative, are you?' I said. 'I didn't see you at the service.'

'No. None of your family knew me. You might say Silas and I had been business acquaintances for a great number of years. I chose to pay my respects privately, since my main purpose in coming to Greenford was to conclude our contract.'

This was odd. I knew my Great Uncle's regular investment contacts these days were exclusively with Mortimer Smith and Joshua Brember, two local men. Both of them had been present at the funeral service. What business could this man have with Silas? He said he'd come to 'conclude our contract'. Herbert might find there wasn't as much money left in his father's estate as he'd been expecting. I smiled with grim satisfaction. It would be good to find out more.

'What was the nature of your contract with Silas? I might be able to help you,' I said. As I spoke, something in the air warned me I should be careful in my dealings with this man.

'I cannot tell you more for the present. Let us simply say he and I made a bargain some time ago. It was the most important business arrangement Silas made in the whole of his long life.'

'Are you saying there is still a debt to discharge?' I said.

'No. Silas has settled in full. Our arrangement was wholly satisfactory to me.'

'Then what are you still doing here?' As soon as I'd voiced this thought, I realised I was speaking out of turn. But he merely arched one eyebrow slightly and answered my question with perfect equanimity.

'I am here to pay my respects, just as you are. And, perhaps, while I am here I would like to see if I can strike a similar bargain with another member of the family. Yourself, possibly?'

Where was this conversation leading? I had nothing to offer. But perhaps he had something to offer me. What other hope did I have?

'You haven't been sent by Ned Whitehouse, have you?' I said.

'Ned Whitehouse? The Bilston Blackguard? No, I have little business with any man of his kind. In any event, I should be far more likely to use his services than he mine. Whitehouse is a mere bully-boy; I prefer to have nothing to do with his like.'

So, this man knew both my Great Uncle and the man whose fingers I could almost now feel tightening around my neck? The two were as different as they could be. The need for caution and the irrational feeling that this stranger might provide an answer to my troubles with Ned quarrelled within me once again. He gave no sign of wanting to say anything further, so I prompted him.

'You were saying something about a bargain?'

The man smiled, and drew up onto his lap a small attaché-case I hadn't noticed before. He clicked open the brass fasteners.

'We can make a bargain here and now. It will benefit both of us.'

'Keeping it in the family, I suppose. What arrangement was it you had with my Great Uncle, precisely?'

'Silas wasn't your Great Uncle. You'd have to put a number of 'Greats' before that title to describe the precise relationship. There would have to be eight of them, to be exact.'

'What on Earth do you mean?' I said. 'I know very well Herbert was his son, and Herbert was my father's first cousin.'

The hopes I was starting to build upon no firm foundation crumbled away. Was I sitting on this seat and talking to someone who was soft in the head? I looked at him again. He merely paused in his task of rifling through the contents of his attaché-case and returned my gaze directly.

'What you say is almost correct,' he said. 'Herbert had some degree of cousinhood with your father and he is the youngest son of Silas. He is, in fact, the sole child of his sixth and last marriage.'

'Six marriages? All the family knew Silas married only once. He returned from Cornwall with Grace as his young bride. I was a young scholar at the time. Silas was already an old man.'

He smiled again, conspiratorially.

'Silas saw no need to give the younger generations of his family the details of his earlier life. He wanted to portray himself as a steady man of business returning to his home village to enjoy his twilight years. Tell me, do you remember much about your Great Aunt?'

'Not a great deal,' I said. 'I was quite young. So was she. And she was very pretty, I remember this much.'

In truth I remembered her well. She was more than pretty. Every contour of her face was etched into my mind as a vision of loveliness. But typhoid had taken her away barely two years after she'd come to Greenford.

Silas had grieved terribly. It had taken years for him to recover his spirit sufficiently to take much interest in his worldly affairs. It was during those dark years that he and I had formed a friendship bridging the generations. As far as I was concerned there were only three generations to bridge. Herbert, fourteen years older than me and a charmless youth, had always resented the easy relationship I enjoyed with his father.

Herbert's mother had died when he was not much above a boy and she had not yet reached her thirty-seventh year. Now he was left with a father who too often showed a preference for the young villain who happened to be from one of the poorer branches of his family.

'And how old would you say Silas was at that time?'

'I don't know,' I said, puzzled by this line of questioning. 'He must have been quite old, even in the days when I was a child. But he'd always enjoyed robust good health. All the family were surprised when he suddenly died a few days ago.'

'Everyone must leave when their time comes. Even those for whom special arrangements have been made must depart when they are called. What would you say if I told you Silas was two hundred and eighty-two years old on the day of his death?'

'I'd say you were mad.'

The man chuckled softly, seeming to be not in the least offended.

'I thought you would say as much,' he said. 'There was hardly anything else I could expect. But it is quite true. That was the nature of our arrangement, or the part of it that most interested Silas, at least. And I can make a similar bargain with your good self today. Is this your wish?'

'You are entirely insane,' I said. 'You're trying to tell me I can live until I'm two hundred and eighty-two?'

'No. In your case the contract would have to extend until you'd achieved two hundred and thirty-nine years of age. Or, if you wish, you can live until you are three hundred and thirty-nine. Or, within the hundred-year rule, anything up to-'

'Go to blazes!' I shouted. 'I'm here to mourn the passing of my Great Uncle Silas and here you are trying to take a rise out of me.'

He was quite unperturbed by my outburst. At first he maintained his infuriating smile, but then he looked at me severely.

'Your choice makes very little difference to me. If you wish you can return to Tipton now and have your throat cut. Or, if you prefer you can skulk here in Greenford and have Ned Whitehouse send his henchmen to Middlesex to deal with you. He'll be sure to extract some additional painful retribution if you put him to so much trouble.'

Then he smiled again. I wanted to ask him how he knew about the fate awaiting me in The Midlands. How had he even known about Ned Whitehouse to begin with, come to that? He'd called him the 'Bilston Blackguard'. As far as I knew this sobriquet was used only in The Black Country. I knew a direct question would only meet with another ridiculous answer, so I played along with this alarming conversation, wondering where it would take us next.

'What is the alternative?'

'That's more like it,' he said. 'As I told you, you can make an arrangement similar to the one Silas made with me. We call it 'The Contract of One Thousand'.

'Which is?'

'You may have sovereigns and years of life to the value of one thousand. You may have five hundred of each if you wish, or this number in any combination of sovereigns and years, subject only to a minimum of two hundred of either and the hundred-year rule, to which I have already alluded.'

'You seem very fond of your rules and numbers,' I said. 'And, pray, what would be my side of the bargain?'

I knew what he was going to say, of course, but I wanted to hear him say it.

'Your signature on a contract is all I would require; nothing more.'

'My signature in blood, I suppose. Tell me, should I open a vein in my right arm or in my left?' I was still trying to treat this situation with the levity I thought it deserved, even if I knew an undercurrent of fear at the knowledge that, somehow, this disturbing man was aware of my dire circumstances.

'Tell me, if you were purchasing a property or entering into any other legal agreement would you expect to sign in blood? No, of course you wouldn't. I have a small flask of ink in my attaché-case. The ink will serve our purpose adequately and rather less messily.'

'But to what would I be agreeing?' I said. Then I said the ludicrous words I'd been trying to avoid. 'You want my soul, do you? You're the Devil. I suppose that's what you'll be telling me next.'

'To say that you'd be signing away your soul,' he said. 'Would be an excessively dramatic way of stating the facts of the matter. Your playwrights have much for which to answer. All you'd be doing is entering into a simple contract of service.

And I would like to assure you I'm as human as you are. I'm considerably older, nothing more. I made my own contract over seven hundred years ago.'

'You'll be telling me your agreement was another of these Contracts of One Thousand, I suppose.'

He answered me as if the two of us had been discussing an entirely normal business transaction.

'In my case I entered into a Contract of Two Thousand. This is very similar to the arrangement I am offering you. Except, of course, the rewards are twice as good and part of my service has to be during my lifetime. Not that such duty is onerous. I need no more than another dozen signatures and then I will have fulfilled this part of my contract.'

'And the other part?' I asked him.

He flinched. He visibly flinched and for a few moments looked unsettled for the first and only time in our conversation. I thought for a moment I'd shaken him out of his ridiculous fantasy. But he quickly recovered his composure and carried on as before, exactly as if he were talking about some minor legal dealing.

'My own cessation clause falls to be met in the summer of the year 2086. This is a lifetime in the future. It would be a number of lifetimes away for nearly everyone who is alive today, in point of fact. My option was for a thousand years and a thousand sovereigns. I made my choice in the year 1086, when I was one of the soldiers accompanying the King's surveyors of property in one of your neighbouring shires. We were undertaking what the peasants even then called 'The Domesday Survey'. The one who offered the contract to me was my Captain. He was born a Phoenician a thousand years before, so he told me.'

He believed every word of what he was saying. He really believed it.

'It's a wonder everyone doesn't go for this Contract of Two Thousand, then.'

'They are very rarely offered. I was exceedingly fortunate to be offered such generous terms. Contracts of One Thousand themselves are seldom offered. You yourself would be a lucky man.'

'Am I?' I said. 'I've heard these bargains are really no bargain at all. Tomorrow I could be struck down by a horse, or meet my end at the hands of one of Ned Whitehouse's men.' I shivered when I thought how likely this was. 'Or,' I said, 'I could limp out the centuries, burdened with an incredible number of years in poor health.'

'I see you are familiar with certain imaginative works of literature,' he said. 'But none of the things you fear is true. The contract would guarantee you a long and healthy life. If you signed, you would not, despite very minor changes in your appearance, age one day between now and the agreed date. You can be assured no kind of accident or violent death would befall you during the whole of the period of the contract. I must emphasise that you would continue to enjoy rude good health, exactly as did your Uncle Silas. He was already eighty-two years old on the day he signed his contract with me.'

I found myself wearying of this game. It had been fun to lead this lunatic on for a while, but now more sombre thoughts were forcing themselves to the forefront of my mind. My own mention of the name of Ned Whitehouse had brought them there.

'And I suppose the fairies will bring me my gold sovereigns if I wish upon a star at the time of the next blue moon. Will they tie them up in silk if I ask politely?'

'You mock, of course. I can hardly blame you. But will you sign the contract? What balance of years and sovereigns would you choose?'

As he said this he started to unbuckle the case. Did he have the sovereigns with him? What had he said was the greatest number I could specify? Eight hundred gold sovereigns? Was that what this imbecile had promised?

'And you'd be prepared to put the coins in my hand now, merely for signing a piece of paper?'

'No. Do you think I'd carry such a weight of gold in this bag? The practice is well established. I'd give you ten sovereigns now as a gesture of good faith. The balance of seven-hundred-and-ninety sovereigns would then be yours within forty-eight hours.'

This madman would place ten sovereigns in my hand now? The rest of his deranged game would be unimportant, if only the coins were real.

'Show me the money,' I said. 'If it is genuine coin of the realm then I'll sign here and now for eight hundred sovereigns and two hundred years.' There clearly was nothing on his side of the bargain beyond madness and delusion. What was there to lose?

'Ah, so you want the doubter's contract as did Silas. Very well; this is what you'll have.'

He reached into the depths of his bag and dropped ten coins into my outstretched hand.

I examined the coins. All of them were bright and newly-minted, showing the head of the new King. These were the first of the new sovereigns showing George the son as our King I'd held, or so much as seen. He'd only ascended the throne earlier this year, after acting as Prince Regent for ten years in the stead of his mad father, King George III. The coins could have been counterfeit for all I knew, but at least it looked as if they hadn't been crudely hammered out in some wayward forger's smithy.

The man acted confidently enough. While I was still examining the money he drew out a neatly printed document from his case, then a bottle of ink and an impressive-looking plume. Afterwards he unscrewed the bottle-top and briskly dipped the instrument into it. This he handed to me along with what he'd called 'the contract of a thousand'. It was all so very straightforward and matter-of-fact. He could have been a clerk in any lawyer's chambers.

I looked at the document. It was printed on heavy, expensive vellum. The characters were neat but closely-set and difficult to read. But what did it matter? If this idiot wanted to drop ten sovereigns into my palm for nothing, I wasn't going to be the one to argue. I signed with a flourish.

'Now it is for me to sign as the witness to your signature.'

He applied his own strokes of the quill almost imperceptibly. I briefly saw his signature whilst he was shaking the sand over it from a neat silver pot and it was tiny, of the same dimensions and in almost the same form as the printed part of the document.

'Now what will happen?' I said.

'Our business is concluded for the time being. May I take this opportunity to wish you well for the next two centuries?'

He clipped his attaché-case closed and rose to leave.

'What about the rest of my money?'

'I've already told you; the remaining seven-hundred-and-ninety sovereigns will be yours within forty-eight hours,' he called over his shoulder. 'And now I really do have to be on my way. I am a busy man.'

Saying this, he rose from the bench and walked down the churchyard path without so much as a backward glance or even the courtesy of a 'Good Day'. I watched him until he was out of sight, noting his peculiar rolling gait and the fact that, although he carried a silver-tipped walking-cane, he didn't need to lean on it for support but rather swung it vigorously in rhythm with his step.

4

I stayed quietly in Greenford for the next day-and-a-half, telling myself that Ned Whitehouse would be unlikely to send his henchmen to find me within such a short time. Although I hadn't actually been invited to attend the reading of Silas' will in the chambers of Messrs Sharpe and Tolman in Ealing, I was family and no-one would be likely to bar my presence.

All the same, it was abundantly clear Cousin Herbert wished I'd chosen to spend the morning somewhere other than in the solicitors' practice. He probably wondered what I was doing in Greenford at all. My cousin probably wondered how I'd managed to get here so quickly from whatever dark realm I'd landed myself in. Herbert was not to know his father's funeral wasn't the thing that had drawn me back to Middlesex for the first time in more than twenty years. The rest of my family, such as it was, didn't know and probably didn't care whether I was alive or dead. Even my Great-Uncle Silas, despite the bond of affection laid down years ago, could hardly have been expected to remember me in his will.

To tell the truth, I was unsure why I was there with the rest of them. I kept telling myself it wasn't anything to do with my strange encounter with the madman, even though my thoughts had returned again and again to our odd transaction by the church. For some inexplicable reason, the thing lodging in my mind most particularly was my last sight of him swinging his way down the churchyard path.

I was as surprised as everyone else when old Mr Tolman read the codicil to the will. The oddest thing was that even Tolman seemed a little bemused when his rumbling tones announced the particulars of the bequest, although the paper evidenced that the codicil had been added only on the day before Silas' death. Tolman himself would surely have been responsible for the legal work.

Naturally, the thing I remember most clearly about my morning in the stuffy solicitor's office was Tolman's solemn announcement of a bequest to me in the sum of "seven-hundred-and-ninety sovereigns, in the coin of the realm". This wasn't only because all my money worries evaporated with the solicitor's words; it was the exactness of the sum that made me try to recall every word of my strange interview.

The fact that Silas had seen fit to leave anything at all to this prodigal son of the village caused all those present to turn their heads in my direction. Mortimer Smith and Joshua Brember regarded me with interest for the first time. No doubt the mercenary minds of these two were already reckoning up investments more to their benefit than mine.

Cousin Herbert looked at me with undisguised resentment. This seemed to be unnecessary; his father's will had already benefited my fat cousin to the tune of several tens of thousands of sovereigns. How greedy some people can be!

The only glance making me think twice about further delaying my return to Tipton was given to me by my cousin Mildred. She was an exceptionally comely woman a few years my senior who'd been widowed during the year before. Silas had already made a bequest to her of two hundred sovereigns. She must have seen a way to warm her bed at the same time as swelling her fortune. I confess I had similar thoughts.

Soon enough, I was happy to put Mortimer Smith, Joshua Brember and at least one of my cousins far from my mind. I knew I should return to Tipton without delay to face a sweeter music than I'd been expecting not an hour before. Although I wasn't looking forward to the prospect of parting with such a large a portion of my new wealth, I reasoned I'd sooner give up this part of my money than my life.

But, before I returned to the Black Country, there was one more thing I wanted to do in Greenford.

5

The Church of the Exultation of the Holy Cross, despite its lofty name, was an unimpressive structure at that time. When I pushed open the heavy church door, I was pleased to find the rector quite alone. He was bent over one of the pews, studying his Bible and I presume making notes for his Sunday sermon. In those days I was very firmly a non-believer, but couldn't help being impressed by the man's dedication, for all of that. He looked up when he saw me and his eyebrows shot up in a peculiar way.

'Ah, Mr Mitchell. Or will you allow me to call you John after so many years?'

I was surprised by his familiarity. Word would not be out yet of my now comfortable material state but even a poor a man is entitled to normal respect.

He smiled broadly when he saw my expression.

'I see you don't remember me. In the old days you and I used to be very friendly. The two of us were young scholars together. We two misbehaved together in this very church. Peter, I am. Peter Perkin.'

Now I remembered him. About thirty years before he had been a boy of my own age, though thin and weakly compared with the robust specimen of boyhood I presented to the world. It would be a gross exaggeration to describe us as good friends, but we used to attend the Sunday service in company. As I recall, I was the only one who misbehaved: even then Peter took his Sunday duties wholly seriously. And a large and enjoyable part of my misdemeanours were devoted to pinching and teasing Peter at strategic points to ease the tedium of the service.

'Peter. Ah, yes. Now I remember you well. How has the world treated you?'

'As you see,' he said proudly, the sweep of his arm encompassing the church about us. 'This was all I ever wanted,' he said. 'To be the Rector of my home parish, I mean.'

'Good for you,' I said. 'So all your wishes have come true.'

'Not quite,' he said. 'They will have done that when there are no more halt, lame or poor in the Parish of Greenford Magna, or anywhere else in our Good King's country. Anyway, don't you recall our old Rector saying we should be careful for what we wish, lest our wishes come true in an unpleasant way?'

I didn't remember such a pronouncement, as it happened. But it was exactly the sort of homily Old Rector Tidball would have mumbled during his Sunday sermons. What Peter said made me ponder the contract I had signed in a way I didn't wish to do. Now the making of it had given me eight hundred gold sovereigns I was starting to take it seriously. But all I did was laugh politely at the rector's words.

'And what of you, John?' he said brightly. 'How have you fared? What has the world laid at your door? You went to the Midlands in search of adventure, as I recall. Have you come back to Greenford to stay?'

'No,' I said. 'I must return to Tipton soon. Perhaps I'll stay for another week or two. No longer.'

Peter beamed. I beamed too. I'd made the decision to stay a little longer on the spur of the moment. In truth my thoughts had returned to my Cousin Mildred's ample charms. It would be very pleasant to call upon her.

'Perhaps we'll meet up again before you leave,' said Peter. 'We could have a chat about the old days.'

'Yes. We might, if there is time.' In truth I didn't want to have a chat with Peter about *anything*. Least of all did I want to talk to him about what he was calling the old days. Already I was allowing myself to believe my best days lay ahead. 'I was hoping the Rector would be able to look up the parish records for me. I wanted him to find out the date of birth of my Uncle Silas.'

'Well, I'm the Rector now. I have been for three years. Silas Mitchell, would it be? Your uncle must have been in his eighties at least. His birth would have been recorded somewhere in the pages of the register for the years 1715 to 1750, I should think.'

I watched as Peter struggled to haul down the large volume from its shelf and place it on the table. Then he started to leaf through the pages. His actions were confident but at the same time he performed them in a peculiarly reverential manner. He'd clearly undertaken a similar task for the relatives of other departed souls before this. I watched with wry amusement as his brows knitted while he searched. Then he examined the pages more closely. A full thirty minutes passed before he gave up and looked perplexed at me.

'This is very odd. First of all I looked at all the baptisms from 1735 to 1750. I felt sure this would be where I'd find him. Then I searched through the whole volume. He surely can't be recorded in an earlier or later volume, unless his was an adult baptism. Are you sure he wasn't born somewhere other than Greenford Magna?'

'I'm quite sure he was born in this Parish. Try looking in the records for 1538,' I said, laconically.

'Don't be ridiculous, John,' he said. 'You're trying to tease me, just as you used to do when we were children. 1538 was the year in which King Henry started to dissolve the monasteries. Such an entry would make him all of – let's see – 282 years old. Anyway, the earliest register we have for Greenford Magna goes back only as far as 1599.'

'Then my information must be incorrect.' I couldn't stop a smile from playing across my lips.

'It must be. Look, I'm busy with my parish duties now, but...'

'Before I go, I wanted to have a chat with you about Mephistopheles.'

'Mephistopheles?' he echoed annoyingly. 'There I may be able to help. I've only recently finished reading Christopher Marlowe's play. Mephistopheles is the best part of the Dr Faustus story. A wonderful invention by the playwright, he is.'

'Invention?' I said. 'Surely Marlowe based his play on an old legend?'

'This is true. But the legend wasn't so old when Marlowe was writing,' said Peter. 'His play was published in 1604, after his death. Apparently, he'd found the idea from German stories much less than a century old at the time. It seems there was a Georgius Sabillicus Faustus living in Germany in the earlier sixteenth century. He was a real man.'

'A real man?' I was incredulous. 'Can you tell me...?'

'I really am so busy with my sermon, John. Perhaps we...?' Peter was going to ask me to come and see him again.

'I've just remembered. I have much to do also. When I am able I will contact you.'

With unseemly haste, I headed for the door.

As luck would have it, I barged straight into my cousin Mildred as I was emerging from the church.

6

Dinner that evening was superb. Mildred was clearly out to impress me with her culinary skills. But she needn't have tried too hard. I was anxious to sample different wares.

I had dinner with Mildred for the next nine evenings. All the meals were good. She proved to be a passionate woman as well as a good cook and, if I hadn't been obliged to travel back to Tipton, I would have been delighted to make her the first Mrs Mitchell. Instead, our final conversation, on my tenth evening in her home, strikes a note that will remain forever sour in my memory:

'I have to leave Greenford in the morning, Mildred. There's some unfinished business in the Midlands to which I must attend. Perhaps tonight I could stay for no more than an hour or so after dinner. Then we could...'

My sentence was deliberately left unfinished. I knew exactly what I wanted, and she equally knew. But I didn't want to offend the ladylike sensibilities she liked to affect. Mildred would cast her pretensions aside along with her clothing soon enough when we entered her bedchamber. I can honestly say Mildred was by far the most glorious woman I've met in all my years on Earth. I'd been looking forward to this last shared evening. But I did genuinely think this was not going to be our last time together.

'You thought to use me once more before you went back to the Midlands, did you? You've probably got a string of whores in the Black Country.'

'No, it's not like that, Mildred, let me assure you. It's a strictly business matter I have to deal with.'

'How am I going to face the neighbours? What am I going to say to our sanctimonious rector?'

'I've told you; it's a purely financial matter to which I have to attend. It's an important transaction, though I can deal with it swiftly. I'll come back to Greenford for you as soon as I can.'

And so it was a business matter drawing me back to Tipton. I was telling her the unvarnished truth. Her mention of Peter, the simpleton Rector, once again, finally turned the scales. I hardly had a 'string of whores' in the Midlands. All I knew were a few girls who'd sell me their favours for far less than eight hundred sovereigns. The argument went on for another ten minutes. I said things I'd have too many years to ponder and regret.

'You needn't think you'll be sharing my mutton stew this evening.' These were the last words she said to me. They are seared into my memory.

I dined on bread-and-cheese in the *Red Lion* inn that evening instead of a fine stew. I did come back to Greenford, briefly, in 1910. Mildred had been interred in Holy Cross churchyard for more than seventy years. Her tombstone was already blackening at the edges by then.

7

The Fountain Inn, on Tipton's Owen Street, was where Ned Whitehouse spent most of his days. But he wasn't anywhere to be seen when I walked in. In fact, although the establishment was normally a busy one, few people were present. I walked up to someone I didn't know at the bar. He was obviously a boatman, and I greeted him. As he turned to face me I could see I'd made a poor choice.

'It's quiet in The Fountain today.'

'Tim Perry, I am. I work on the boats.'

'John Mitchell. Allow me to buy you a pint of porter.'

Working men usually talk far more freely when they have a pot of ale in their hand. I wasn't sure I wanted Tim Perry to talk too much, although I did wish him to tell me what was going on in the town. He seemed to be far more intent on supping his ale. The tankard I bought him was soon emptying at an alarming rate.

'They always serve a good pint here, don't they?' I said. Tim Perry was already getting towards the bottom of his pot.

'All the Tipton folk are over at Coseley. John Meek is fighting somebody from Darlaston. I don't know why they bother.'

'I don't either.' I didn't care for pugilism, cock-fighting, bull- or bear-baiting or any other of the working man's amusements. But I glanced down at Tim Perry's scarred knuckles on the bar and could see he held a different philosophy of life. I thought it wiser not to expand on my statement.

'They can see better fights on the canal bank between us boatmen. There's not many as gets into a lock ahead of Tim Perry.' Here he studied his giant fist with affection.

'Let me get you another porter.' I thought this would be the diplomatic course of action. None of Ned Whitehouse's men were present in The Fountain to look after me.

'John Meek? I don't think so.'

'It is indeed very quiet in here today.' I decided my safest course of action would be to make a little more small talk and then leave The Fountain Inn as quickly as I could. Tim Perry had clearly taken more blows around the head than were good for him in prize-fighting.

'John Meek? Why, my boy William could thrash him, and he's scarce above a yearling.'

This confirmed my thought. It would be more sensible to beat a retreat than remain and listen to more about Tim Perry and his bare-knuckle baby. All I was trying to find out was if he could tell me whether Ned Whitehouse was likely to be found somewhere else. A big pugilistic event at Coseley would be exactly the sort of thing Ned and his men would relish. I ventured a suitable question, even though I had the distinct impression John Meek had humbled Tim Perry in a prize-fight in the recent past.

'Is Ned Whitehouse over at Coseley, do you think?'

'The Tipton Slasher. It's what all the folks will be calling my little boy twenty years from now. William Perry, The Tipton Slasher.'

I didn't exactly know what to say to this. 'Let me get you another,' was what I did say.

'Ned Whitehouse? He dropped dead a week or more ago, at this very bar while he was supping his porter. Seen it myself. His gang went their separate ways afterwards. Most have gone to Dudley or even as far as Birmingham, from what I hear.'

I hastily mumbled my thanks and withdrew. Hell is where you're supposed to go when you sell your soul, but

Tipton, with its cinder banks, smoking chimneys and yellow skies must be very like the underworld. Now I was free and could escape this Hell-on-Earth. I realised I could go anywhere I wanted with near to eight hundred sovereigns in my pocket. So that's what I did.

8

Probably for no better reason than this was where I knew Uncle Silas had been before returning to Greenford, I chose to go to Cornwall. The last place I thought I wanted to go to was my home village where Mildred, if she forgave me, would be too ready to claim a husband and his eight hundred sovereigns. This was what, in my vanity, I really believed on the day I left the Midlands for ever.

The first place I stayed in was Newlyn, far to the west of Cornwall. I must have had it in my mind to place as much distance as I could between myself and both Greenford and Tipton. At first, I was happy in the Cornish village, even though it was small enough. Judicious investments in the fishing industry quickly doubled my eight hundred sovereigns. I bought a small house and married Sylvie, the first of my five wives.

To be honest, I cannot at this distance of years remember Sylvie's face. But I do remember she was a pretty thing and more than twenty years my junior. For the first few years our marriage was idyllic. She was energetic and attentive, always keen to learn from me. But, almost before I knew it, the years started to take their toll on both her temperament and her looks. Meanwhile, my own appearance and interests didn't change in the slightest degree. Sylvie was acutely aware of this. At root, this was what the constant bickering of our later years was all about.

I stayed with Sylvie for twenty-nine years. They were twenty-nine very long years. She aged so very badly. From the bright young thing she'd been when I married her, she soon settled into being a crabby woman, old before her years. Always she was whining and worrying about money. Why this should be, I had no idea. I had plenty of it.

Finally, I could take it no more and upped sticks, after taking steps to ensure that Sylvie had enough of the money that was all she ever really cared about. My new home was in the town of Lyme Regis, in Dorset. I entered it anonymously and, after readily amassing another fortune, became a respected member of local society. Then I married again. This time I chose a bride who had already reached her early twenties and again I had to watch the years grow upon her. The night before Lizbet's fortieth birthday, once again I quietly moved further east and there began a new life.

The pattern had been set and I maintained it right through the rest of the Victorian and early Edwardian years. Claire was my wife in a small Hampshire village for sixteen years and I stayed with Melissa in Marlborough, Wiltshire for fourteen.

All of them I left as wealthy women: they can have no justifiable complaint. None of my wives presented me with a son or daughter. I can't say I was particularly sorry; it would have made for an additional complication.

9

When I reached Chiswick, in those days a small riverside town in Middlesex, everything was in uproar. All the public houses seemed to be full but I decided to go into one of them. It was called *The Three Tuns*. This I still remember clearly. Even now, I can picture the sign swinging outside in the August breeze: three golden barrels on a dark green background. Excited people were thronging the bar. I spoke to one of them, a young working man in overalls and one of the broad caps they all seemed to wear at the time.

'What's happening? Why is everyone shouting so much?'

'You been on the Moon or something, Matey?'

In fact the young man wasn't so far from the truth. Of course I hadn't been on the Moon but for six weeks I'd been closeted in a hotel in Charing Cross, in the centre of London. I hadn't so much as spoken a word to any of the staff. They had strict instructions not to speak to me.

You might say I'd been hiding away from the World. As the twentieth century got into its stride, this was something I felt the need to do regularly. Being free to go anywhere I wanted and to do more or less anything I chose while I was there might sound very grand but, let me tell you, it can grow tedious when one place is so much like another.

Of course I didn't say any of this. To the young man I merely smiled and mumbled something in the hope he might tell me more.

'You know the Huns have marched into Belgium?' he said. 'They're raping nuns and skewering babies on their bayonets. Laughing while they're doing it, too, from what I've been told. Well, our Government is not going to stand for it. They're sending an army to help the Froggies beat them back. Pint?'

10

"The Huns", as I found out soon afterwards, were the armies of the German Empire. Much had been happening while I'd been lying low in the Charing Cross hotel. This might not altogether explain why on the first day of July 1916 I found myself in a trench in Picardy as one of the soldiers of General Allenby's Third Army. We were making ready to advance on three German lines of defence.

Since that day, over a century ago now, I've often thought about what took me to Northern France. The only answer I can honestly come up with is it was the pint of porter bought for me by Arthur – that was his name – in *The Three Tuns*. Arthur introduced me to his two friends, Tommy and Albert.

Soon the four of us were laughing and joking as if we'd been friends for years. Three of our number had. Arthur, Tommy and Albert had been to school together in Chiswick. I'd been born well over a century before any of them and all the schooling I'd had was paid for. Naturally, I didn't want to tell Arthur as much. But, do you know, this was the first time since my youth anyone had offered me spontaneous friendship?

It was a short step, both literally and metaphorically, from *The Three Tuns* to the recruiting office hastily set up in the town hall. After this the four of us followed a seemingly endless period of training. To start with, we didn't even have a rifle between us.

Never mind about 'Gallant Little Belgium': soon enough almost all of it was under German military rule anyway. Our chief worry was that the war would be over well before we set as much as a foot in Europe. The overwhelming feeling possessing us on that July day was one of relief that we'd at last made it to Picardy. Finally, we'd be getting to grips with the enemy.

More important than any of this to me was the fact that Arthur, Tommy, Albert and I had become great friends over those two years. We hadn't been parted for as much as a day during our training. I suppose I could have easily become a subaltern with my background but I wanted to be an ordinary private like my friends from Chiswick. Even when we were about to face the Germans, we stood shoulder-to-shoulder in the trenches.

'Hey, Johnny!' whispered Tommy to me. 'Albert says you're to call him King Albert from now on.'

'What?'

'There's a place up ahead of us called Albert. Only the Froggies can't say it right. They call it 'Al-bear' or something daft like that. King Albert says when we march into the town he's going to make all his new subjects bow down before him and learn to say his name properly.'

'We might not get as far as King Albert's Town today, Tommy.'

''Course we will. Don't you remember what the Officer said?'

There had been a long artillery bombardment, intended to cut the barbed wire and knock the stuffing out of the enemy. The Officer, in his pre-battle speech had said, *"When you go over the top, you can slope arms, light up your pipes and cigarettes, and march all the way to Pozières before meeting any live Germans."*

But Tommy and I didn't get a chance to continue our conversation. The sergeant blew the whistle as a sign we should go over the top.

11

The Officer's words proved to be even hollower than I feared they'd be. King Albert didn't get a chance to claim his crown. I saw his last act on Earth. This was to fall face down, not twenty yards after leaving the trench. I didn't even see the end of Arthur and Tommy.

Later, I learned that no fewer than fifty-seven thousand of our soldiers had died on that July day. It was the opening of what later came to be called The Battle of the Somme. Our unit, which afterwards I discovered wasn't even part of the main attack, fared even worse. The casualty rate amongst our boys was ninety-five per cent. Everyone I knew had been killed. Except me.

12

I stumbled through the rest of the war years as if in a daze. After The Somme, I fought at Vimy Ridge, Messines and Passchendaele. In August, 1918, I was involved in the Battle of Amiens, regarded afterwards by most people as the beginning of the end of the war. I was unscathed; I received not a scratch in all those years in uniform. But inside, I was as one of the walking dead.

After the deaths of Arthur, Tommy and Albert I made no more friends. Word got around about my knack of staying alive when those around me were killed or maimed. The other soldiers avoided me. Who can blame them? They stopped calling me 'Johnny' and gave me the name of 'Jonah', even though this was supposed to be a naval nickname. When the war was over in November, 1918, I didn't join in the celebrations. In fact, glad as I was to find the hostilities were at last over, I'd have put a bullet through my own head if only I could have found the courage. Would it have even have ended the misery of my life, anyway?

Tom East   198

13

When I was discharged in 1919, I couldn't face going back to Chiswick. What would I have said to the families of Arthur, Tommy and Albert? So I went to Reading. There wasn't really any place I could call home. The nineteen-twenties was my darkest decade, up to that point. In many ways this was a worse time than the war years.

Then, in 1930, I met Maud. To be honest, I only noticed her because she reminded me so much of my long-dead Mildred. Like Mildred when I met her again during my adult return to Greenford, Maud had been widowed the year before and was childless. She was also forty-one years old and very fetching. The money in her bank account would have to be counted in thousands rather than hundreds. Still, her fortune was nothing as compared with my own. But I'd have willingly laid every last penny of what I possessed at her feet.

We married on a bright July day only months after we'd met. The ceremony was a simple one, but still it featured in all the local newspapers. My cash may have been an attraction for Maud but I'm absolutely sure I'm not flattering myself when I say there was a strong physical attraction on her part as well as my own. After all, although by this time I was not far off one hundred and fifty years old, I looked several years younger than my bride.

The two short years of our marriage were the happiest of my life after I left Greenford in 1820. Our last evening on the river bank at Sonning, where we'd set up home after our marriage, gives me pain to remember:

'What they say isn't true is it, John?'

'What do they say?'

To tell the truth, I couldn't have cared less what anyone said. There were some moorhens close to the river-bank making their peculiar shrill call. It had been a fine summer day and the early-evening haze was beginning to settle on the calm surface of the water. I was with Maud; I was supremely happy.

'Oh, it's only one of these washer-women's rhymes. Don't even think about it.'

'Tell me what it is. Then we'll forget about it together.'

'I feel so silly now I'm talking about it. The rhyme goes, "*Change the name but not the letter; change for worse and not for better.*" When I met you I was Maud Martin. Now I'm Maud Mitchell. It sounds ridiculous when I say it.'

'So you were MM,' I said. 'Now you're still MM. Maud, you'll always be *Mmm* to me.'

It was lame, but it was the only thing I could think of on the spur of the moment. For some reason, Maud found my weak joke to be hilarious and was soon laughing uproariously. Her laughter was infectious and before long we were both falling about like schoolchildren. Suddenly, I stopped laughing.

I thought I'd seen a lone figure walking along the opposite bank. It seemed to be that of a man with a peculiar rolling gait. Unless I was mistaken, he carried a silver-tipped walking-cane that seemed to be glinting in the last rays of the setting sun. From what I saw, the man didn't lean on the stick but rather swung it vigorously in rhythm with his step. When he drew level with us the figure stopped and turned to face us for a moment. His form was in the evening shadow cast by the trees behind him but I swear he was looking in our direction. Then he seemed to slip into the deeper shadows along the river-bank and I saw nothing further.

Maud didn't notice my sudden silence or what had caused it but after a moment more of noisy laughter she fell quiet herself. My wife stayed that way for a long while. She was happy in the approaching dusk. When Maud at last spoke she murmured very quietly and I didn't catch her words.

'What was that?' I said.

'I said, I'm sorry, John. We'll have been married two years tomorrow and I'd quite forgotten my anniversary gift for you. Whatever will you think of me? But I know what I was going to get for you. I'll be going into Reading on Saturday and I'll buy it then. I am sorry, John.'

'Never mind, Maud. You'll just have to be extra nice to me until then.'

'John; let's go home now. I've got something else you like.'

14

Of course, I knew exactly what Maud had in mind. We had a very physical marriage. But I never received either of her intended gifts. On our way home she developed a mild headache. Before long, this had become severe. By midnight, she was dead.

I cannot begin to tell how dark it was for me in the months following Maud's death. Officers of The Berkshire Constabulary even suspected I'd poisoned my wife. I had to endure their clumsy investigations and innuendos until Maud's passing was finally attributed to "death from unknown natural causes". I wouldn't really have cared if the police had laid the crime at my door. I'd have been glad to meet my end swinging from a hangman's rope, if only some kind of magic rope could have despatched me. After Maud's departure I felt my days to be over. I could never quite shake off the belief that in some way I was responsible for her death, anyway.

Somehow, I recovered sufficiently to act out a semblance of normality. In a matter of years after Maud's death Europe and the world were plunged into another war. This time I wasn't so foolish as to don a military uniform: I paid for a false identity and spent the war years pretending to be a rich 49-year-old trying to avoid the bombs and living in some comfort. Many remarked that I looked younger than a near half-century. In fact my age at the time was nearer to a century-and-a half.

After this second war, the years sped by swiftly. My money ensured I was untouched by the post-war austerity and a quarter-of-a-century later I saw on television the first (and almost the last) steps of Mankind on our Moon. The firework displays greeting the new Millennium spoke of a rekindled enthusiasm but this mood lasted for no more than months for the population at large and minutes for me. Soon my fellows were bickering more than before. All the time I did nothing much but watch my fortune grow and remember Mildred, Arthur, Tommy, Albert and Maud.

15

When the autumn of 2020 came around I returned to what so long before had been my home village of Greenford. When I saw this bench, exactly where I remember the old one being sited, outside Holy Cross Church, I knew I'd have to go straight to it. In truth, despite a trick of the light and weather, I knew from the first I'd arrived on the right day.

My antique fob-watch tells me it is now five-to-two. What it is really saying is that in five minutes time I know I'll see a man coming up the path to join me. He'll be walking with a familiar rolling gait and will be carrying a silver-tipped walking-cane. The man won't need to lean on the stick but will be swinging it vigorously in rhythm with his step.

I fear the sight of this man, because I know he'll be coming to bring what he calls "the cessation clause" into effect and claim what I airily signed away two centuries ago. Icy fear will grip my bowels when his jaunty figure comes into view. The sensible thing would be to put as many miles between myself and Greenford as I could, rather than sitting and waiting for my fate.

But, although my legs are still strong, my heart is tired.

Myfanwy

Now I don't have a job at all, I realise the best I ever had was the one with Scopestars. It gave me the opportunity to travel the length and breadth of the UK. For what other reason would I have gone to Inverness? Selsey Bill would have been no more than an amusing name to me if not for the company. My travels for work took me as far east as Lowestoft and as far west as Penzance. I've seen so many other places.

About the only place the job didn't need me to visit was my home village of Llywel, at the head of the Usk Valley. But then nobody ever goes there: it's too small and there's never been any work unless you're a farmer. I was only seventeen when I left Llywel for good.

Scopestars gave me the perfect job in other ways, too. I was the company's chief installation engineer and my own boss. Most people who bought telescopes set them up for themselves but if anyone needed a hand, the company would send me out to do everything from laying the concrete base to making the final alignment of the telescope drive and lens. They charged for my services, of course.

Still, I was good at what I did and the customers were always pleased with my work. Most of the time, I was finished in three days at the outside. Even the very occasional big telescopes – twelve- or eighteen-inch reflectors are weighty beasts, let me tell you – would take me no more than four days with the help of local labour I recruited myself to help with the manhandling. Otherwise, I did everything by myself and rarely failed to complete my three-day target, even when this took in the weekend.

My best job? I'm not sure but without hesitation I'd say one of the simple four-and-a-half-inchers I set up in Bristol was definitely the most special. Let me explain.

*

This happened over ten years ago, back in the autumn of 2001. I know the dates precisely because, only a few weeks before, terrorists had crashed those airliners into the World Trade Centre, killing thousands of people. The world took an ugly turn on that day and it's still not running straight and true. Well, you could hardly expect it to be, could you?

The job was the complete set up of a telescope in the enormous back garden of a newly-retired churchman named Father Green. A decent old guy, he was. As usual, I did as much of the work as I could on a hectic first day, a Saturday, laying the foundation, erecting most of the stand, and completing as many of the other, often troublesome, preliminary tasks as I could manage. I liked to keep the other two days free for the more delicate stuff. It's the way I always used to work.

Father Green had told me of the quiet, partly riverside, walk I could take all the way back to my digs. These were only a mile away from his house, a big old place. This suited me very well: once I'd done my delivery on that first morning, I could leave the van parked outside my lodgings. I always found it preferable to walk whenever I could. This was more relaxing after a busy day.

Father Green's advice was good. Although Bristol is a typical city, you'd have sworn you were in the country once you took to the path. The shrubs lining it were beginning to show the yellows and golds making that time of year so special, and the still of the evening air lent a peaceful quality to everything.

Then I heard it. Only the opening line filtered through to me at first: '*Pa ham mae dicter, O Myfanwy*'.[1] In an instant, I found myself transported back to my childhood home at the head of the Usk Valley. Now, I might be biased, but I swear *Myfanwy* is the sweetest, saddest song in any language. It's not too much to claim that the song always reaches directly into some deep crevice in my soul.

The footpath arced around at this point. Soon I could hear the song quite clearly: '*Pa ham mae dicter, O Myfanwy, yn llenwi'th lygaid duon ddi..?*'[2] It is strange how this simple lyric, written a century-and-a-half before by Joseph Parry, describing a young man's puzzlement at the wrath of his sweetheart, could work the spell it did, but I was immediately entranced. Perhaps it was the mere fact of hearing it sung so well, without any kind of accompaniment, in what was almost the centre of an English city.

There was a high stone wall to my left, and the singing was coming from the other side of it. The end of the song was reached, '*...dweud y gair ffarwel*'[3] but almost immediately it started again. Four times more I listened. I could see that, by walking a dozen yards further along the path, I'd be able to look over a lower section of wall and see the wonderful singer of the song for myself.

I didn't do this. For reasons I can't now properly explain, I was afraid. Whether I was afraid of anything more than shattering the magic of the moment, I'm not sure. At all events, what I did was duck my head as I came to the lower section of wall, and then continue to follow the footpath back to my lodgings, the strains of *Myfanwy* echoing behind me.

The Sunday evening followed the same pattern. When I got to the wall, I could hear the strains of the song. Again I listened to the singing five times. Once more I ducked my head down as I passed the low section of wall.

On the Monday, I'd more or less finished my work by lunchtime. Father Green was pleased with the result. I talked to him about my wish to take a boat on Bristol's River Avon. The Avon at this point is not really 'touristy' but he was able to give me the name and work address of an old friend of his. Father Green told me that this friend would take visitors out on the river for a special cruise. He'd just retired from his full-time job and was now very keen to expand his waterway business. I'd be one of his first customers. The Churchman wrote all the details down on a piece of card for me. I have it still: I keep it as a memento of that time.

And I had every intention of going for a boat cruise on my final afternoon. It would have been a good way to round off my three days in Bristol. In the event, all I did was potter around in Father Green's garden until dusk started to fall. The truth was, I suppose, that I wanted to hear the singing for one last time.

On that final evening, I at last found some spine. I listened to the singing three times more but, instead of ducking my head down as I passed the low section, I looked over the wall to see who was making this beautiful music.

I saw a small church- or chapel-yard. Most of the gravestones were old and weathered, but there was one, barely a dozen yards away, of newer appearance.

By the side of this sat a woman, in her sixties I suppose. Her attention was fixed on an old-fashioned portable record-player, placed actually on top of the flat part of the grave.

As soon as the song finished, she pulled the arm of the record-player over to start it again. She did this in what seemed to be an automatic way, as if she were quite oblivious to my fascinated gaze. But, half-way through the song, she looked directly at me with eyes as dark as those in the song. There was no wrath to be seen in them, though; only gentleness.

'Are you going to gawp over the wall all evening, young man,' she said, 'or are you going to climb over that wall and join me? It's low enough for you to get over, isn't it?'

What could I do? I clambered over the wall and sat self-consciously on the opposite side of the gravestone. She smiled at me briefly, then turned her full attention back to the record-player again. *Myfanwy* was played once more. I thought it was high time for me to say something.

'Huw Rowlands,' I said. 'I've never heard *Myfanwy* sung so beautifully.'

'Thank you,' she said. 'Tomos would be pleased. He had the record especially made for me a few weeks before he was taken from us. Myfanwy Morgan I am.'

Myfanwy. I should have guessed. I started to read the tombstone: '*To the memory of the singer Tomos Morgan, aged 64, who died on the Millennium Eve of 31st December, 1999, after a long illness...*' There was a little more to the inscription, but soon Myfanwy Morgan was speaking again and I didn't have the chance to read it.

'And where do you come from? You're not from Bristol. You're not even from England, are you?'

'No. My home was a small village in Brecknock. It's called Llywel. You wouldn't have heard of it.'

'Ah. That's where you're wrong. My home was just on the Carmarthenshire side of Mynydd Myddfai. I used to live in the village of Myddfai itself.'

'We could have almost been neighbours.'

'Your mother and I could have been, perhaps. It's all of forty years since I lived in Myddfai.'

'*Dw i'n gallu siarad Cymraeg,*'[4] I said. It had been a long time since I'd been able to hold a conversation in my own language.

'We might both be able to speak Welsh, but we're in England now. We should speak English.'

An odd response, I thought. Still, I didn't want to argue. So we had a long conversation, in English. She was bright and cheerful throughout; although it was clear to me she missed her late husband terribly. All the time we were speaking she played *Myfanwy* without a pause. This didn't disconcert me in the slightest; she turned the volume lower and I love the song so much that it made a wonderful background to our conversation. I'll always remember that evening. Darkness started to fall quickly, almost before I realised it.

'Goodness,' I said. 'Is that the time? I must be on my way.'

'So soon?' she said.

It wasn't 'soon' at all. I'd been sitting and talking to her for well over an hour. For a moment, she looked disappointed, but then she returned my smile.

'Goodbye, Mrs Morgan. It's been a real pleasure.'

'*Mae'n amser ffarwelio,*'[5] she said, speaking Welsh for the first and only time.

It seemed to me that 'it's time to say goodbye' was an oddly formal way for her to bid me farewell. I didn't say anything. Instead, I hopped over the wall, and resumed my busy life as Scopestars' Chief (and only) Installation Engineer.

*

The world, and my life, changed a great deal over the next ten years. I'd had no occasion to visit Bristol during this time, even though by the end of it I was living in Taunton, not far distant from the city. The biggest change from my own point of view was that by 2011 I no longer had a job. Scopestars still limped along in an unhappy, downsized form, now importing all its telescopes from Asia. The company had no room for an installation engineer of its own and I'd been "factored out". That was the expression I overheard the new Managing Director using on one of the dark days towards the end. It made me shudder.

Looking for a job was the reason I was in Bristol on the 1st October, 2011, a Saturday. I can be precise about this date, too. As well as it being not much more than ten years since I'd finished my work on Father Green's telescope, the day was a phenomenally hot one. All temperature records for the month of October were broken.

There was to be no Indian summer for my working life, though. After enduring all the formalities and rituals of the employment world until mid-morning, I knew the light engineering company wouldn't be offering me any kind of employment.

They had the nerve to call the event a "weekend human resource seminar", would you believe? They did this so they wouldn't have to pay any travelling expenses, I'm sure. It's a wonder *they* didn't charge *me* for attending. Anyway, by eleven o'clock I found myself wandering disconsolately along the right-hand bank of the River Avon.

Before I'd come to Bristol that morning, I'd put the card Father Green had given me ten years before into my jacket pocket, promising myself that, if I landed the job, I'd treat myself to a cruise on the river as a reward.

But I was so down that I fished the card out of my pocket regardless, even though I knew I couldn't afford the luxury of a river trip.

*

Captain John, as he styled himself, proved still to operate from the spot on the riverbank where the crumpled card given to me by Father Green ten years before said he'd be. He was ready for business, and, although far from young, was active and cheerful into the bargain. I enjoyed the first part of my private cruise along the River Avon.

'How long have you been doing this?' I asked him conversationally.

'Just over ten years ago it was when I started,' he said. 'Though I have to admit I nearly gave it up after my first day on the river.'

'Why was that?' I asked. He looked like a man born to the water, although he'd probably worked at some more mundane job before his retirement. His answer told me I was right in my guess:

'On my very first morning, the Monday after I'd retired from my job in insurance at the end of September, I had a very nasty experience. It still gives me the horrors whenever I think about what I saw.'

'Oh,' I said. 'Tell me about it.'

He looked at the water, plainly not wanting to answer. I don't really know why I'd asked; I'd spent money I couldn't afford to come on the river with the aim of giving my depressed spirits a lift, not to hear some downbeat story.

'See that bridge ahead?' He spoke suddenly, pointing to the structure half a mile or so down river. 'On that Monday morning I was just about to pass under it for the first time – I'd only been out on the river for half-an-hour – when I found a body, floating in the river. Seems the woman had taken her life by jumping in. It was all so sad.'

His words made me recognise this part of the river from ten years ago.

'Drop me off at the bridge if you would.'

'Why? You've a way to go yet, you know.'

'Please, just drop me off.'

'I can't give any refund against prepaid fares.'

*

Although I was the one who'd be losing out through my impetuous action, I did feel bad about it. Captain John was a good sort. Still, I hope I managed to mollify his bruised ego with a few words of reassurance. But now, standing on the river-bank, I didn't really know in which part of Bristol I was. It didn't now seem to be in the area of Father Green's house.

Some notion of seeing the old churchyard again had entered my head, I suppose. I even had the vague idea of seeing Myfanwy once more, unlikely as this would have been ten years later. Unfortunately, I have a very poor sense of direction and wandered around aimlessly for hours.

Dusk was beginning to fall by the time I heard the voice:

'*Pa ham mae dicter, O Myfanwy...*'[1]

That was all I heard before the strains of the music died away on the evening breeze, or in my imagination. Nevertheless, I set off at once in the northerly direction from which I'd heard them. Soon, I found myself on a familiar footpath I'd not travelled for ten years.

Although it was the first of October, the leaves were still hardly yellowing on the bankside trees even though, elsewhere, the colours of autumn had begun to set in a few weeks ago. Despite the hour, the warm air made it feel like a summer evening rather than one of autumn. Before long, I found the church, not far from the riverbank. All was silent; no strain of *Myfanwy* could be heard.

The low section of wall was unchanged and I scrambled over. No one was there; there was only the deserted graveyard. I stood by the side of the gravestone I'd last seen in 2001, ten years before. It was still the newest-looking stone, though now it bore the marks of the intervening years. I read:

"*To the memory of the singer Tomos Morgan, aged 64, who died on the Millennium Eve of 31st December, 1999, after a long illness. A resident of Bristol, his heart was always in his native Myddfai.*"

And then, underneath this, an addition had been carved in the stone:

"*Also sacred to the memory of his wife Myfanwy, aged 63, who came when she was called on 1 October, 2001.*"

NOTES

[1] *Pa ham mae dicter, O Myfanwy* - Why is it anger, O Myfanwy [the name is derived from *f annwyl* – my beloved – and is pronounced Muv-Ann-Oy].

[2] *yn llenwi'th lygaid duon ddi* – that fills your dark eyes.
[3] *dweud y gair ffarwell* – to say the word farewell.
[4] *Dw i'n gallu siarad Cymraeg* – I can speak Welsh.
[5] *Mae'n amser ffarwelio* – It's time to say goodbye.

Causeway of the Legion

This was meant to be no more than a stroll across the gentler slopes of Fforest Fawr. The idea was to give Steve a final chance to have a few hours alone to quietly think through his decision of whether or not to sign as a full-time soldier. He'd accumulated years of experience as a Terrier. It looked from the newspapers and television as if there were going to be the chance of some real military action in the Middle East, so why not go for it?

He hadn't walked far before the light mist thickened into a dense fog. This shouldn't have been *too* bad. Steve was used to the mountains; he prided himself on his navigation skills. If the worst came to the worst he could simply wait here by the menhir for the weather to clear. As he always did, he carried warm clothing and emergency food and drink in his light knapsack. But the last thing he'd expected to see half-emerging from the swirls of mist before him was what looked like the armour of a soldier from ancient times.

Before the fog blanketed everything again, he was ready to swear he'd clearly seen a Roman legionnaire in full uniform.

Instinctively, he ducked behind the menhir he'd been examining. In truth he'd only been looking at the stone so closely because, frankly, by now he feared he was lost in the clingingly damp air and wanted to keep close to something familiar. Worse, now he'd discovered that, like a fool, he'd left home without his compass. What carelessness! Always, he'd been meticulous about that sort of essential. Now he had little hope of even finding his way back to Sarn Helen, the old Roman road, with the weather like this. Even so, there was still no need for panic. Steve was confident that, sooner or later, the weather would clear sufficiently to allow him to find his way back to his planned route to Ystradfellte.

So there'd been plenty of time for a leisurely examination of the stone of Maen Madoc. This was something he'd never properly looked at before, although he'd passed it at least a dozen times. What on Earth did the worn lettering mean: *Derva Filis Iusti Ic Iacit*? Was the inscription written in some sort of eccentric Latin?

Now the carving could hardly be his main priority. The strange figure, once again partly visible, was approaching closer to his hiding-place. He looked more than ever like an ancient legionnaire. Steve crouched down further behind the rock, irritated at his unwonted display of fear. The situation was ridiculous. Hiding from a Roman soldier at the beginning of the twenty-first century? Come on! Still, he felt cautious about showing himself and was glad the newcomer didn't seem to have caught sight of him.

After a minute or two the man came close enough to allow Steve to study him properly. He looked mean and thin with his aquiline features and scowl. And he was dirty, not at all like the pictures of the clean-cut military men he'd seen years before in school history books. His face bore a greasy film of sweat. His tunic was torn and dishevelled. His armour was no longer a shining bronze but dull, almost green in colour.

'Are you going to hide there as though you were a scared deer all of the day, Briton? Humilus of the Second Imperial Legion commands you to come out to help him find his way through your accursed island mist. Quickly now, or you'll be feeling the weight of my *gladius* across your shoulders.'

With a start, Steve realised he could after all be seen. He guessed by 'gladius' the man was referring to the short sword he'd drawn and was now wielding in a threatening manner. He felt ridiculous in doing as he was told, but thought it unwise to argue. Not when he found himself alone here on the southern slopes of Fforest Fawr confronting an armed madman.

'Look, there must be some mistake,' Steve said, emerging from behind the standing stone with his hands high in the air. The situation felt surreal. 'I'll do what I can to help you, but I'm afraid that ...' Steve's voice trailed off. He was bemused and didn't know what else to say. And the man dressed as a legionnaire seemed eager to put his sword to deadly use. But the hardness of his eyes changed to a look of wonder when he heard Steve speak.

'You speak Phoenician as if you were one of my own people! It's the first time I've heard our tongue spoken since I was sent to serve the Emperor in the backward lands of Britannia. Where could a barbarian Briton have gained such knowledge?'

Steve blinked. Clearly the man was alarmingly disturbed. He didn't know what he should do or say in a situation like this. And this "Humilus" was still waving his ... his ... what had he called it? ... *gladius*. He tried to smile. The expression felt uneasily crooked and lopsided on his face.

'Yet your garb is not that of a Phoenician,' the madman continued. 'Nor is it that of a Briton. Where are you from, stranger? Are you one of those Druids we've been warned about? Keep your incantations away from me or I'll despatch you to your Heathen god!'

'No ... no ... I'm not a Druid. I'm ... I'm from Swansea.' Steve couldn't believe he was saying these words. He wished this maniac would stop accompanying every word he spoke with an alarming motion of his sword.

'I've never heard of any village of that name. No matter, you can direct me to the camp at Nidum. But first, do you have food in the strange red bag across your shoulder?' The man cast his eyes greedily at Steve's knapsack. It was almost as if he could smell its contents.

Nidum? Steve didn't have a clue where this could be. Nor where anywhere else could be, for that matter. He was disoriented by more than the fog. But he was relieved to be able to say: 'Yes, I have food. Here, I'll give you some. Take anything you want.'

His hands were trembling from more than the cold as he fumbled with the straps of the knapsack. It seemed an age before he could hold out one of his two long, crusty rolls.

The man snatched the bread and looked at it doubtfully. Suspicion and hunger were competing in his eyes. At last, hunger won the uneven battle and he crammed a good portion of crust into his mouth. He chewed fast, revealing uneven rows of blackened teeth as he did so. He bit off another mouthful. Almost as quickly he tore off another.

At last he paused for breath. 'Good, good. This is a fine loaf. I've not seen bread quite like this in any part of the Empire. And what is this inside? Some sort of *caseus* made from fermented ewe's milk, I'll warrant. But what are these dark, fiery things within it?'

It was nothing more than a roll filled with peppered cheese. He'd hastily put this together before he came out this morning. 'Pepper,' he said. 'Do you want the other one?'

'I am hungry,' said the man, snatching the remaining roll without another word. Steve couldn't help noticing that the soldier – he had to think of him as a soldier – reeked strongly of stale sweat, and felt his own stomach churn. He had been looking forward to eating those rolls, but couldn't have touched them now.

Not that he'd have a chance to eat anything. The second roll was being wolfed down even more quickly than the first.

'Drink?'

'Ah, wine. I could do with some to get my blood flowing again.'

'No, not wine.' Soldier or not, he was mad, no mistake. 'It's coffee. I'm sorry; it's got lots of sugar in it. I like my coffee to be very sweet.' He poured a plastic cupful from his flask and handed it over. 'Careful; it's hot. Sip slowly.'

Humilus didn't put his mouth to the cup, but sniffed at it cautiously. 'This smells like Druid's work to me. Poison. You drink some first.'

Steve took the cup back and sipped at it. Normally he loved sweet coffee, but this time it had an unbearably sickly taste. He had to force himself to drink as if with enjoyment so as to try to reassure his unwelcome guest he wasn't offering him – what was it the Romans were supposed to fear? – a cup of hemlock?

'Here,' he said, satisfied he had swallowed enough to prove his point. 'This is yours now. Drink it all.'

Humilus put the liquid to his lips, wrinkling his nose as if to show he was drinking only through the call of thirst. When he had finished he did not, as Steve dreaded, demand to be taken to this Nidum place, wherever it may be. Instead, he leaned back against the stone and closed his eyes lazily.

'I think I'll rest here for a short while before we press on,' he said. 'It's been a long time since I've been able to rest with a full belly.'

Steve carefully noted the 'we' in that sentence and resolved to make the 'short while' last as long as he could. 'Can you read Latin?' he asked. 'What do the words on that stone say?'

'You ask me if I can understand the language of the Empire? Do you test me to see if I am able to read? I am no ignorant native. This stone is inscribed in poor Latin. It's hardly the work of a scholar. The words are supposed to read "Dervacius, son of Justus, lies here". Who Justus and his son may be, I have no idea. This stone wasn't here the last time I came this way. It was probably erected by you Britons, trying to mimic the Imperial ways.'

'Why do you think so badly of the local people?' asked Steve. He thought he'd found a way of spinning out the conversation. He didn't want it to touch on this 'Nidum' place again. Where was it? Surely it couldn't be the town of Neath?

'The Britons? Without us they'd still be painting their faces blue and dancing in forest clearings. That's what my centurion Antonius Blearius says, and he listens to Tribune Dubius who knows all there is to know. Dubius tells him we are here to bring to the benighted people of these islands the benefits of Imperial civilisation.

'If we should freely take our pleasures with the native girls or sometimes kill one or two of the tribesmen this is a small price for you barbarians to pay in return. What's more, there are minerals and the ores of precious metals lying neglected in the soil, so Dubius informs Antonius Blearius. You wild natives would only leave them in the ground to waste away.'

Steve was aghast. What Humilus was saying told him the Roman Empire displayed an even more contemptuous attitude than that of any conqueror in later centuries. The delusions of the man, whether Roman soldier or madman, were complete. Alarmed as he was, Steve still tried to prolong the conversation. He wasn't sure of his theory about "Nidum" and Neath was a long way from here on foot. And the man was still waving his short sword around dangerously. 'Tell me about yourself, Humilus,' he said.

'There's little enough to tell,' replied the soldier, mellower now. 'My name is Humilus Militaris. I was born in Phoenicia, far to the south and east of this cold, unwelcoming land. For a few years I farmed with my family, but then I chose to become a soldier in the Imperial Guard. At first I served in Gaul but then my leaders forced me to come to these benighted islands. As I told you, I am with the Second Legion, though for many days I have been separated from Blearius and my fellow legionnaires.'

This was not good, thought Steve. Already the conversation looked as if it would soon be leading back to this

Nidum place. He'd managed at most five minutes. Automatically he rolled up the sleeve of his parka jacket to look at his watch.

'What devilry is this?' demanded Humilus, starting and leaping back violently. 'You wear a magic amulet on your wrist. You are a Druid, or else one of their creatures. You have come to ensnare me!'

'No ... no,' stammered Steve. 'It's only a wristwatch.'

Humilus was ignoring his words and pointing his *gladius* at Steve's chest. More than ever he looked eager to use it. But in that moment a ray of sunshine broke through the mist. It shone directly on the spot where they faced each other. Curiously, Humilus seemed to become transparent and insubstantial in the pool of light.

'You're fading away!' shouted Steve.

Humilus tried to mouth something. No words could be heard. The rays of the sun were falling more strongly upon them and the soldier's form could now hardly be made out.

Steve wasted no time in wondering. He turned and ran, panting, up the hillside. With the skies now rapidly clearing, he was able to find the track of Sarn Helen without trouble. He didn't stop running up the path until he reached the car park a mile or so distant. By the time he stumbled to its perimeter there was no more than a trace of mist remaining in the whole area.

Breathless, he found his car and was more than glad to see its reassuringly solid outline. As he fumbled in his pocket for the keys he suddenly remembered he'd left his knapsack where it lay on the ground next to Maen Madoc.

For a moment, he thought about going back for it, but decided it would be better to come again tomorrow. And, if there were the slightest hint of a mist on Sarn Helen, *Sarn-y-lleng*, Causeway of the Legion, he knew he'd turn right around and go home.

He'd decided something else, too. He wouldn't be joining any army. Of that much he was certain.

Dream Honeymoon

The noise of the whirring fans in the hotel dining room reverberated through his skull. He stumbled as he made his way to the table he shared with Laura, not seeing Mrs Hobbs until he'd almost walked into her.

'Whoops, steady as she goes. Everything all right this morning, Mr Robinson?'

'*No, I feel sick,*' he thought. '*I feel as if I've been on several route marches across the Sahara*'. But he managed a smile for the old lady:

'Not so bad, thanks. I had too much sun yesterday, I'm sorry to say. You're looking so well yourself. The climate in the tropics must agree with you.'

His answer brought warmth to her face and a light to her clear grey eyes. He was not merely being polite. She really did look so much brighter than last night when he and Laura had chatted to her in the hotel bar.

'Well, I must get back to Laura. She'll be complaining about me bringing her cold coffee otherwise.'

As he approached their breakfast table, Laura looked up at him, an anxious expression on her face. It was the same look she'd worn when they woke this morning. He sat down without speaking, passing her the coffee cup. She thanked him with a twitch of a smile but her expression didn't change beyond this. Minutes passed before his new bride broke the silence. He knew exactly what she was going to say:

'Jon, darling, don't worry about it. It could have happened to anyone.'

Yes, but that's not the way it was. It had happened to him. And on their honeymoon; the dream honeymoon for which they'd scrimped and saved so long.

'I think I'll go for a sauna after breakfast. Why don't you go and have a swim, Jon?'

'No, I still feel tired. Maybe I'll just have a laze on one of the sun-loungers.'

*

It was only when he eased his limbs on to the warm canvas of the sun bed that he realised how stiff and tired his aching frame had been. His neck muscles and shoulder blades felt as if they'd been pummelled with an iron rod. He closed his eyes, grateful for the balm of the tropical sun.

Slowly he drifted off into something akin to sleep. Yet he was still conscious. He was able to watch with a species of detachment as fragments of his dream of the night before drifted by under the gaze of his mind's eye.

The dream... he was there on the bed in the honeymoon suite of the hotel. Laura lay beside him, in a heavy slumber. Everything was pitch black, save for the bed with its lustrous satin sheets, and the gossamer white curtains wafting in the breeze against the moonlight as it filtered through the open window.

Then he saw her. The woman. She came toward him, arms outstretched. In that moment he was lost. All he could think of was the fullness of her soft, engulfing nakedness, the oddly cool touch of her flesh. The flesh... it was the same colour as the moonlight beaming through the window. Finally, he knew again the utter exhaustion he felt after spending his passion upon her.

*

The next morning, he had been awoken by Laura's playful touch:

'Jon, I'm sorry I fell asleep so quickly again last night. I must have had too much to drink.'

'Don't worry, Laura love. I felt a bit tired myself.'

'Never mind. We don't have to get up yet, do we?'

He groaned inwardly as she gently teased him with her lips and tongue. Her small hand moved slowly, expectantly towards his manhood. There was no response. He could not respond. She was upset, as any woman would have been. Then she'd tried to reassure him. That had only made things worse ...

*

'Darling.'

'Uh - What!'

'I'm sorry if I startled you. You'd fallen asleep on the sunbed this morning, just as you did yesterday. My sauna was great again today. Makes you feel fresh and alive. How about you? How do you feel after the rest?'

'Oh, I'm OK now. Let's go for a dip. We'll take it easy for the rest of the day to get over the remainder of our jet-lag and then – what do you say to an early night tonight?'

'I think that's a marvellous idea.' Her face brightened.

'So do I. Everything will be absolutely fine tonight. I'm sure.'

*

But things weren't at all fine. Neither on that night, nor on any in the painful week following. The days he passed in weary idleness, lounging on the sun-bed, or splashing lazily in the pool for no more than a few minutes. Laura spent her time reading thick novels, or going on long walks with Mrs Hobbs, whose husband was fortunately away on business somewhere. The old lady herself seemed younger and livelier with each new day.

Between the pair of them he was persuaded to talk to the hotel doctor, whose speciality seemed to be the cultivation of an air of professional gravity. After a ponderous consultation, the doctor pronounced in a tone admitting no dissent that Jon was suffering from post-viral syndrome. He handed him a box containing vitamin pills. If anything, Jon's fatigue increased after the visit.

The evenings were the worst. He fought against tiredness, mainly to put off for as long as he could the need to go to their room, to endure the painful minutes when Laura would lay beside him, looking up at the ceiling, saying nothing. Then she would turn her back to him with an audible sigh. She always fell asleep surprisingly quickly.

On the Thursday night he realised with a jolt he was actually willing Laura to fall asleep so that once again he could enter the world of his dream. It was always the same... the darkness of the room; the smoothness of the satin sheets; the full ripeness of the woman as she came to him; the touch of soft flesh so curiously bathed in the colour of moonlight.

There was the rising passion; a frenzied desire coming in wave after wave, each more powerful than the one before, until he felt his whole being was going to fragment. Then he knew oblivion rather than sleep until morning. After this was another day of fatigue and an ever-growing barrier between himself and Laura.

So came the last evening of their honeymoon. They were sitting in the hotel bar. Laura was trying to make some sort of conversation. He was finding it ever more difficult to keep in touch with the world of his waking hours; Laura's world. His reality was becoming the one of his dream; of the cool embrace of the woman whose face he could not remember but whose body he knew so well.

He had the strange impression he was peering out from somewhere in the darkest recesses of his skull, as if looking through a narrow window at a distant scene he could recognise but of which he was not a part. There was a blurring, a darkening, at the edges of his field of vision. Only slowly did he realise someone had joined them in their corner of the bar.

'Hello, Mrs Hobbs. 'We've not seen much of you over the last day or two.' Laura's voice held a note of relief at the prospect of livelier company.

'That's because I've been busy. I've been making one or two very special arrangements.'

'Really?'

'This place is doing me so much good. I want to stay for another week. I've rented a bungalow on the far side of the island. My husband will be joining us in the middle of the week. He's still away on business. And I want you to be our guests for the week.'

'Oh, that would be lovely. But I'm afraid we have to get back to work.'

'No you don't, Laura. Our poor Jon certainly isn't ready to go back to drudgery yet. Another week will see him right. So I've been pulling a few strings. The doctor has already drafted a letter for Jon's company. That tour-guide lady says she'll be able to arrange things with the airline. There'll be no trouble at all. They only need a word from you.'

*

On the first night on the quieter east coast of the island, Jon slept a dreamless sleep. Although he still felt drained when he awoke, the extreme fatigue of days past had left him. The bungalow Mrs Hobbs had hired turned out to be spacious and set in beautiful grounds. He and Laura were able to spend a pleasant afternoon simply walking, examining the tropical flora and looking out to the blue and silver shimmer of the sea.

After dinner they had drinks with Mrs Hobbs on the veranda.

'I think, Jon, that what you and Laura need tonight is an early night.'

'But, Mrs Hobbs, it would be unforgivably rude of us,' said Laura. 'We're your guests and the very least we can do is offer you a bit more of our company.'

'No, I won't hear of it. You really must start calling me Cassandra. The three of us have become good friends, haven't we?'

Jon said nothing and she favoured him with her warmest smile. Despite the weakness he was still feeling, he tried to return the smile.

She was a sweet lady. Quite handsome too, in a mature way. Her eyes were clear and vital, and she moved with a stately grace. She must have turned a few heads when she was younger. Not that she looked so old now. Odd how badly he'd misjudged her age when they'd first met.

'Cassandra is right, Jon. We could both do with some extra rest.'

*

They had not made love but they'd talked for some time, more easily than at any time since their arrival. Laura still turned away from him when she was ready to sleep, but there was a subtle lessening of tautness in the way she held her shoulders and in the manner she lay her neat dark head on the pillow. He kissed her lightly on the cheek. Within minutes he'd drifted off to sleep himself.

*

He first became aware of the gentle movement of the curtain. Then, slowly, he was conscious of another presence in the room. She was there, waiting for him. Tonight she was more magnificent, more voluptuous than even before. The woman was the ultimate temptress; the embodiment of all things sensual. His body ached for the touch of hers. Tonight their passion would reach new heights.

She came to him, and soon he was enfolded in her yielding flesh, the cool nakedness that was so indefinably bound up with the moonlight now bathing the whole room. So tightly was he held in the grip of his aching desire that he did not feel the stirring of the slender form beside him.

'Jon! Jon!'

These were the only words that Laura could gasp before her voice became a low moan of disbelief, then a choking scream of dismay at the sight of her husband locked in a carnal embrace with Cassandra Hobbs. The woman's features, if indeed the creature could be called a woman, were twisted into a demonic mask as she urged the young man on to a passion he'd never come near to reaching with Laura herself.

Jon was not aware Laura had awoken, still less that she had fled screaming from the room. All he knew was the nearing moment of ultimate ecstasy. He knew he had to reach out and claim the moment, no matter at what cost. And he was aware what the cost would be...

As the young man poured the last of his life force into her before going limp in his final stillness, Cassandra, the demon, the succubus, gave a smile of pleasure. She stroked his lifeless body with something like affection. He hadn't been bad, this one: he had fire in his loins. The life force she'd taken from him would be good for some time before she needed to seek new prey.

It was a pity they'd disturbed Laura. She'd promised her mate that this fine young woman would be lying there in readiness for him when he returned. Now he'd have to go out into the forest to take her. But then, perhaps in this way he'd enjoy the experience all the more: the priapic chase through the undergrowth; the screams of the young woman as her husband the incubus claimed her. She laughed, clinging to her the dead form that had once been Jon Robinson. Yes, her mate would be sure to enjoy his own night.

Reconstruction

'What do you have planned for today, then?'

'Mainly business.' My answer was terse. I thought to fob off the over-cheerful landlord with a brief answer but then I relented. His smiling face was a big improvement over the unfailing misery of the landlord I remembered from the sixties and seventies. Before I got down to business, I had a more personal mission in mind. 'But that's for this afternoon,' I said. 'This morning I'm free. I thought I'd take a stroll down Ruislip Road.'

'It's hardly strolling country,' he said, surprised. He must have had me marked down as a casual visitor, or a retired gentleman of leisure. No-one would want to come *here* to see the sights.

'Is the primary school still there on the other side of the road?' I asked. 'It was already dark by the time my taxi pulled up at the pub last night so I couldn't see.'

'The old place is still there, although entirely rebuilt and modernised since my time,' he said. 'Used to go there myself once upon a time, don't you know? You were a teacher at the school, were you?'

'Something like that.'

'Maybe you taught me? Geoff Smith? I was a pupil during the nineties. Long time ago now.'

'Not so long to me. The nineties were well after my time.'

They were forty years after my time. And I wasn't a teacher.

*

My humble origins were far behind me. So I had mixed feelings from the beginning about returning to my childhood home in West Middlesex for my latest, no more than modestly profitable, money-making project. In the end something like nostalgia won the day.

I had to suppress a smile of satisfaction as I left. My legal people had received the last letter yesterday. Now I'd be able to give that company the go ahead for their reconstruction and expansion. Then all I'd have to do would be to watch the money filter into one of my bank accounts. All it takes is to pull the right levers and to apply a bit of gentle persuasion.

In the end it had been too easy. That old couple had no idea of land values in this part of the world. They were even pleased with my final offer. It would be a quick deal and then they could retire to a little cottage in the country with roses around the door. Everybody, except their employees who'd be unlikely to find such soft jobs again, will soon be happy. Well, I'll be happy, anyway.

I must have taken leave of my senses to have checked into this commonplace pub for a night. Not that anyone in this anonymous suburb would recognise me these days. The old barman I remembered so well would be pushing his century by this time. If he was still around he'd be long gone from the pub. More likely he'd jumped off the planet years ago.

My planned stroll was pure nostalgia on my part, I knew that. If I'm honest, I'd have to admit the deciding factor was the idea in the back of my mind that if I stayed in *The Fox and Hounds* overnight, it would give me the opportunity to take a morning walk along the road past my old primary school. I wouldn't have dreamed of trying to go inside. All the teachers I remembered would be long gone.

Still, I'd entertained for some weeks the foolish notion of walking this short distance along Ruislip Road. Short distances are all I can manage now. Somehow I must have convinced myself it would, for a moment, be exactly like the old days. But what they say is right. You should never try to go back.

*

I suppose I'd been lulled into even more of a sense of false security by the appearance of the old pub. It might have been very different inside but, from the outside, it looked exactly as it did in my younger days. My mood was almost jaunty when I began to walk along the other side of Ruislip Road.

The appearance of the school was a disappointment. The scenes of my youthful waywardness were no longer housed in a collection of ramshackle wooden buildings, thrown up haphazardly around pre-war brick classrooms. This was what I'd been unthinkingly expecting to see, despite what the landlord had told me. Instead, a purpose-built glass-and-concrete structure met my gaze.

I tried to tell myself the modern building would be better for the young pupils, but caught myself muttering the single word 'character' under my breath. 'Sentimental old fool', I tried to tell myself. My reaction had been of the same order as those I'd witnessed in so many others I'd mocked in my financially-productive working life as a property developer.

Even beyond this, something still seemed to be wrong. I quickly realised what it was. The field had gone. The words of the Head on bright days in summers of the nineteen-fifties had always given a special thrill to me: 'You may use the field today, children.' That simple message always delivered on its promise of rough-and-tumble games on the grass; of joys only youth can know. On most days of the year the damp or cold had confined us to the smallish squares of asphalt and concrete where the height of our physical endeavours had been to chase around a bouncing leather football.

On those kinds of days, the favoured game of my classmates had been a nasty one. Our gang would shout taunts at two old men who, on at least two occasions each week, would traipse along the narrow strip of pavement where I was now. This was separated from our precious and now non-existent summer field by yards of ten-foot high chain-link fencing. If we were lucky, their walk would coincide with the end of our 'playtime' or lunch, when the school whistle would be blown to order us back to the classrooms.

The reaction of the men to the blast of the whistle was always dramatic. As soon as it sounded, the shorter of the two, a balding, hatless man, would fall down and crouch low on the pavement. His companion, a straight-backed, tall man who wore a cap and scarf in summer and winter, would bend over and implore him, amid much arm waving, to get to his feet. We never saw the shorter man rise from the pavement. We'd always be ushered into our classroom by our scolding teachers before the drama could be concluded.

They were cruel, those boys. I should have said something; tried to stop them. But you don't, do you? 'Peer Pressure' is what it's called, isn't it?

*

This memory of times past was why I found myself to be, well over half-a-century later, once again on the school side of Ruislip Road. I admit I was in something of a daydream. Thinking too much about the past can do unaccountable things to the best of us.

Then, quite suddenly, my World became out of focus. I blinked, trying to force the uncomfortable sensation to pass, then pulled out my handkerchief to cover my eyes. When I looked ahead of me again through watering, half-closed lids, I saw two men of about my own age. Why had I not seen them before? I wasn't far behind. Both wore the long gabardine mackintoshes of an earlier era. One was short and bare-headed. The other was tall and straight-backed.

'Oi! Granddad! They'll be playing your tune in a minute!'

I looked to my left. In place of the modern building there was now a collection of ramshackle huts around neater brick-built buildings. The voice had come from a gangling boy standing on the edge of the school field. He was wearing grey shorts, braces, a dark-brown pullover and long woollen stockings.

It was me. I couldn't believe it. It was definitely me leading the mockery.

'Put your show on for us then, old man.'

Some of the others surrounding the boy – surrounding me – were pulling at his shirtsleeves, as if trying to get him away from the borderline between asphalt and green field. But they were half-hearted about their persuasion and laughing. They were sharing the joke.

'Come on! We haven't seen you in action yet this week!'

At that moment a tall woman in the schoolyard put a silver whistle to her lips and blew a long, shrill note. The effect on the shorter man was immediate, as I knew it would be. He fell to his knees, covering his head with his hands. His tall friend stood over him, shouting in an effort to make him stand up. Then the wind gusted, and a piece of grit entered my eye, quite painfully.

I used my handkerchief once more to dab at my watering eye, ineffectually at first. For reasons I can't explain – it was only a piece of grit, after all – I stumbled forward to my knees, at the same time closing my smarting eyes. At the same moment I heard loud explosions and cries of pain all about me. Frantically, I continued to dab at my eyes. An intense smell of burning keened my nostrils.

At last, I managed to look about me. I was no longer in Middlesex. I was in the midst of a scene that could have been taken from Hell. There were bursting shells all about me. Men, shouting and screaming, were all around. The quieter ones, those who were not lying face down on the muddy, foul-smelling ground, were either cursing softly or whimpering like babies as they stumbled forward. The landscape about us consisted entirely of churned mud and pools of water, save for a few blackened stumps of trees.

There was thickening, choking smoke, through which I could barely make out the forms of the others, although I could see they were all dressed in military uniform. I looked down at my sleeve and saw it was a grey-powdered khaki, with brass buttons. Ahead of me, I recognised the two men from Ruislip Road. Only now they too wore uniform and were years younger. I watched them only for a few seconds before they disappeared into the cloud of smoke ahead of them.

I slithered a few feet further forward in the mud, alarmed and confused.

'Get up soldier! On to the enemy positions! Pick up your rifle! Be a man!'

I looked behind me to see a man, angry and red-faced. He wore the stripes of a sergeant.

'Oh, it's you again, is it?' he said. 'It was hard enough to get you out of the trench. Get up!'

I struggled to my feet. But I couldn't stand on my wobbly legs and did no more than slip face-down into the wet mud. I tasted its bitterness in my mouth.

Then I blacked out.

*

'Are you all right, Sir? You've had a nasty turn.'

'What happened?'

'You passed out in the Ruislip Road. At first they thought you'd had a heart-attack but the doctors are now saying it was probably not so serious. You must have fainted off or something. Rest easy for a moment.'

'Doctors?'

Only slowly did I realise I was tucked up in a bed in a hospital ward. The young woman speaking to me was a nurse in uniform.

'Try to relax, Sir.'

'But I have an important business appointment.'

'That will have to wait. There'll be more tests to run. And you need to rest.'

Perhaps the nurse was right. I felt terrible. My head ached and my vision was still blurred. The property deal could be finalised next week. First of all, I needed to do some reconstruction on my own account. Some things might be more important than the quest for more money. And what they say is definitely right. You should never try to go back. You might learn more about yourself than you could have imagined.

Sleep-vampire

At one o'clock the Demon knocks,
or at two or three or four.
Though it's a sin to let him in,
he'll still slip through the door...

Mac couldn't think why this verse was plaguing him. At least once an hour that annoying first stanza was thrusting itself into the forefront of his mind. Far too many of those hours had been waking ones of late. All his problems, big and small, were being exacerbated by the debilitating insomnia he'd known for months. Of late, things were becoming worse.

When had it started? He couldn't remember. Was it when he'd left Rosa? No. He'd been justified to leave. She was never right for him. All she'd had to offer was her youth. A young girl falling for him had been flattering but he knew from the first she'd always hold him back.

Even if it hadn't been easy to leave her asleep with their baby son, it was the right thing to do. He'd left an envelope full of tens and twenties. More than that, he'd opened a bank account in her name and set up a hefty standing order. It was more than generous, wasn't it? No, his insomnia couldn't be anything to do with Rosa.

He looked at the clock-face on the dashboard of his Mercedes. The time was only a minute or two after six o'clock. Still, it would be safer to stop the car now and lay up for the night. His original plan had been to drive as far as the town he'd marked on his map. It was called Llandrindod Wells. That would have given him no more than a short run tomorrow after breakfast to sign off the deal in what looked on the map to be an even smaller place called Rhaeadr.

There was no chance of his plan to drive further north materialising now. Not the way he was feeling. Even at this early hour his eyes were starting to feel sticky and heavy. He knew he was only a few miles north of Brecon. Fortunately, he'd just passed a reasonable looking inn. It should do for one night.

Telling himself he'd feel more alive in the morning, he stopped his car in the lay-by, with the idea of performing a U-turn. The A470 was a busy road, and vehicle after vehicle zoomed by him. After a few minutes of waiting, impatience got the better of things.

Impulsively, he swung the Mercedes out as soon as he saw a tiny gap in the traffic. But he'd cut it much too fine. The traffic in the southbound lane was forced to brake sharply, and the driver of the supermarket lorry coming in the opposite direction blared his horn and flashed his lights in a theatrical fashion. But what the hell. He was through, wasn't he?

*

'Good evening, Sir. In what name has your booking been made?'

'McSpadden. No booking. I want your best room.'

The girl at the reception desk blinked at his directness.

'I'm sorry, Mr McSpadden. It's booked. The couple who've taken the Benybont Room will be arriving within the hour.'

'Tell them there's been a mistake. It happens all the time in the hotel business. I'm well up on these things.'

'I can't do that, Sir. They know me. I made the booking for them.'

'Look, I haven't got time to fool around. What's the cost of the room?'

'Ninety pounds. But...'

'I'll give you a hundred and fifty. No questions asked. That means you can do what you want with the odd sixty. The extra doesn't have to go in the till. Get the message?'

'It's not at all ethical, Sir, but... Have you driven a long way?'

'Never you mind from where I've driven. I'm not in the business of soothing consciences. Now tell me – why is this one your best room?'

'It's larger than the others. And it directly overlooks the Benybont Gardens.'

'Is it quiet?'

'All our rooms are quiet. Especially so at this time of year.'

'That's the most important thing. Now, give me that key.'

*

Jerked into alertness by the incident on the A470 and feeling much better after a shower and shave, Mac strolled into the restaurant. Everything about its decor spoke of the outer provinces; of an establishment trying too hard to be up-to-the-minute and only succeeding in looking silly in the process. At least the menu looked tolerable and the waitress was at his table minutes after he'd taken his seat.

'I'll have the whitebait for starters and *Poulet Normand* for main course. Oh, and I'll take a half-bottle of your *Pauillac* and a carafe of plain water with plenty of ice and lime.'

Mac knew he should have ordered white wine with fish and chicken but thought this more likely to give him insomnia than red. He hoped a good red would drowse him more effectively.

'Do you want bread, Sir?'

'Don't you serve bread as standard? Huh! You'd better get me some then.'

For a moment a flicker of annoyance passed over the waitress's face, but it was quickly replaced by her more usual mask of professional obsequiousness. Mac smiled to himself as she left. This young woman wasn't cut out to be a waitress.

*

'Was the whitebait to your satisfaction, Sir? I told the chef to take extra care with your *Poulet Normand*.'

'Don't worry; you'll get your tip. I always leave a decent trip for triers.'

'What? I'm not interested in the tip. We always do our best to provide good service to all of our customers.'

'I'm not...'

Mac didn't finish his sentence, which would certainly have been a barbed one. As he started to speak he looked at her more closely. She was rather attractive. Dark hair, wide eyes and a good figure into the bargain. Wasted in a hotel. This waitress was made in exactly the way he liked his women. The package was set off exhilaratingly by the flush of anger on her face that seemed to be genuine.

He smiled in what he hoped was a friendly way. Better let her go now. But when she came back with the coffee...

*

'The meal was superb,' he said. 'And the service was absolutely first class.'

'Thank you, Sir.'

'What time do you finish here?'

'At midnight, Sir.'

'What are you doing after that?'

'I'm going straight home. I have two young children.'

'This is for the excellent table service tonight,' he said, laying a ten-pound note on the white cloth. 'Your real tip will await you in the Benybont room at midnight. Shall we say a hundred-and-fifty pounds?'

'I don't know what you mean.'

'You know exactly what I mean. Make it a hundred-and-eighty then, if you insist on driving a hard bargain.'

She flounced off, leaving the ten-pound note on the table.

*

Lying there, alone, in his big feather bed, Mac cursed himself. A hundred-and-fifty? A hundred-and-eighty? What on Earth had he been thinking? He might as well have offered her a straight two or three hundred instead of trying to bargain with her as if she'd been a Marrakech whore. Even five hundred would have been worth it if he could get a good night's sleep afterwards.

Now it was twelve o'clock; the exact time she'd said she was going off duty. He'd already been lying in bed, staring at the ceiling, for a full two hours. He could look forward to at least two hours more of fretful wakefulness before his nightly sleep of no more than two or three hours arrived. He couldn't go on like this.

Dr Montague's words kept coming back to him. And they'd called Monty "the best in Harley Street". Hmmm. "Overwork. Nervous tension. Blah Blah." Utter rubbish, really. Monty had prescribed sleeping pills.

But Mac had tried this sort of thing when he'd had milder trouble a few years ago and all they'd done was upset his stomach. He'd thrown the prescription away. No, he wouldn't be resorting to drugs in a hurry.

*

Something, Mac couldn't have said what, made him spring fully awake. He stared at the too-bright orange figures on the face of the bedside alarm. They read one-twenty-one;

tonight his period of rest must have started and ended earlier and have been even shorter than usual.

When had this pattern started? The same old question came unbidden into his head. Not too long before, he could rely on undisturbed sleep. A dog barked in the distance, to be answered by another closer by. Mac broke into a sweat. A dog – that was what had started it. Soon after he'd left Rosa, it was. He closed his eyes, visualising the scene.

It was late one night in the previous summer. A quiet country lane just outside a Midlands village. All right, so he'd been driving a bit too fast and he might have had a drop too much to drink. The animal appeared from the shadows. An elderly woman was plodding after the animal, heedless of her surroundings. Mac swerved at the bend, mounting the pavement. He narrowly missed the woman but the dog crumpled softly into a black heap.

The woman rushed over to the stricken animal. He slowed down but didn't stop. There was a row of houses nearby. She could get help there. It wasn't as if he'd run her down, as he might so easily have done. Better get away from the place.

More of the odd verse slipped into his mind:

At one o'clock the Demon knocks,
or at two or three or four.
Though it's a sin to let him in,
he'll still slip through the door.

His choirs are the dogs that howl and cats that yowl.
The harshest rhythms of the moon
are the songs you'll hear from far and near;
the daylight will be with us soon.

By yellow light you'll watch the night
and feel the air grow colder.
You'll learn the touch of Hellish burn
before the night grows older.

As if on cue the first cat began to mew softly, only to raise its volume quickly as it was joined by at least a dozen others. Then the nearby dog howled mournfully again. Several others, sounding as if they were close at hand, answered. Mac leapt out of his bed and looked below him from the window into the Benybont Gardens. He saw a circle of dogs around a male figure.

No; it was a female. The waitress from the restaurant... No; it wasn't her. Was it the man waiting to meet him in Rhaeadr? Was it the young wife he'd treated so badly? Was it even human? They and others skipped through his memory as he looked.

Somehow, the beast, whatever it was, bore the features of every man, woman and animal Mac had done, or tried to do the dirty on, over the years. Even those of the father and mother he'd abandoned in Dundee all those years ago, when they most needed him. Then it seemed that what he could see was more like a huge, slavering dog. It turned its head towards him, unmistakeably grinning up in triumph.

Mac jumped back from the window and quickly closed the curtain. He was trembling, and lay on the bed, his heart thumping. Slowly, very slowly, his natural assertiveness started to regain control. What he had seen could be no more than a group of animals playing around a tall figure for some reason. Probably it wasn't even a human figure: a stray black bin-bag or two provided a more likely explanation. Moonlight could play funny tricks on the eyes, especially when someone was as light on sleep as he was. He began to breathe more easily.

Grimacing at his foolishness, he tried to smile as he felt the ambient temperature drop sharply. Soon he could see his breath condensing into icy clouds before him. Then he heard a soft padding sound coming along the passage and up to his door. There it stopped. He remembered the final stanza of the verse:

But if he should come at half-past-one
and wait outside your door
you'll feel cold breath across your shoulder,
and know you'll sleep for evermore.

Not Quite Paradise

You asked me to note everything down exactly as it happened. I don't know why you wanted me to do this. Is it because you want to write another of your books? Or do you just want to tease me more?

Anyway, you wouldn't believe what I said when I told you the first time. I suppose what you really want to know is something to do with that young woman. You know, the nurse you can't find and keep on to me about. Is it?

*

I was out strolling, doing nothing special and going nowhere in particular. It's something I used to do often on the outside, but do little enough of now, with all the damned rules you're so fond of in this place. For me, walking was always a real pleasure. When I was out on a pleasant day, I always felt at peace with the world and with everybody in it. Perhaps it was only because I was feeling like this it could have happened at all – the first time, I'm talking about, not what happened later.

The only way I can describe it, even now, is to tell you that all at once I found myself in two places at the same time. That is, I was still walking along the river bank in exactly the way I'd been doing before. And I was entirely aware of walking and my normal surroundings in exactly the same way as usual.

But I was also, at precisely the same time, and pace for pace, walking somewhere else. The 'somewhere else' seemed to be situated physically above the head of my normal self. And, although this place bore some resemblance to the river bank I knew, it was also very different.

At first I had no more than a shadowy impression of the other world. Gradually, though, it became more substantial and I could only gasp at its sheer loveliness. It was, I suppose, the colours I was aware of more than anything else. They were so much more intense, so much more brightly-hued than I'd seen or even dreamed about before that moment. After a time, my presence in this other world became the dominant one and I was only aware of my normal self in the everyday world by looking downwards and concentrating hard.

Then I suppose I became frightened by the experience. My mood or whatever it was suddenly shattered and I found myself merely walking along the river bank as before. I tried to make a conscious effort to return to my enhanced state but I could find no way to do it.

And that was it. I wish I could better explain what I saw and felt. The whole thing probably lasted for fewer than thirty seconds but during that half-minute it was the most powerful experience I'd ever had. Up until that point it was, anyway. I have tried to reason for myself exactly what happened. Was I merely day-dreaming? Did I pass, momentarily, into some disembodied state? Had I imagined the whole thing?

No, it was none of these things. I am satisfied that somehow I slipped through a gateway into another world, one that exists in parallel with our own. And I say this: the other world was so beautiful, so enriching to the soul and the senses it made our own world seem very ordinary, even drab, by comparison.

*

You really want me to write about the second occasion, don't you? The one all the fuss has been about. I know you people.

I was ambling along the river bank, precisely as before. Of late, I'd found myself walking there many times. It doesn't take a genius to guess I'd been hoping to re-enter the world I'd so tantalisingly glimpsed. Nothing had resulted from these attempts. My body and mind had remained stubbornly below and all I could see when I cast my eyes upward were the clouds scudding across our familiar sky.

So, I'd all but given up my efforts to recreate the magical experience that had briefly been mine. Already it was starting to acquire the status in my mind of nothing more than a very special and private memory. It wasn't the kind of thing I wanted to talk to anyone about. Least of all did I want to say anything to you or to any of the others in this place.

My earlier experience seemed to me something I'd been privileged to enjoy once but was unlikely ever to know again. You'll understand, then, that I was more than a little surprised, to say the least when, once again, I found myself in that other world.

This time was different in that I seemed to enter the other world more quickly and more fully. I was hardly aware of my ordinary being, though I vaguely knew and accepted this was on the river-bank below. I tried not to look downwards or to give way to feelings of panic again. My hope was to prevent shattering the spell, or whatever it was that had brought me to this place.

Trying to keep myself calm, and to prolong what I at first feared might once again be only the gift of a moment, I tried to breathe slowly and deeply. It seemed to work. Before long, save for a slightly dreamlike feeling, my presence in that higher world felt altogether more stable and assured than previously.

It was as wonderful, probably even more wonderful, than I remembered. Sensations crowded in on me until I nearly cried out. I could almost taste the air, so thick and full of life did it seem.

And the creatures! There were small, fluttering things among the trees making a sound so beautiful I could only think of it as singing. But, as before, it was the new colours I could see that had the greatest effect on me. Looking more carefully, I realised they were almost the same colours as I knew in our world. And yet they were not.

True, the sky could still be called blue and the grass green. But our bluest sky was grey in comparison and the greens of the new world were so intense it would be a mockery to call them by the same name.

There was a running river by my side, exactly as in the world I had left behind. Only now, for the first time, I became truly aware of its music. This seemed to come from a thousand different voices, all singing together to create a perfect harmony. This had such depth and substance that I felt I could reach out and grasp it.

The assault on my senses was so great that for a moment I had to cover my face with my hands to prevent my mind from becoming unhinged.

'Are you all right?'

Slowly I took my hands from my face and looked to see who had spoken these words. It was a woman. I do not say that she was lovelier than any woman I had ever seen before. But she was so *different*.

She was so much more rounded, so much larger, so much more vivacious than I had thought possible. I was too overwhelmed by the mere sight of her to answer. She spoke again.

'Excuse me, but are you well? I couldn't help but notice you didn't seem quite... calm. Have you come from the hospital?'

'Er, yes…I think so.'

I didn't know why I had answered in this way. Perhaps it was from sheer fright. I could see she was advancing purposefully in my direction. It terrified me to see such a large person bearing down upon me. But, as she came nearer, I was surprised to see that the top of her head was level with my shoulder.

'Let me show you the way back. I'm a nurse.'

I knew what a nurse was. We have many of those on our world. It surprised me to see so many ways in which this other world was similar to our own. I had no difficulty in understanding what she was saying. Perhaps she would be able to answer some of the questions fermenting in my brain.

'What is this place?'

'We're only down by the river. Not far from the hospital. You must have been here many times. Which ward have you come from?'

'I think I'm no more than a visitor.'

She said nothing, but gently linked her arm in mine and guided me along the towpath. No woman in our own world would have acted so boldly. I didn't know what to think.

'It's so pleasant down here by the river, don't you think? I sometimes take a walk here when I'm off duty. That's not often enough, sadly.'

'Yes, it is beautiful.' I had to agree with what she was saying. Then I saw something in the water that alarmed me. 'What's *that?*'

'Oh, it's only some effluent from the factory around the river bend. It's a terrible shame they can get away with polluting the river so blatantly.'

Floating with the slime on the river surface was a small, dead fish. It disgusted me. Then, as we rounded the bend in the river a large building came into view. This must have been the factory of which the woman had spoken. I was astounded to see a dark purplish fluid being pumped directly into the river, which bubbled and steamed at that point. The most prominent feature of the building was its dark and very old-looking chimney. From this a plume of yellow-grey smoke was spewing into the sky.

The air about the factory was heavy with a sickly, sweetish smell I couldn't quite identify. It thrust itself deep down my nostrils and throat. A wave of nausea coursed through me. I shook myself free of the woman and turned to face her.

'How can you people do such awful things to this beautiful world?'

*

The last sight I remember from my time there was seeing the woman's blue eyes growing rounder and wider. At the same time her mouth started to open and close as if she were trying to say something to me. But her efforts were pointless. Already she was beginning to fade away from my vision and I could hear none of her words.

Needless to say, I've never been back to the other world. Nor have I tried to return. I've even avoided going anywhere near to the river. I don't want to go there again, ever.

It was a beautiful world. This is one thing I've never changed my mind about. I confess I often try to recreate its beauty in my mind's eye, although I know memory is a feeble thing compared with the intense reality of what I saw.

Never again will I try to reach that world. Our own may be a poor and dull place by comparison, but at least we know how to look after our world and the people in it.

You will keep looking after me, won't you?

Mercenary

'Do I still please you, John? Oh, sorry. General, I should remember to say.'

'You certainly should address me by my proper title. Let's have some respect around here. Don't get ideas above yourself. And I haven't time now for another of your soul-searching witterings. I have some tactical planning to do before I make my rounds of inspection. Just be grateful to find yourself on full rations.'

'Do you want me to be back at the usual time so you can enjoy my belly?'

'Seven o'clock this evening. Not a moment earlier or later.'

Samantha Howell departed, closing my bedroom door as quietly as the timid mouse she was. In truth, I'd had enough of her. She was too young to be more than a temporary amusement. Really, I should find a more vigorous girl to warm my bed. There'd surely be a one somewhere among the Townies.

Probably it was no more than the maddeningly coy way in which she used that odd expression, "*enjoy my belly*" that made me keep her on. It really got to me. By six o'clock each evening I could hear her silly girl's voice running through my mind and I'd start looking at the wall clock every couple of minutes.

In truth there wasn't much in the way of official duties to keep me occupied. "Tactical planning" may have been how I described the way I spent my mornings to Samantha and my soldiers. But what "tactical planning" was possible when you were pinned down with fifty troops in a fortified small town? The Government forces could march in and sweep us away at any time. The only reason they didn't do it was that too many Townies would be killed in the process. It would be easier for them to starve us out.

In fact I spent the mornings doing nothing more than idling the time away in my private quarters before it was time for lunch and my dreary round of inspections. "Private quarters" was a bit of a joke, too. These consisted of a few shabby rooms above a pub. Two years ago they'd have held B&B guests who couldn't afford anything better. Now there were two of my riflemen posted by the door at all times.

*

The first call on my afternoon inspections was to the radio duty room. Whenever someone new was on I liked to come up to him quietly after tipping the wink to his companion on armed guard. Soldiers need to be kept on their toes, especially when their situation was as dire as ours. This man, though, seemed to be alert enough. His head was bent over the radio and he was listening to the drone of static caused by the Government jammers as if it were his favourite music. He saw me coming and sprang to his feet, saluting.

'Sir!' he said.

'At ease, soldier. Make your oral report.'

'Sir! At eight hundred hours the jamming on the communications device stopped for thirty-eight seconds in total. I picked up some music and a partial news report.'

I warmed to this flush-faced boy. The way he looked down at the transistor radio and referred to it as a "communications device" with a perfectly straight face was the kind of thing I liked. We'd confiscated all the other radios in the town and kept them locked up. There was no need to encourage low morale, or deplete our small stock of batteries, by letting people listen to Government propaganda.

'And what did you pick up from the news broadcast?'

'I recorded it in full, Sir, as per my orders. And I made a note of the music. It was...'

'Just give me the news in your own words for now. Was there any mention of us in the news bulletin?'

'Yes, Sir. At the end. I didn't pick up much but they were referring to a rebel stronghold in our town. They were saying we were one of the last holding out.'

'Rebel stronghold, eh? File your report, soldier.'

So, they were still calling us a "stronghold", were they? It didn't feel like that to me. Least of all did it feel like one when I made my inspection of the troops. There were only about fifty of us left. A month ago there'd been sixty. Ten soldiers and twenty Townies had taken their chance and made a break for it. Fools. Most of them had ended up with one of our bullets in them. The only way to escape to Government lines was for them to run across open country with their backs presented as easy targets. It was worrying that so many had taken this chance.

*

Captain Strong was always my final call of the afternoon. I tried to pretend I saw him last for some military reason, though in reality it was because I put off seeing him for as long as I could. He was so depressing. I'd have replaced him if this were not such a crucial time and if there were a worthwhile replacement.

If any man had been mis-named, it was my second-in-command. Strong was the last thing he was. If it were left to him he'd have surrendered like a shot. I always tried to explain that the Government forces would have us both up against the wall in two shakes if they got their hands on us. He seemed to understand but then two or three days later he'd be again spouting the same defeatist claptrap.

He wasn't really a Captain, any more than I was a General. I'd been a Sergeant and he'd been a Corporal. But we might have been the last unit of a rebel army that had once held the whole of Western Britain. After our Lieutenant had been killed six weeks ago I reasoned that, since we were now the most senior soldiers, we should take whatever titles we chose.

'Make your report, Captain!'

'General.' I hated the conspiratorial grin Strong always flashed at me when he called me by my title. 'Two things to report. The first is the state of our rations.'

'Yes? Go on then.'

'All soldiers are on full rations. Most of the Townies are on two-thirds rations. At that rate I calculate that we have enough food for three weeks.'

'Only three weeks?' This didn't really surprise me. 'Put all Townies on half-rations. Better keep the soldiers on full rations. There aren't so many of them and we need to retain their loyalty.'

'All the Townies, General?'

'Better keep the Mayor on full rations. We might need him.'

'All the Townies except the Mayor, General?'

'You swallowed a parrot or something?'

'But what about...'

'You heard my orders. The Mayor is the only exception.'

I guessed Strong had been expecting me to exempt Samantha as well. Well, I wasn't going to.

'You said you had two things to report, Captain.'

'Yes, General. The Mayor's been to see me again. He asked for an audience with you. But I wouldn't grant one. He was saying...'

I groaned, interrupting Strong.

'He wants to try to persuade me to throw in the towel, does he?'

'Mayor Preston has had proper legal articles of surrender drawn up. The report he's given on our treatment of the Townies is very fair. His signature is already on the document. So is mine. All it needs now is for you to sign it. I told him I'd...'

'Give it to me, Captain.'

'Are you going to sign the paper?'

'I am not. Tomorrow, I'm going to take this over to the Mayor and give him an audience he won't forget in a hurry. Then I'm going to come back here and try to explain things to you one more time. I've had enough for today.'

*

It was well before six by the time I returned. An hour before Samantha came. What a miserable day! For a moment I thought of calling for the girl and my food earlier, but this would never do. My troops would see it as a sign of weakness. So might she.

Was I right? Should I keep trying to hold out? I jumped as I realised there was a stranger in my room.

'Who are you? What are you doing in my private quarters?'

The woman had breezed in as if she were paying a casual visit. But how had she walked past the guards?

'I'm Maria Howell. I've come to talk to you.'

'Don't you know all communications from Townies are supposed to be made through the Mayor?'

'Townies?' she said.

Who was she? All the Townies knew we mercenaries called them that.

'You do belong to the town don't you?' I said. 'That makes you a Townie.'

'I was born here, yes,' she said.

'Look, I've wasted more than enough time. I'm very busy.' I couldn't help noticing how attractive she was. This was why I didn't immediately call in the guard and have her shot. 'Look, go and talk to the Mayor and we'll say no more about you breaking the rules.'

'I want to talk to you about something private. It is not for the ears of the man who calls himself the Mayor,' she said. 'I've come to offer myself to you for the night.'

'What?' I said.

I looked properly at Maria Howell for the first time. She was certainly beautiful. Voluptuous, and with depthless dark eyes. And here I was, preparing myself for a night with the half-grown Samantha. My throat went dry at the prospect of a night with this woman.

'It is very simple,' she said. 'I will come back at eight o'clock this evening. I will be yours for twelve hours and in that time will do anything you wish. All I want from you is your signature on the document of surrender. It has already been signed by your second-in-command and the one who claims to be the representative of the townspeople.' How did she know of the existence of the document? It was nothing more than a fancy piece of paper without my signature.

'You will only be bringing the inevitable forward by a few weeks,' she added. 'And I will be yours tonight...'

'You've got this wrong' I tried to laugh. 'What makes you think you can swan in and do exactly what you like?'

'My body. But, for the moment, this makes me think it,' she said.

In her hand she held a pistol. Its shiny black barrel was pointed at my forehead. Where did she get the gun? I could swear she wasn't holding one when I first saw her.

'Now look, be sensible...' Inside, I was terrified. She could have put a bullet in my brain in a moment. I knew many of the Townies would be happy to do the same thing. Was this the end? I calculated to see whether I should leap over and wrestle the gun from her before she pulled the trigger. She wasn't quite close enough for me to take the chance.

'Let's not waste any more time,' she said. 'You want me. Come on; admit it. In turn, I want your signature on the Articles of Surrender to go with those of your deputy and the so-called mayor. It is as simple as that. I am a very desirable woman. Let me show you.'

Still holding the gun, her other hand moved to the silver studs on the high-necked dress she wore. Four of the studs popped open. She was fabulous.

'How do you know the Mayor and Captain Strong have already signed? What guarantee do I have that you would come back at eight o'clock?'

'Let me say only that I know. You have my word about my return.' She licked her lips. It seemed she was looking forward to this night as much as I was.

'I am willing to do this for my daughter's sake,' she continued. 'She is too young for the demands you make upon her and...' Her voice quavered. 'I do not want her to die of starvation. She'll be on half-rations. Soon afterwards there will be even less than that.'

How did she know? Samantha didn't. I'd only given the order to Strong a few hours ago.

I stared at Maria. She was some woman. And what she had said earlier was true. What did I have to look forward to if things went on as they were? I would only be bringing the inevitable forward. Our food supplies would rapidly diminish over the next few weeks, no matter how much I tried to husband our resources. During that time, sickness among the already deprived Townies would increase. Some of them would probably rise up against me in anger or desperation. Fifty troops might not be enough to control them. On the other hand, I could have a night with Maria...

'I'll sign,' I said, surprising myself with the suddenness of my resolve. I slid the document across from the other side of the desk and hurriedly applied my signature in the space above those of Strong and Preston before I could change my mind.

When I looked up, Maria no longer had the gun.

She quickly picked up the signed Articles of Surrender and walked to the chamber door. Then she turned and gave a wave. I waved back; I knew she'd return. Eight o'clock; I could hardly wait.

I strained my ears to listen for the sounds of the outer door opening and closing but heard nothing. Surely one of the guards should have challenged a stranger? Someone was going find himself on a charge or worse in the morning. But that was for tomorrow. Now I could settle back and wait for my meal. My dessert tonight would be a special one.

*

At seven o'clock the door opened and Samantha walked in.

'What are you doing here?'

'This is my time. The guards admitted me as usual. You wanted me to come.'

Hadn't her mother said anything to her?

'But...'

'Are you not ready for me? Would you prefer it if I came back later?'

'But – your mother?'

Her face became ashen. It was as if I'd struck her a physical blow.

'I am no more than a poor girl of the town,' she said after a moment. 'Please do not mock me.'

'I don't understand,' I said. 'Your mother has been to see me. Has she not spoken to you?'

She sobbed. I said nothing. At last she spoke.

'My parents died in a hail of bullets. This was a month before you and your men took over the town. I was with them at the time. It happened before my eyes but I was unharmed. They were mutilated by the bullets. It was horrible. Every day since then I wish I'd died with them. My mother was my best friend. I miss her so much.'

Her words chilled me.

'You'd better go,' I mumbled. 'I have no use for you tonight.'

As she left, tears were still streaming down her cheeks.

*

It is now not quite eight o'clock.

Had the earlier visit of Maria Howell been nothing more than a dream brought on by the disillusions of the day and my fears for the future? Or had it happened? It seemed so real. Exactly what was going to be in store for me as the clock struck eight?

Soldat

1

'Monster!'

This word, the earliest I remember hearing, was forever on the lips of Klemens. At first I thought it was my name.

In fact most people knew me as Heinz Müller. As far as I know I was born around 1900 in what used to be Manzow. At its height no more than a hamlet and a few surrounding farms, it was barely fifty kilometres east of Berlin. This was what they used to tell me. I've never been to the city myself. It might as well have been on a different world. Few people came to our bleak corner of Der Oderbruch.

The surname Müller was given to me because I spent my first eight years in the ramshackle workplace and dwelling of the miller, Klaus Klemens. The name of my mother is uncertain, though many in Manzow liked to nod sagely and say she was Bertha, the miller's daughter. In truth, almost everyone said this, except Klemens himself. She died before I was two years old and I have no memories of her, not even as a warm shadow. The nearest I can claim to a real memory of Bertha was from one autumn day when I was around six years old.

I'd ventured into the miller's bedroom. It was one of the places in the mill forbidden to me, but all was quiet and I thought I'd get away with it. I knew he kept a picture of his daughter by his bedside. All I wanted to do was to look at it properly for the first time and try to discover what the other boys meant when they said the special word: *Mother*. I tiptoed into the room and was soon cradling the cracked wooden frame in my hands.

I gazed at the picture with reverence. I have to admit it couldn't have been a very good likeness. The focus was poor and already the image was starting to fade. Bertha was so young in the photograph and had a sad, moon face. Even though I'm the very last person who should utter such a thing, I have to say that, even then, I recognised she was no kind of beauty. Still, this picture could be of my own mother and I gazed at it wonderingly. I didn't look for long.

'What do you think you're doing?' Klemens was framed in the doorway.

'Mother.' This was the only word I could get out.

'My daughter was not your mother! You've been listening to the tales of those wicked farmers.'

In two of his great loping strides, Klemens was across the room. He snatched the wooden frame from my hands and cuffed me with it, grazing my ear and causing it to bleed.

'She was not your mother,' Klemens repeated. 'One day she found you lying naked in the hills and brought you home with her. Why she did such a thing, I'll never know. She should have left you to die. You were always a little freak. I rue the day she brought you into my home. Now, I'm going to have to destroy the only memory I have of my daughter to stop you repeating those evil stories. Get out of my room!'

I didn't need telling twice. A bleeding ear was a small thing but I'd felt the fury of Klemens' boots and fists many times before. I crept to my space behind the millstone in the big room and tried to sleep. At the time I didn't know this was the last night I'd be permitted to sleep in the mill. Always after this, I'd be locked in the woodshed whenever the miller didn't need me to work. But, on that last night of comparative comfort, I could hear him sobbing softly behind his door and couldn't help wondering once again about some of the things I'd heard. Who really was my mother? Who could my father be? There were all sorts of stories of my sire. All of them were unpleasant. I'm not going to repeat them. I have to accept this is something of which I will never be sure.

*

None of this really matters; Klemens died not long before I became nine, I think it was and I was set free. He'd rented the mill from a landlord who lived somewhere in Schwedt. Suddenly, I found myself with nothing in the World. I couldn't sleep in the mill, nor even the woodshed close to it, because they were locked up from the day of Klemens' death until one night when they were destroyed by a storm. Nobody wanted to take on the mill in the years it still stood. There would be no profit in it.

Somehow, I survived and grew. Later, I became known through the whole area as the Wild Child of Manzow. In many ways it was better to sleep in barns and odd corners. I'd find my food wherever I could. The scraps of food the miller threw to me had been barely enough to keep me alive, anyway. I found it preferable to be left to fend for myself. Some of the farmers were good to me as a child. They didn't call me names like the others. A few of them, Old Siegfried especially, even gave me money when I did things like chop wood for them. His son and the young man's wife were always considerate, even saving me leftovers from their poor table.

Despite my deformed hands and other problems, no-one could deny that I came to know every inch of the land better than any one of them, especially the wilder parts of our terrain where few people went. Although I spent so much of my time in the low hills, the place I liked best of all was Die Bratfpanne. This was in the centre of the lowest plains, a small depression set right in the middle of a ring of boulders. Even on the blusteriest of days – and we had a great many of these in Der Oderbruch – it was always calm and windless inside Die Bratfpanne itself.

I would lie in its deepest part for hours at a time doing nothing but looking up at a sky that was normally iron-grey, listening to the song of the few birds venturing near. On a few days the sky would even become a luminous blue. These were the times I liked best: I'd watch the clouds scudding above me and pretend the pictures they formed were of a better world than the one in which I found myself.

But I shouldn't complain too much. I made not too bad a life for myself. I taught myself to read well, once Siegfried's daughter-in-law had shown me the rudiments. I even learned to write, despite the difficulties with my hands and the problems I had in finding pencils.

Soon I came to know most of the books in Manzow and around. There weren't many volumes to be seen within a radius of ten kilometres, in fairness, but I knew every word of each of those I was allowed to read. Word of my knowledge of the land and my expertise as a guide spread beyond Manzow itself. People travelled from the bigger villages some distance away and would endure my appearance so I could reveal to them the hidden delights of this place. Even so, I always kept Die Bratpfanne as my own special refuge. Every man should keep something special and private to himself.

*

All this was to change when I stood on the threshold of manhood. It was then our Fatherland found itself at war with the Russians and the people of some other nations I'd never heard of before that summer. I do not understand the details, but Siegfried told me some of the arrogant ones in other lands had insulted our Emperor in Berlin. The main thing this war meant to me was that fewer people now sought out my services as a guide. I relied more on chopping wood and casual work on farms when I could get it to survive.

Naturally, I walked as far as Schwedt to offer my services to the Imperial Army. They wouldn't take me. They said I was too young. This may have been true in the early years of the war, but they also said the same thing in later times. I walked all the way to the recruitment office in Schwedt three times more over the next years. They might have been saying I was too young but what they meant was I was too ugly and malformed. Too ugly to serve the German Empire!

I'm sure I would have gone mad but for a conversation I had one day with Siegfried.

'Isn't it exciting?' he said.

'What is exciting?' I said, grateful for the chance to rest the axe and my aching shoulders for a while.

At that moment I was at my lowest ebb. Any kind of excitement was the furthest thing from my mind. The Imperial German Army didn't want me; I could see no future ahead for myself. My belly was empty and would have to remain so until I'd finished chopping this pile of logs for Siegfried.

'The news about your friend Walter, of course; it is that I'm talking about.'

'I don't know anyone called Walter.' I didn't add there was no-one I could count as my friend, except Siegfried himself.

'Yes you do. Walter Schickel, from Kirchnow, is the man I'm talking about. Last year you acted as a guide for his family. You were chock full of stories about young Walter afterwards.'

I remembered the Schickels now. Their son, whom I'd naturally addressed as 'Master Schickel', was named Walter. He'd shown me a few acts of kindness and treated me as a normal human being. Afterwards, I'd told Siegfried about him. The young man was about six years older than me. Never before or since have I seen anyone take so readily to the outdoor life.

This was hardly enough make him my friend but, from that day forward, Siegfried and I devoured every scrap of news we could discover about Walter and his doings in the war. It was true he was the only Imperial Soldier I knew – all the young men in Manzow itself had left long before the outbreak of hostilities – that was the expression people liked to use – and it soon became second nature for me to see his exploits as my own.

Imagine our delight when we heard one day Walter Schickel had been awarded the Iron Cross, Second Class, after the Battle of Gorlice-Tarnów. Everyone in Manzow and all around also took pride in the way Walter and his fellow soldiers drove the enemy deep back into the dark lands of Russia. It made it all the harder for us all to accept what they told us only a few years later. Germany had lost the war!

Why this should have been is a thing I never will know. One day all the stories were about brave victories on the field of battle; the next there was only one story about something they called an Armistice. This had something to do with a piece of paper being signed in a railway carriage somewhere in France. France! This was a country on the far side of the World. At the time, I even doubted such a land could exist. What this story had to do with any of the people far to the east in Der Oderbruch was beyond me.

*

Times were very hard for the first ten or fifteen years after this Armistice, whatever it was. Siegfried, an old man even before the fighting started, died only a few weeks after its end. Many of the remaining families in Manzow left their farms and sought better land further west.

But the things I heard from other parts of our country were also not good. Our Emperor had to flee abroad and our unworthy new government wanted to pay vast sums of money to the people in other countries, who had been our enemies only a short time before. At the same time, so it was said, a poor man had to pay a suitcase full of banknotes for a loaf of bread.

Slowly, things did start to improve for Germany, though they never did for Manzow, which had been dealt its death blow by the war. There were fewer families left as the years passed by. In time, though, I even found myself guiding occasional parties over the hills again, mainly by using exaggerated signs to point things out. Many seemed to enjoy my antics, though I hated the restrictions upon me. Sadly, many fewer visitors came after the war, especially in the early years.

Then, one day, we were told our country was at war once again. Naturally, my first instinct was to report to Schwedt as soon as I could. Walking into the recruiting office, I was greeted with an unfriendly chill.

'Yes?' said the recruiting sergeant. The bald man looked up from his papers. He was old but tried to exude an air of importance in his new soldier's uniform. He looked at me doubtfully.

This time I was better prepared. Although it was a balmy September, I wore a thick scarf that had once belonged to Siegfried. This I'd wrapped tightly around my neck and pointed to my throat to suggest I'd lost my voice. I didn't want these people to hear me speak in my stumbling fashion and think I was an imbecile.

Then I stepped forward to place my piece of paper on the desk in front of him. Siegfried's daughter-in-law had copied out the words I wanted in very neat printing. The note read: '*My name is Heinz Müller. I live in Manzow. I am willing to serve the Wehrmacht in any capacity*'. Capacity! This fine word should prove to them I was no idiot. The sergeant looked at the words for a long time. He probably didn't know what 'capacity' meant.

'What's this? We're only looking for young, fit men here.'

I stepped forward again and turned the paper over. He looked at it critically.

'It says here you were born "about 1900". That's no good. It would make you around forty. Where's your birth certificate?'

At this point a tall young man stepped smartly through the door of the office. The sergeant looked up, all his attention immediately upon the newcomer. Fearing that my chance would be lost, I pulled from my pocket the pencil I'd especially borrowed and brought with me – even if I'd hoped not to use it – and scrawled '1905' on the piece of paper. Unfortunately, the difficulties with my hand have always made it hard for me to write quickly. This time, the figures were large and barely legible, like those of a child in the early years of kindergarten. The sergeant looked at what I'd written with barely concealed contempt. His prominent moustache twitched.

'What's wrong with you?' he said. 'Are you …' Then his eyes alighted on the young man again. '*This* is the sort of soldier we want: young and fit. You're too – old.' With that, he lost all interest in me and I slunk out to the street.

*

This time, they'd told me I was too old. Too old to serve the Fatherland!

For a long time, all the news reaching us about the war was good. It made all of us in Manzow – though few were left now – proud. But, as the years passed, the tide turned against our soldiers once again. I heard that our enemies were reconquering this country called France and, even here in the East, the Russian armies were knocking on the door of Poland, close to my home.

Then, on Friday, 22nd September, 1944 – I know the date exactly because he told me what it was and from that day forward it was burned into my memory – I had an unexpected and very special visitor. It was Walter Shickel. I can remember every word of our conversation. I can recall every word said by Walter, at least. He probably couldn't understand many of my own. I will always be grateful for the way he looked me in the eye and carried on speaking as if I'd been able to answer properly. He even smiled, warmly, at me.

'Well Heinz, my friend, this war is not going at all well for us. The Russians will be at our borders before long. In the West the enemy has been laying siege to Aachen for weeks.'

Friend! He had called me his friend! This hero was treating me as an equal. After the first war he'd joined up as a regular soldier and now wore an officer's uniform. What sort of officer he was I couldn't say, but after all these years in uniform a man as bold as he was must have reached a high rank indeed. Although Walter looked tired around the eyes and parts of his uniform were worn and dirty, to me he was still the young man who'd won the Iron Cross at Gorlice-Tarnów. He was a true hero of our nation.

'This is why I am here. You will, as a proud German, understand this. The Wehrmacht has a special job for you. Will you be brave enough to take it on?'

The Wehrmacht wanted me to serve my country! At last! My words in response came out as babble. At first Walter must have misunderstood what I was trying to say, because he continued:

'Oh, I know what you're thinking. The Wehrmacht turned you down before. I've heard all about this. But that was when you wanted to be an ordinary soldier in the ranks. It is a special, very important task we have in mind for you now. You, Heinz, are the only man who can accomplish it. I remember how well you knew the land. When I found out what was needed, you were the one I thought of immediately. So, I suggested your name to my superiors and was sent here to talk to you. My unit is nearby for the moment; soon we will be marching north. We want you to be a corporal in the Wehrmacht. You will be on special duties. Will you do it, Heinz? Will you do it for the sake of our old friendship and for the Fatherland?'

A corporal in the Wehrmacht! This time, I didn't trust myself to speak. I nodded my head. Walter smiled and placed the bag he was carrying at my feet.

'This bag, Heinz, contains your uniform. There are also twenty-four rounds of ammunition in the side compartment. And this,' – here he held forth the weapon he'd been carrying – 'is your soldier's rifle. Now, will you put on your uniform before I leave?'

Quickly, I discarded my rags at my feet. I'd never wear them again. The uniform was frayed in places and the neat hole beneath the left hand chest pocket, especially surrounded as it was by a pale brown stain that hadn't quite come out with washing, told me more than I wanted to know about the fate of its original wearer. Still, at that moment I was immensely proud. My pride swelled even more when Walter Schickel gave me a smart raised arm salute.

'Welcome to the Wehrmacht, Corporal Müller! You will do your duty like a brave German; I am sure of this.'

I was confused. I didn't know how to address him. Major Schickel? Captain Schickel? Some higher rank? Unknowingly, I must have put my question into some sort of words. He must have understood what I was saying because he answered:

'When we are alone together like this, Heinz, you have to call me Walter. Of course you must. We are both men of Der Oberbruch. Now, it is for me to return to my unit. We are marching north-east to Königsberg.' Here he patted the holster hanging from his belt. I wanted to ask him to take the pistol out to show me but didn't dare.

'We are to join with the forces of General Otto Lasch. Our orders are to hold the Soviet army at the city. But, in case we should fail and the Russians march through here on their way to Berlin, your job will be to hide in the hills and to kill any Russians you see. A small force of Private soldiers will be sent to support you in about a week. They will be yours to command. I know you will not let the German people down. So, I bid you farewell, my friend!' He offered me his hand.

He had called me his friend again and shaken my hand. There was none of this shouting the Leader's name in the way even a few of the farmers left in Manzow were wont to do. This was the moment in my whole life I most treasure.

*

I saw no Russians. Not one round of fire did I let loose in anger. None of my promised command arrived. Nevertheless, I did my duty. Even when the last of the farmers packed up and left the area, I stayed, living off the land, gathering wild fruit and trapping small animals. In time I saw no need to cook the animals before I ate them. Their warm blood had more flavour this way. The winter following Walter's visit was very cold in its later stages and the thin uniform offered little protection from the elements, so I was grateful for the small amount of heat my diet brought to me.

My existence itself became unreal and tied in some way I didn't understand to the land. There were times I thought I'd perish, forgotten, in the hills. But I had my orders as a soldier of the Wehrmacht. I meant to follow them. I would do my duty.

2

Die Wahre Spiegel, 29th August, 1969

The local government authorities have issued a categorical denial of reports of sightings of what is claimed to be some kind of supernatural creature around the former settlement of Manzow. This area has been entirely unoccupied since the end of the war and does not lie on the route to anywhere.

It is considered that these stories must have been spread by the institution claiming for itself the title of The Federal Republic of Germany. This is nothing more than a low attempt to undermine morale in our Democratic Republic. Such actions contradict and perhaps give a true insight into the more sinister motives behind the positive messages now being issued by the Federal Republic under the banner of 'Neue Ostpolitik'.

The area is considered to be wholly unsuitable for redevelopment for agricultural use of any kind. The decision has been taken that, as soon as the financial situation allows, work will commence on making the area suitable for leisure and amenity. Before the war, a secondary use of the area was exactly this, albeit in a hesitant and primitive way. All of us, especially the people of the eastern part of the Democratic Republic will be proud to know that plans now being drawn up are infinitely more ambitious than anything that would have been envisaged earlier in the century.

Meanwhile, immediate steps will be taken to clear the area of the few wooden structures remaining from earlier land use. The condition of most or all of these is poor and presents a real danger to the public. While this preparatory work is going on, therefore, our citizens are strongly advised not to enter any part of the area. The Public Authorities repeat that they are unable to take responsibility for anyone who does so.

3

27th July, 2023

'There it goes!'

'Lukas! You're imagining things again.' Renate laughed, but she looked nervous in the encroaching gloom. 'This is the third time since lunch you've told us you've seen your creature. Neither of us has seen a thing.'

'I think you made too much of that old newspaper report you turned up on line,' said Jannik. 'More fool us for following you out to a place like this. But, this time we'll know for sure whether you're seeing things. There's no way any kind of creature could come back out from that group of boulders without us seeing it. After we've taken a look we'll call this nonsense off. I've had enough of all this trailing around this sort of countryside. I'll be pleased to get back to Hamburg.'

'Ah,' said Lukas. 'This time I do have proof. I filmed the thing on my Linker. The three of us will be able see it now. I had a clear view for at least ten seconds.'

The other two stood on each side of him and watched the small screen on his wrist. Despite the doubts expressed by their words, their faces betrayed an eagerness that was almost a match for that of Lukas.

'Here it comes. Just at this point now,' he said.

The three of them scanned the tiny screen worn on Lukas' wrist. Their expressions soon changed to disappointed puzzlement.

'There's nothing to see. Nothing at all. Your eyes must be playing tricks. Or is this no more than wishful thinking on your part?' said Jannik.

'Perhaps there wasn't enough light?' said Renate, trying to be the diplomat. She sensed the boys were on the verge of yet another argument. She knew that, at root, she had been the cause of the tension between them. When they got back to

Hamburg she wouldn't be having much to do with either of them again. Lukas was a bit too interested in his technological gimmickry and Jannik's surface jokiness concealed more than a tinge of nastiness.

'No, I tell you I had a good view. This linker is the latest model. It uses the latest version of VS9 technology and takes moving pictures to the equivalent of the old 1SO 2000. And there's nothing wrong with my eyesight *or* my imagination. I vote we press on. The circle is only a kilometre ahead.'

'OK,' said Jannik. 'We'll take a closer look. But if we see nothing, that's definitely the end of this business. We go back to Hamburg tonight and there's to be not another word from you about this so-called Monster of Manzow. Agreed, Lukas?'

'Agreed.'

'Are you both sure we should go any further?' said Renate. 'The light is really beginning to fade now.'

'And the light will be gone altogether if we don't get a move on,' said Jannik. 'Come on, we don't want Lukas to be nagging us to come back to a place like this tomorrow.'

*

'They're coming,' said the thing that had once been Heinz to himself. 'This time they're not soldiers. They're not even Russians, to judge by the look of them. For goodness' sake, one of them is a girl. What is this war coming to?'

*

'It's a bit creepy here,' said Renate. 'I hope you two don't plan to stay for hours.'

'We won't be here for long.' Jannik looked meaningfully toward his friend, who was marching ahead of them. 'We'll take a quick look around to humour Lukas and then we're off, that I promise you. Anyway, we won't have to wait much more. Look ahead of you. These are the boulders.'

Soon the three stood on the lip of the depression in the ground. Years before, it had been called the Bratfpanne, or frying pan, but the three young people weren't aware of this.

'Nothing. Nothing at all. There's not even a shrub the smallest animal could hide behind.'

'I'm afraid you're right, Jannik. This feature has been in the plain sight of the three of us for the last fifteen minutes. Nothing could have climbed out without us seeing it. I'm sorry I've wasted your weekend.'

'Don't feel so bad about it, old friend.' Jannik's sardonic pose had deserted him. 'This weekend hasn't been so bad. Anyone could have…'

'_!'

Renate had thrown a small stone. Its flight had been straight and true at first. Then it had seemed to suddenly bounce in mid-air. None of the young people realised it had been deflected off the weaker leg of Heinz.

'Why did you throw that?' said Lukas, turning to Renate.

'Sorry; for a moment I thought I saw something. It must have been a trick of the light,' she said.

'It's funny; when you threw the stone I thought I heard an odd sound. It was like the cry of some kind of creature in pain,' said Jannik. 'Anyway, there's nothing there now. It can only have been my imagination. I think we should get out of this place as soon as we can. We're all starting to see and hear things. By the time we get back to Hamburg there'll be time for no more than a few hours' sleep before we have to go to work.'

'Yes,' said Renate. 'Let's go. I don't like any part of it. This Bratfpanne is the worst of all.'

'Bratfpanne?' said Lukas. 'Why do you call it that?'

'Well, it reminds me of a frying pan. I'll be getting out my real one in Hamburg before I go to work in the morning. You can be sure of that.'

The Crystal Spirit

Ted had already been feeling every one of his almost eight completed decades, even before the time he crossed the rolling dunes of Ross Links in the half-light of pre-dawn.

It hadn't been wise to leave the warm bed in his daughter's house at Belford just so he could say he'd stood upon the desolate Ross Back Sands before breakfast on the shortest day of the year. He knew this: age was catching up with him faster than ever these days. But images of Lindisfarne at one end of this vista and the looming presence of Bamburgh Castle at the other had invaded his dreams. Those dreams wouldn't let him rest last night. So, here he was, on the beach at last, seeing these sights in reality.

He'd visited these sands a half-dozen times before this morning but those occasions had always been in broad daylight with at least some sunshine. Today was different.

Always he'd had a hankering to know what it was like out here at this early hour. Well, now on this morning of the Winter Solstice, he knew. It was gloomy and cold. In the extreme north-east of England the darkness seemed, if possible, almost tangible. Ted hadn't seen a soul on his long walk from the village. Not a single creature was in evidence; no bird had so much as ruffled its wings. He was alone.

Ted was painfully aware of his aching limbs as he made his way slowly across the wet sand of the beach. The walking stick he'd only recently started to use wasn't much help.

Even if he couldn't have stayed in his snug room, he knew he shouldn't have come so far this morning, not on his own at least. Still he'd discovered two years ago on his first visit to his daughter in this distant part of England that it was a beautiful, desolate part of the world. Today, he'd lost all track of time and distance. Already he'd spent twenty minutes at least blinking through the half-light to watch this fine silver-white horse racing across the beach.

What was such an animal doing out here, alone and riderless? What was the odd dark red-brown mark on its neck? These questions had been the reasons why he'd stood so long on a piece of wormholed driftwood. There he'd stayed until the tide was lapping around his feet, hoping for the horse to come near enough to allow his misting eyesight to focus on the unusual sight.

In the event, it had not once approached near enough for him to make out what it could be. Eventually, the animal had turned and galloped away to the south with a shake of its head, as if flaunting its freedom. Ted watched its graceful movement until it was lost to his fading vision.

Wait a minute – was this the same horse, now galloping back towards him? This time, could he make out a rider on its back? Not many moments had passed before he could see the answer to both of these questions was "yes". Before long, he could see the rider was a young woman with dark flowing locks.

Rider and horse were soon upon him. The woman rode as if she were born in the saddle, although Ted noticed there was no saddle on the horse. And she was beautiful. There was no other word for it. She smiled briefly at him. He smiled back, more broadly. For a moment he forgot his years, his aching legs and back.

'I'm looking for my father,' she said. 'He's in a boat. Have you seen him?'

She was an absolute vision of loveliness. Her simple shift was pure white, contrasting with her raven hair. Her skin was pale, but the red-brown scarf across her left shoulder and chest added colour. It must have been the coloured scarf he had seen earlier but failed to properly make out. The thing he noticed most, now she was close, was the finery draped around her neck, over the scarf. It was a lustrous, fine chain with a glittering crystal suspended from it.

Ted couldn't answer the girl's question at first, so stunned was he with the sight that greeted his eyes.

'No, there's been no-one else here,' he eventually managed to say. 'Either on the beach or out at sea.'

She dropped easily down from the horse and gracefully walked over to him.

'You look tired,' she said. 'Rest a while.'

Saying this, she lifted her right hand toward his face. Instinctively, Ted closed his eyes as two of her cool fingers delicately touched the lids. When their gentle pressure was removed, he tried to open his eyes, but found he couldn't do it. He heard footsteps crunching away across the small patch of shingle set in the otherwise unbroken sands. Now he felt no urgency to force his eyelids apart. Instead, he stood there contentedly listening to the wash of the surf around him.

Gradually, he did manage to look ahead. His eyes felt refreshed and light when he opened them. The girl was no longer there. Before him stood the horse, alone. It looked exactly as it had before, save that its white coat now radiated a brilliance that couldn't have been natural. The horse seemed to look directly at him for a few seconds, pawed the ground, tossed its head, turned and galloped away. Ted could see that on the side of the creature's neck was indeed a dark patch. Was this, after all, what he'd seen earlier? Had he only imagined a rider?

He didn't have time to ponder this question. Behind him he heard the furious yapping of a small, energetic dog. Turning, he could see it was racing toward him. Soon it bounded over to where he stood and started to leap up at him excitedly, wagging its tail. It was friendly, over friendly.

A young man was running towards them.

'Chum!' he called, breathlessly. 'You naughty boy. Stop that!'

Chum took little notice. Now he was running around Ted in mad circles, making darting runs towards him and then back towards its owner. Eventually, the young man panted up to his side.

'I'm sorry, Sir,' he gasped. 'Chum gets carried away with himself sometimes.'

'Never mind,' said Ted. 'He's friendly enough. Get your breath back.'

The young man whistled through his teeth, then rested his palms on his knees and drew in gulps of air.

'Really sorry about this,' he said, after recovering his breath. 'Chum doesn't usually see anyone at this early hour. I…Where's he gone now?'

Chum was running in widening circles around the pair of them. He barked excitedly as his feet splashed through the waves on the shoreline. They both laughed.

'Lee.' The young man held out his hand. 'We'd better go up the beach a few yards, before the incoming tide engulfs us.'

'Ted,' he said, taking Lee's hand. 'Your dog is a handful.' Ted felt an extra stiffness in his limbs as they took a few paces away from the shoreline.

'He certainly is. It's odd to see anyone here. Normally there's nobody when we're out at this hour of the morning. Not at this time of year, at least. The visitors we do have in this part of the world, especially the Australians and New Zealanders, usually go further north to Staithes. In search of Captain Cook's birthplace, sort of thing.'

'There was someone here a short while ago. You must have seen the woman. She was a young girl really. Younger than you I'd say, Lee.'

'A girl? I'd have noticed.'

'Well,' said Ted. 'Perhaps she'd gone by the time you arrived. But you'd have seen her horse, for sure.'

'A horse? I've been coming here for five years and never seen anything but another dog on this beach at this hour. The only horse I've heard of that has anything to do with this part of a coast was the one in the old story my Grandfather used to tell me. Silly stuff it was really. Still, I often think of it in the mornings when I'm out here with Chum. It makes me think of my Grandfather... Sorry, I didn't mean to... He died two years ago.'

Lee's expression softened.

'I'm sure your grandfather wasn't young,' said Ted. 'Neither am I. Would you mind telling the story to me?'

'I remember it very well,' said Lee. 'My Grandfather used to tell it to me at least once a week when I was a kid. It was supposed to be true – something that happened more than two hundred years ago.'

'Go on, then'

'This girl and her father, they wanted to make the journey from Berwick to Newbiggin to buy a horse the girl had been saving all her sixpences for. They travelled in his small boat. The story was that she always wore a scarf. When she'd bought the horse she was going to tie it round the horse's neck and ride all the way home. No saddle, bridle, or anything like that. There was something about some sort of jewel the girl wore around her neck, over the scarf.'

'A crystal?'

Lee looked at Ted questioningly.

'That's right. How did you know that?'

'Only a guess,' said Ted.

'It wasn't worth much. It was nothing more than a home-made bauble. But it had been in their family for centuries.'

'It sounds a pleasant enough tale.'

'Not all of it is.'

Lee fell silent.

'Aren't you going to tell me the rest?'

'There's not much more to tell,' said Lee. 'They never made it to Newbiggin. They drowned – nobody knows quite what happened, but it was on this stretch of coast. Goodness!'

'What's wrong?'

'I should be going home to get ready for work. This morning I'm running a bit late as it is. But Chum likes – where is that dog? Chum! Look. There he is, worrying away at that bit of driftwood. It looks like it's from the prow of an old rowing boat. Chum! It's nearly as big as you. Let it be, will you?'

But the dog wouldn't leave the piece of wood alone. Ted watched, fascinated, as mighty canine efforts were made to pull the wood to shore. Eventually, Lee waded into the shallows to lend a hand.

'You won't give up, will you?' said Lee to his dog. 'Look, there's something caught on the wood.'

Lee bent down and fumbled for something.

'It's only a bit of old metal. Been in the water for ages, by the look of the rust. Some kind of necklace, I'd say. There's a clasp at the bottom. Looks like it might have held some sort of jewel at one time. Well, there's only one place for a bit of junk like this.'

He bent his elbow, as if to toss it back into the waves.

'Wait!' shouted Ted. 'Don't you want it?'

'Of course I don't want it. It wouldn't be worth a bean. Would you like to have it? It'll be a sort of memento of this morning, eh?'

'Yes. I'd like very much to have it.'

Lee handed over the object with a wink.

'Look, I'm sorry. I've got to make tracks. Work and all that, you see? Great to have met you, anyway. I've enjoyed our chat.'

With that, Lee turned and jogged off in a northerly direction, Chum at his heels. Ted turned to face the south again. In the distance he saw a figure. It was as if in constant motion, a kind of graceful, dreamlike motion which didn't seem to be bringing whatever it was any nearer to where he was standing.

Unmistakably now, he began to make out the figure of a white horse. He glanced northwards, thinking of calling after Lee to tell him to look, but the young man and his dog were already some distance away. Ted suddenly felt all the weight of his years on his shoulders.

He looked back towards the south. The white horse was now approaching quickly. There was definitely a rider on its back; he could even see her smile. She had flowing dark hair and was dressed in white. As he watched she seemed to fade from his vision. Then he looked down at his hand. It was holding not a string of tarnished metal, but a shining chain. At the end of the chain was a glittering crystal.

ELDRITCH

'Eldritch' is a word of of uncertain origin. Nowadays it means 'otherworldly' in a general sense. However, it probably derives from the Germanic 'elf reich', reich meaning realm –i.e. 'the realm of the elves'.

This book is the a new edition of the first Eldritch collection, *The Eve of St Eligius*. The second, *Wish Man's Wood*, will appear very soon. Other recent writings by Tom East are:

FICTION

Dimension Five

The Gospel According to St Judas

The Greenland Party

Tommy's War: July, 1914

POETRY

Scenes from Seasons

Charge of The Light Verse Brigade

Lyrics, Polemics & Poetics

Extracts from Reviews
of the first edition of *The Eve of St Eligius*

...They say that electricity in our houses destroyed the ghost story which belonged to an age of guttering candles and gas light. This collection confirms this as a platitude and, more importantly, as a falsehood. The ghost story – if that is what these are – is alive and kicking, decidedly kicking...

Phil Carradice, historian and author of over 50 books.

...Although the stories are described as 'dark'—and many are—not every one ends badly for the protagonist. Take 'Before the Kettle Boils', for example: I found this to be a nostalgic look at the differences between big city and rural living, an uplifting tale despite the appearance of a ghost...

Sam Kates, author of *Earth Haven* and *Elevator* trilogies.

...His knowledge of so many obscure historical facts, particularly those pertaining to Wales, its culture and geography was very impressive. But most enjoyable for me was the story telling talent that kept me turning the pages...   **James W**

...Perhaps the sheer range of the stories is the most impressive feature. My favourite is 'Before the Kettle Boils'. A 300-year old legend may be important to the storyline but in every respect the action and characters are right up-to-date...   **JE**

...Tom East's collection of stories is far from simply frightening its readers. The author's skill in building a credible plot around an incredible event goes deeper, giving the readers the intellectual satisfaction provided by a well-balanced narrative, the care for detail, the variety of stylistic devices, and the round, dynamic protagonists involved in suspenseful situations that are often open-ended, inviting the readers to fill in the blanks...   **Petru Iamandi**, translator of over 100 books

Printed in Great Britain
by Amazon

11561531R00169